WHEN HELL FREEZES OVER

SIN DEMONS

MILA YOUNG

HARPER A. BROOKS

DEDICATION

To the magic cat who has endless sparkles.
-Mila Young

To the talking goat that slipped in at the end.
-Harper A. Brooks

CONTENTS

Sin Demons Series   vii

Chapter 1   1
Chapter 2   8
Chapter 3   15
Chapter 4   28
Chapter 5   39
Chapter 6   50
Chapter 7   60
Chapter 8   73
Chapter 9   85
Chapter 10   95
Chapter 11   105
Chapter 12   116
Chapter 13   126
Chapter 14   137
Chapter 15   150
Chapter 16   160
Chapter 17   174
Chapter 18   190
Chapter 19   201
Chapter 20   212
Chapter 21   229
Chapter 22   245
Chapter 23   256
Chapter 24   272

Hell on Earth   283
His Haven   287
About Mila Young   289
About Harper A. Brooks   291

SIN DEMONS SERIES

Playing With Hellfire

Hell In A Handbasket

All Shot To Hell

To Hell And Back

When Hell Freezes Over

Hell On Earth

Snowball's Chance in Hell

CHAPTER ONE

MAVERICK

"The path to paradise begins in Hell." — Dante Alighieri

I can't believe what I'm seeing.

Aria, the small, meek-looking woman I so easily tricked, is gone. She's not human. Definitely not human, and what stands before us is a creature of immense power. With eyes a cloudy white, wisps of shadowy smoke surrounding her, and sparks of light emitting from her skin, she's quite an unsettling sight.

What the hell is she?

I've seen my share of fucked-up shit in the underworld, but this is new. And from the horrified looks on my brother's, Dorian's, and Elias's faces, I'd say they're just as stumped. And scared. I don't think I've *ever* seen Cain frightened before. Not even by our father, and he's one terrifying S.O.B

"Aria, please," Cain begins, his voice surprisingly calm

despite the chaos. He holds up his hands and takes a slow step towards her. "You can't let Sayah take over. You have to fight her—"

The creature's laughter booms, sounding manic against the eerie silence of the night. "You have no idea who you're talking to, demon. She can't control me. Not anymore."

A shiver shoots up my spine at her words. Aria's voice is woven into the shadow creature's, sounding too raspy and strained to truly be hers.

"Well then, who are you?" Dorian shouts back.

Aria's head tilts and her brows pinch in annoyance. "I am the darkness. Ever consuming and never ending. I am the nightmares that keep you up at night. I am the beginning and the end."

"And a bit dramatic..." Dorian whispers under his breath.

Her hand lashes out, and a shadowy tendril shoots from it, wrapping around his middle and lifting him into the air with ease. Aria holds him there, feet above the ground, her eerily white eyes focused on him, and him alone. The symbols across Dorian's chest glow brighter and his long fingers try to rip Sayah's grip from him, but he can't seem to get a good hold.

Cain and Elias take their opportunity to run in opposite directions and loop around, trying to take Aria down from behind.

Still homed in on Dorian, Aria throws her hand out, and the shadow mimics her action. He's tossed yards away, like he's nothing more than a rag doll. He lands with a hard thud in the icy snow. At the same time, Cain and Elias rush her from behind, becoming nothing more than blurs of color in their speed. But somehow, she senses them and whips around, swiping her shadowy arm their way. It nails them both in the stomach and sends them hurtling across the yard, too.

I can't just stand here. Whatever Sayah is, it has Aria trapped inside her somewhere and I need to get her out. Even if that means slicing open the shadow creature and pulling Aria out with my bare hands.

I unsheathe my daggers, aim for the monster's chest, hold my breath, and throw one Sayah's way with deadly accuracy. It whirls through the air, whistling as it flies with incredible speed right for its target.

Again, to my amazement, Sayah's able to track my weapon and snatch it right out of the air by the handle. She holds it there, with the blade pointed at her heart, only centimeters away from piercing the flesh right between her breasts, and lifts her head to meet my gaze.

My cock jerks in response. Shit. This is not the fucking time to be turned on. But there's something so damn sexy about a deadly fight. I don't know how to explain it.

In one fluid motion, she twirls the knife around her wrist like a weapons expert and throws it tip down into the dirt.

I rush at her, my other blade held firmly in my grasp. But she doesn't run. She comes at me, meeting me the rest of the way in seconds. I swing my dagger, but she ducks and twists herself out of harm's way with ease. Using all my speed, I try to swipe at her middle, but she manages to block my attack.

Staring at our crossed arms, I'm stunned. Most demons in Hell can't even match my combat skills, yet here she is, doing so without even breaking a sweat.

She smirks.

My other fist flies, aimed for the side of her face, but she blocks that one as well. Again, I'm dumbfounded, frozen in place from my astonishment.

"Do you want to play together again?" Sayah asks through Aria's lips, and the sound of it grates on my nerves. With every strike, she's able to either stop me or avoid contact, and suddenly we're performing some strangely fluid dance across the grounds, me trying to find an opening to land a hit and her easily evading all my attacks.

"What… do you… mean?" My reply comes in quick gasps while I try and catch my breath.

Spinning, her arm goes out, snakes around my head before snatching my other dagger right out of my grasp. In a flash, the blade is at my throat and her other hand is seizing my arm and wrenching back. The pain in my elbow is immediate from being bent in the wrong direction.

My body stiffens, the sharp edge biting into my flesh enough to draw blood, and I realize she means replaying the moment in Lucifer's throne room. Only she's the one who has me pinned.

An eerie grin splits her lips, and it sends my pulse into overdrive. Even though her eyes have lost their color and are a milky white, I can see the dark intentions behind them. She wants to kill me, but she wants to play with me first.

My cock stiffens to the point of pain, too restricted in my pants. It doesn't help that she's gorgeous, completely naked, and covered in blood. An all too tempting sight. I have to ignore it now, though. I'm all for a little knife-play, but now's not the time for this. Aria's in real danger, and I have to remember this isn't her. Not really. It's Sayah, the shadow creature; she's got me by the balls. Almost literally.

She pushes my straightened arm even more, causing me to hiss in pain.

"You like that, demon?" she asks and starts to run my own blade up and down my neck. The skin burns, yet the pain not only makes me angrier but hornier. And from her narrowing gaze, she senses it, too. "You like when it hurts."

The moment she loosens her hold on me—even just a little—I'm either going to knock her out or bend her over. Right now, I'm not sure which.

Leaning in close, her lips brush against my cheek when she whispers, "She wants you, you know. I can see her darkest desires. Her most secret thoughts… and she longs for you to fuck her. Hard and raw."

Her words ignite a fire in me, and I'm suddenly sweating all over. Is the creature telling me the truth?

She licks the side of my face, and then murmurs, pleased with what she tastes. "But she's loyal… Loyal to…"

She jerks back, her head whipping to the right. From the corner of my eye, I see Cain sprinting towards us, leathery wings tucked tight to his body and inky-black gaze full of determination and fury.

I take those few seconds of distraction to wrench my free arm up and shove the knife away. Then I duck, twist, releasing my arm from her grasp, and quickly seize her by the wrist to spin her at the same time. Her back slams against me, and I trap her in place with the blade now at her neck. Her bare breasts are soft against my arm, and the curve of her ass presses against my groin. I growl.

Pushing my nose into her hair, I inhale deeply. Hell, she smells so good. Like vanilla and cinnamon and… untamed *power.* It makes my head fog.

Cain halts in front of us, his expression an intimidating mixture of fury and fear. "Don't fucking move," he bellows. His fists glow a fiery red. "You hurt her and you hurt Aria."

"And?" I snap. "We have the creature. What does it matter what happens to Aria? She's just another soul."

He hesitates.

Could it be? My oldest brother actually cares for an

earth woman, and not just because of the dark entity inside her? At first, I thought he might be keeping her around to harness her power, but now… I just don't know.

Hell may just freeze over.

"Let her go, Maverick," he says, pronouncing each word to emphasize the threat behind them. I can see the distrust lingering in his eyes. He's afraid I'll pop out of here and bring her back to Hell.

And maybe I should. Father would be happy about it. He'd even reward me. But is it worth it?

No. Lucifer's admiration only lasts moments before turning into boredom or disgust. I'd learned that the hard way.

I'm done pining for his attention. No more.

If I am going to finally be free of his oppressive hold, I am going to have to kick his ass off the throne. And that means teaming up with my brother and the other two Hell rejects.

I throw the dagger at Cain's feet to show my allegiance, but his gaze only hardens on me.

"Let her go," he repeats as his wings spread wide. The sharp talons at the ends spark in the light of the moon. I spot Dorian rushing over to us, down the hill and toward the yard, and I'm sure that if I turn around, I'd find Elias trying to sneak up from behind me again.

None of them believe that I'm here to help, and I don't blame them. I wouldn't trust me either.

"C-Cain?"

I freeze.

It's coming from Aria. But the voice has lost the shadow creature's inflection. It sounds like her now. Just her.

Cain's eyes widen, and when I glance down at the woman in my arms, the smoke surrounding her is gone, the flickering orange lights extinguished.

Is Sayah gone? Just like that?

Cain's expression softens, his wings folding in and the black veins disappearing from his skin. "Aria…"

Then her entire body goes limp in my arms. Her head rolls to the side. Unconscious.

CHAPTER TWO

CAIN

I lift my gaze to Aria lying in my bed, looking so peaceful. Her breaths are shallow; Sayah's possession took its toll on her body. Everything about Aria is beautiful, yet what lies inside her is terrifying. It took us all off guard and that was our mistake, to not take into account how Sayah would react during the ritual.

My worry comes from an inability to protect Aria.

I move to stand by the bed and brush a loose strand of hair from her forehead.

Voices cleave through the absolute silence, along with heavy footsteps striking the floorboards out in the hallway.

Dorian enters first, his sights set only on Aria and he marches over to her other side. He runs the back of his hand over her cheek, his lips thin, shadows crossing his face. "Fuck, this is bad, and we've been through a lot of shit already. This isn't fair to her."

Elias shoves Maverick into the room, then pushes him down into a seat before tying his wrists behind the chair, and then his ankles together. Neither say a word, but their gazes are on Aria.

A somber, harrowing silence falls over the room once more, and how far away Aria feels from us right now. At how insistent Sayah was that she was now in control.

Memories of what just happened tear through me, refusing to leave me alone.

"What now?" Dorian demands, wrenching me from my thoughts.

"I say we begin with killing Maverick," Elias growls.

"What the fuck did *I* do?" my brother answers. "You three are responsible for the ritual, which brought out that thing from inside her."

"Are you kidding me? This is your damn fault. I bet if you didn't take Aria to Hell, Sayah wouldn't have grown so powerful," Elias persists.

"You can't prove that? Do you even know what *it* is?" Maverick snaps back, disdain on his face.

"Do you, Brother?" I turn on him, my voice like acid, and I close the distance between us. "Because if you do know, that is the best way to save yourself here. Or maybe I'll just feed you to Elias." Anger surges through me. I'm tired of the games.

He's shaking his head. "If I knew, I would have eradicated it back in Hell. But whatever the fuck it is, it's trying to conquer Aria."

A shudder races down my spine, consuming me. I know this, but to have seen it in action, to hear it from my brother who hasn't been around Aria as long as us, fills me with fear.

"Let's not let anger blur our decisions," Dorian says, the calm one among us, which isn't how this story goes. I'm the one in control, except I feel like I *am* losing control. One thread at a time, everything is slipping through my fingers.

Aria.

Command over my territory on Earth.

My goal is to return to Hell and eliminate my cold-hearted father.

But it feels so far out of reach, like I'm losing touch with myself. Aria has distracted me with emotions I never should have felt. Yet, despite that, she is now my priority and if I have to reshuffle my other priorities, so be it. But I can't lose my head in the process or else everything will go to hell.

There's no stopping the onslaught now. We're in the thick of it, and we'll fight our damn way out, even if it means tearing through everyone to get it done.

Sucking in a deep breath, I let go of the tension bunching up my muscles and turn to my men. "Okay, what do we know so far? The ritual definitely worked because we all sensed the connection with Aria. So I doubt anything strange happened there."

"Except for the fact that your ritual aggravated that thing to come out and possess her," Maverick adds, his voice grating on my nerves.

"I'm fully aware of the situation," I growl, not looking at him as I speak. My hands curl into fists. I'm the one in control, but today I'm ready to detonate from the fury burning through me. Refocusing on Dorian and Elias, I continue, "Sayah has grown stronger over the past few weeks, and whatever happened out there, it gave her an opportunity to finally take over. Which begs the question, will Aria be herself when she wakes up, or will we confront Sayah?"

No response from anyone at first. Dorian steps around to stand at the end of the bed. "Sayah is a parasite that's latched onto her, so there is only one way to get rid of it. Exorcising it out."

Maverick clears his throat. "I'm going to agree with

pretty-boy over here. At least he's making sense." He glares at Elias.

"Can I throw him out the window now, chair and all?" Elias snarls, his gaze locking on my brother.

I glance over my shoulder at Maverick, and imagine how much pleasure it would give me to see him flying across the room, but I also don't want him out of my sight.

Maverick lifts his head to face me. "Are you willing to risk Aria dying during an exorcism? It could kill her when we don't know what we're dealing with."

"If she's had that thing cursed into her from a young age, it's true. We could end up hurting her rather than helping," Elias suggests. "I've seen it happen. Those bastards are close to impossible to remove from people."

My throat clenches like a fist at the possibilities. Jumbled thoughts crowd in my head, suffocating me, while the urgency of the situation presses down. We don't have time to waste.

Maverick shrugs. "So, what's the plan then, Brother? Wait until she wakes up and kicks all our asses again? Or are you going to try another ritual?" The sneer in his voice leaves me furious.

"The plan is for you to shut the fuck up," Elias snarls, while Dorian sighs heavily.

"Tying her up won't work with Sayah," he says. "So, we need a plan B in case she doesn't wake up as herself."

"Agreed." Maverick steals the words from my lips. "I mean, we all want her back. I can still taste her."

His words seize me, and I wrench my head toward him, fire erupting in my chest. "What did you say?"

The smirk on his face is enough to drive me off the edge. The jolt of anger is instant, scorching hot, and I'm lunging at him before reason settles in my mind.

I crash into him so fast, he's thrown backward, and the chair he's in snaps and breaks beneath our weight.

Two hits to his face, I drive a third to his head because it makes me feel so fucking good to just smash something. The bastard just laughs, pinned beneath me, blood smearing his chin from his busted lip.

His shoulders curl the moment I pause and he head-butts me right in the nose, blood instantly in the back of my throat, catching me off guard.

I get up off him, kneeling beside him and wipe the blood from my nose. The thought of tearing into him bellows in my mind, as do the eager expressions from Dorian and Elias watching us. They're waiting for me to tag them in, to get their chance at Maverick. He's still on his back, hands still tied behind him, but he's smirking.

Something about the look in his eyes, a vulnerability I'd seen once before, wrenched me into a past memory, one where Father had Maverick tied to a chair, torturing him. I knew he'd kill my brother that day. I felt it in the air. I hadn't seen Father that furious before, that dangerous. Something overcame me that day, and I helped my brother. I put myself at risk to aid him. He may piss me off, but I loathe Lucifer a lot more.

That memory remains an unspoken event between us, and now that same expression crosses his face. One where, despite his words and actions, he's asking for help. Why else would he have left Hell and walked out on Father when he knows Lucifer's wrath as well as I do?

I get to my feet and reach down to grab Maverick by his shirt. I yank him to his feet.

"Thanks," he says softly.

I nod and turn back toward Aria and my men, who don't say a word. Family is fucking complicated, and they know it better than me, having seen all the shit with my father and brothers back in Hell.

Our world is falling apart around us, but that doesn't mean I need to fall alongside it.

I crack my neck. "Alright, we need a plan."

"Father's diary mentions Aria's name a lot," Maverick says, his voice no longer carrying the edge of arrogance it had earlier. "When I flipped through it, he had written some notes in Latin I could make out about holy water and theorized its effects on her. It's part of the reason he wants her back, so he can experiment on her, uncover what's inside her."

"So, he's thinking of exorcising her with holy water?" Dorian states the obvious. "Except, holy water doesn't work on demons. That's only in the movies."

"That's because the stuff from churches isn't the real shit," Maverick adds. "From what I've deciphered in the diary, holy water needs a special cross dipped inside it, along with salt, and then blessed with prayer by someone pure of heart. And we all know many priests are far from being pure of heart."

"So, why would Lucifer want to be with Sayah?" Elias asks.

"You're talking about the Lord of Hell," Dorian answers. "What has he always wanted? To grow his power and control everything. Sayah is a new toy for him, and he wants to understand and own it, is my guess."

Dorian isn't wrong. Remnants of my life back in Hell still linger in my mind of all the crap Father pulled, all the deaths, all the anger toward anyone who held a secret from him or threatened his position. Nothing has changed about him. Not a damn thing.

But now he's got Aria in his sights, and that's just not going to work for me.

I stare at Aria for a long moment. "Watch over her. I need to study the diary and see what else I can find in it." I grab Maverick by the shirt. "You're with me."

"Um, what's the deal with Maverick then?" Elias demands, as I turn toward the hallway. "Is he now just staying with us because he said so?"

I twist around to both Dorian and Elias, who stand near Aria's bed, waiting for an explanation. They looked pissed. They hate Maverick as much as me, but what if he's an element we can use? What if he's finally come around and seen the truth of what our father is?

"Can we really trust him?" Dorian asks.

I tighten my hold on my brother. "You're mistaken if you think I trust him, but I'd rather have him by our side than in Lucifer's ear." I look at Maverick. "If you're telling the truth, then we can use another soldier in our war. If not…" I lift my gaze to my two men. "He takes one step out of line, and I give you both permission to take him out."

Maverick stiffens in my grip, but instead of fighting me, he says, "That's fair." His voice is stiff but abiding. "I only want to keep Aria safe and stop Lucifer. So we have a common goal."

Except, a goal without a plan is just a wish…

With Maverick in my hold, we march out into the hallway. I'm determined to find an answer in Father's diary to help us with Sayah so we aren't blind-sided again. And if Maverick proves to be a thorn in my side, I will take him out myself.

CHAPTER THREE

ARIA

My eyes open suddenly and inhale a loud gasp, as though I've burst free from beneath the water's surface. As if I've been drowning and finally I've found a way to breathe again.

I sit up, finding myself in a large bed. I scan the room... It's Cain's, but I'm alone and there's no sound. The light pours in from the window while snow feathers outside so peacefully.

I don't move, trying to still my racing heart, and think back to the last thing I remember.

Darkness.

Overbearing pressure.

Cold... I remember feeling so cold... and then there was Sayah.

I felt every bit of her taking me over, her grip cruel, squeezing, wrenching me within, anything to suppress me.

My palms grow slick with sweat with the memory and knowledge that I stood no chance. And I received no notice of her rushing out of me. One second, I was bliss-fully drowning beneath the pleasure of my three lovers, and the next, the monster within me had shown her face. Then things got blurry.

Only snippets of what happened around me stick in my mind, mostly Cain and Maverick facing Sayah, but beyond that I was drowning. Within my head was nothing but my panic and its echo. The dread that I would forever be trapped inside my head, lost to the world, lost to my men.

My heart thunders harder just at the thought, and I shake so hard that I'm not sure how I'm meant to live with such a thing inside me. She's gotten worse, and I knew my time was running out quickly.

What if I can't stop her… will I disappear forever?

I close my eyes and the room seems to tilt around me. Breaths refuse to come… my entire life I lived with Sayah but I never once believed she was such an ominous being who wanted me out of the way.

The clack of something striking the wooden floorboards erupts in the room, and I open my eyes to Cassiel leaping up on the bed. He's so big, fluffy too, snow dusting his coat, and his two front legs bandaged up, yet he's moving around like he's fine.

"Cass." I throw my arms around him, needing him, wanting to just forget my own horror. He settles in against me, his head in my lap, and he's breathing heavily like he's been running upstairs to see me.

I run my fingers through his thick fur. "I can't tell you how good it is to see you. You scared me half to death when you were thrown out the window." My chest clenches at the memory that almost killed me.

Movement in the doorway draws my attention to Elias, leaning a shoulder on the doorframe, his hands deep in the pockets of his jeans. He's wearing a black hoodie and looks so human. Well, with exception to how ridiculously handsome he is—no mortal could ever look like him with his strength in such ordinary clothes.

But I like him like this. It makes me feel… normal.

The light hits him just the right way, his bronze eyes are especially light today, and that smile almost breaks me. He looks at me as if I'm everything in the world to him, and it's almost terrifying to know that this is what's at risk if I let Sayah win.

"Hey, little rabbit. Good to see you're awake. How are you feeling?" He strolls into the room, his shoulders moving back and forth with his lazy walk. His gaze never leaves me, and behind his eyes I see the agony he's holding back. The pain of seeing me… Was he expecting Sayah to return?

"Get over here," I tell him, needing to touch him, to have him against me.

He's so quiet, which is unlike him when he always has a smart-ass comment to make, especially with Cassiel around. But instead, he takes a seat on the side of the bed and reaches over, ruffling the fur on the lynx's head.

Then he takes me into his arms, abruptly and hard, like it took every ounce of strength he had to not run over to me the moment he stepped into the room.

"I missed you so much," he whispers, his voice breathless.

His hold is perfect. It's everything I crave, so I bury my face into the curve of his neck, his skin so warm, so inviting. And when I inhale his scent, it floods me. Masculine, woodsy, with a hint of wolf. He's everything, and I grip him harder, wanting to bury myself in him.

He rubs my back with one hand, the other on the back of my head, holding me, knowing exactly what I need.

To escape from the horror I've been through.

I'm a complete mess. When I finally come up for air, I

lift my head and kiss him, desperate to fill myself with him rather than the monster residing in me.

His lips are gentle, as if he's scared of hurting me, yet his kiss is that of a man who knows how to rekindle my passion with the tenderest of touches.

Our foreheads touch and we stare at each other.

"Cassiel is okay now," I say randomly, and pull back to scratch the little guy still keeping his head on my lap. He's making a purring sound, loving the attention.

"It took a lot of lying and a little threatening to the local zoo's vet, but yeah. He made it out okay." He glances at Cass with a cocky smirk. "I thought cats were supposed to always land on their feet anyway?"

On cue, Cass hisses at him.

I laugh. "Not always. Anyway, it means everything to me that you did." Giving him a lopsided grin earns me a kiss on the nose.

"What about you? How are you feeling?"

"Confused. Lost. Scared. It's ridiculous right, but I've lived with Sayah my entire life, yet the moment she flexes her muscles and shows me her real side, her real intent, I'm all chicken shit."

He cups the side of my face. "You are the strongest person I know, having gone through so much, and you never give up."

I half chuckle. "Seriously, if I could find an exit button right now to just give up on all this crap, I'd be tempted."

He's shaking his head. "I wouldn't let you. I know you too well. You'd hate yourself for it later."

I can't help but smile. "I know you're right, but I hate always being public enemy number one. I need a break."

"How about this? We get through all this shit, then we'll take you anywhere you want. Anywhere. It'll be an Aria-all-request vacation."

I smile and wipe my eyes, before yawning. "Yeah, I'd like that."

"How about you get some more sleep? Cassiel will watch over you and I'll be just outside, alright?" He holds the sides of my face and kisses me softly.

I nod, and as he climbs to his feet to leave, I slide in under the blanket. Cassiel snuggles in beside me, and a heavy sleep already pulls shut my eyes.

When I wake up, there's a calmness in the room, along with a gentle scent of lavender. I crane my head up to see that someone placed a candle in my room, and it smells beautiful. Cassiel is by my side and snores like a beast, but there is no sign of the men. Though my throat is as dry as sandpaper and as rough when I attempt to swallow.

"Don't move," I whisper to Cassiel and slide out of bed, finding myself dressed in one of my long tee-pajamas. This one has a cute orange kitten on the front, one paw hanging off a clothesline with the words, 'Hang in There.'

I laugh to myself, wondering which deadly demon put me in it. My guess is Dorian, since he loves pushing Elias's buttons. Especially when it comes to cats.

And I realize in that moment that I am no longer covered in blood as I had been during the ritual. Which one of the guys won that challenge to clean me up? Though, when I look at my fingernails, there are still traces of red underneath. A shower is a must.

On bare feet, I cross the room and step out into the hallway. There's no one around and it's quiet, which is reassuring. I love the quiet more and more these days, as it means one thing—no major drama is unfolding.

Once I head downstairs, a whisper of a voice comes from the open basement door. My thoughts go to the three guys, and I want to see them all, my pulse kicking up a notch at the thought of having them surround me. My feet skim the floorboards as I quicken my pace and climb down the creaky wooden steps.

At the bottom, more voices drift down the long hall. It smells like damp earth down here, and that's because of all the bags of dirt lining the way. I remember first finding Elias down here hauling in the stuff and not understanding why. Now knowing that it can help amplify or bind certain magic, it makes sense why the demons would keep it in their home like this. They're always up to something.

I follow the whispers and come upon a room with its door cracked open. Cautiously, I peer inside.

In the middle, Maverick sits back on his heels, his head dropped forward, and he's humming a song to himself. It's a soothing ballad I don't recognize, yet my heart goes out to him, seeing him like this.

Not only are his hands tied behind his back, they're chained to the floor. Blood drips from his mouth and there's a nasty bruise under his eye. A circle of white powder, most likely salt and dirt surrounds him, which I assume are to keep him from vanishing.

I recall him vaguely from last night at the ritual, fighting alongside Cain against Sayah.

Though so much about Maverick leaves me confused. He's an asshole, but he also saved me. I don't trust him, yet when I'm in his presence, my heart thumps in my chest harder. I crave his attention, but I also don't know where his true allegiance lies. I'd seen the way he engaged with Lucifer, the hatred between them, but then again, aren't all demons in Hell similar?

"You can come in," he says, and lifts his head, offering

me a saccharine smile. His lower lip is split and blood drips down his chin.

I push open the door and step inside.

"How are you feeling?" he asks me.

"I should be asking you the same question," I respond.

"Just dandy," he responds. "My brother isn't exactly in a trusting mood, so I've been allocated my own room. Like it?" His sarcasm has me smiling at him.

"Why are you really here?" I ask him. "I remember you appearing last night, but then what? Cain captured you and tied you up?"

"It might surprise you to know that I volunteered."

"To be tied up?" I gasp.

He grins. "Not that part. But to stay here. To help you four against Lucifer."

I narrow my gaze on him. "What gives? What do you really want out of it?"

"Can't a guy just finally sort out his shit and realize he's fucked up by choosing the wrong team?"

"A normal guy, maybe. But you? I don't think so."

That overly sweet smile is back. I don't see any ill intent or hidden agenda behind his expression or in his eyes.

Though he might be the world's biggest liar for all I know too.

"Why don't you be a good girl, come over here, and help me out of these chains?" he says, twisting around so I can see his tied-up wrists.

"Not a chance."

We stare at each other, and he pulls a leg out from under him, then pushes himself to his feet, so he's no longer looking up at me. His brown eyes soften, and I find myself staring at him too long, at his lips and remembering how incredible they felt against mine. "I'm not sure if Cain told you, but the contract I held over your friend, Joseline…" He pauses and clears his throat.

"Yeah?" I prod him along.

"It's null and void. I canceled it."

My eyes seem to widen on their own at his words, and I feel myself almost leaning forward. "You did?"

"Take it as a peace offering."

I swallow past my dry throat. "Thank you," I say at once, relieved in all honesty to know Joseline is free from under the demon contract. That means everything to me. Though, I'm still not sure what to make of Maverick or the emotions he rouses within me.

"What made you change your mind?" I ask, struggling to believe it's all in good faith. Sure, I want that to be the case, don't we all want a world of rainbows and unicorns? But that's just not going to happen. I've fallen for three demons, and I'm letting a fourth get under my skin too because I am a sucker for punishment. But I am also a realist and know that there's motivation behind everyone's decision.

But the creak of floorboards outside the room distracts me and I turn, forgetting my words as Elias steps into the doorway, his brow furrowed at seeing me.

ELIAS

"*Y*ou had me worried," I say, storming into the room, not even paying attention to Maverick. I pull Aria into my arms, holding her tight. Seriously, when I found her missing from Cain's room, a streak of panic overcame me.

"I was thirsty," she tells me.

"And you ended up in the basement?"

"I heard voices. I thought it was one of you three."

I wave it off. It doesn't matter anyway. "Come, and I'll get you a drink."

But before I can guide her out, Dorian and Cain both enter the room abruptly, suddenly stealing all the space.

"Oh look, we're having a party," Maverick jokes. "Did anyone bring cookies?"

"What are you doing here?" Cain asks Aria. Everyone is ignoring Maverick.

She shrugs. "I was thirsty and on my way to the kitchen, but I heard voices. They led me down here and I found him, expecting you."

"These will be his accommodations while he stays with us," Cain instructs, while Dorian slips out of the room.

"He's staying?" she asks, her mouth kind of half hanging open, while staring at Cain, then over to Maverick, who winks at her.

I narrow my gaze at him, wanting to knock him flat on his back.

"It's complicated, but we're sorting out a solution," Cain says.

"Oh, Brother, can't you ever talk straight. Honey pot, I left Hell and am here to join your little band of demons."

A growl erupts past my throat, my attention locking on Maverick. "Over my dead body. Cain would never—"

"That can be arranged," the asshole replies. Everything about him makes me burn up with fury. One minute he's on Lucifer's side, doing his bidding, the next he's suddenly chummy with us and no longer on the devil's side. Does he think we were born yesterday?

As if he knows what I'm thinking, Maverick holds my stare. Tempting me. He has a way of getting under my skin with a single look. I sometimes wonder how Cain and his six brothers can be so different.

Whispers from Cain and Aria draw my attention, and I twist my head to see that they've moved closer to the door, talking quietly. I lift my head, ears pricked, and I catch the tail end of what they're saying.

"At the ritual, you said you loved me. D-Did you mean it?" she asks, and her words strike me hard.

Love? Cain, Lucifer's very son, had said he loved her? I never thought he was even capable of such an emotion.

How could I have missed it when I was there?

Then again, I was a *bit* preoccupied.

Dorian abruptly strides into the room, carrying a tall glass and pitcher of icy water. He goes over to Aria and pours her a glass, interrupting her and Cain from finishing their chat.

"We'll talk about it later," Cain reassures her as she accepts the drink and gulps it down.

Aria has been on my mind endlessly, and I can't get her out of my thoughts. I crave her, worry for her, want her by my side every second of the damn day.

Shit!

Does that mean that I… Do I… love her too?

"Well, this is a happy reunion," Maverick drones on, drawing me out of my thoughts. "And I see you didn't bring me a glass of water. Incredibly rude. So, are we here to talk about Lucifer's diary again, or are you going to hash out your plans to take over the world?"

"Shut the hell up," Dorian snaps.

"What diary?" Aria asks.

"Maverick stole our father's diary, and I've been trying to decipher it." Cain explains.

"Lucifer's developed quite an obsession with you," Maverick chimes in, which only has Aria's face blanching.

"What does it say? I want to see it," she insists, and I wouldn't expect anything else from my little rabbit.

"I'm still trying to work it out. It's written in a strange language I don't understand."

"That's easy then. We will find someone who can speak that language and get it done." She pushes past Cain and approaches Maverick, standing inches from the line that keeps him locked in. "You must know what language it's written in right?"

But Maverick's shaking his head. "If I did, I would have translated it already."

I step closer to Aria and place my hand on her arm. "There are bits in Latin that talk about testing holy water on you."

"What for?" she asks, her voice almost squeaking with shock. "To eliminate Sayah?"

"Fuck, Elias, why the hell are you scaring her?" Dorian blurts out.

I face him instantly. "She has a right to know everything we do. No more secrets," I reprimand. "That's what got us into so much shit before. We're now a team."

"I can take it," she says. "Elias is right. No more secrets, please."

"Can we talk about translating the diary first, before we bring up any crazy theories? I'd rather know for sure." Dorian glances at Cain. "If none of us can figure it out, then we'll need someone who can. Let's get some help."

"Oh yeah? From who?" I ask.

"Miranda. The seer from the Storm markets," Dorian states. "One thing her gift allows her to do is *see* more from things or people. Maybe she can see past the language barrier and decipher it."

"That sounds like a long shot," I grumble. "And besides, can't she not see anyone Hell-born?"

"This is an object, Elias. Not a person." He taps the side of his head in a gesture for 'think about it.' "It's a loophole."

"Stupid."

"Hey, it's worth a try. I don't see you coming up with anything better."

"You trust this person?" Maverick asks, butting into the conversation again.

When Dorian nods, he turns to me next. I shrug. "She has an extreme love for incense and perfume, but that's really it," I say.

"Dorian is right," Cain starts loudly, regaining all our attention again. "Time is not on our side, so the sooner we know about Lucifer, the better. She deciphers the diary, and we expedite finding the last remaining relics."

"And seeing that we are sharing," Aria states as she fills her glass of water. "A few days ago, when Dorian and I went to the library, I discovered something that might be of interest."

Every eye in the room is now on Aria as she finishes drinking her water and sets the empty glass on a small table near the wall.

"I read that each of Lucifer's seven sons were created when he needed help to rule his dominion, and he found a way to rip apart his soul into those seven pieces and turn them into his sons. One for each of his sinful attributes, hence the first sin demons were born."

"We all know the history lesson." Maverick's head throws back as he laughs.

"Don't you get it?" she asks him, but it's Dorian who steps forward.

"Aria's onto something here. Lucifer wanted to rule his dominion by finding a way to split his soul into seven pieces... He split his *own* soul."

My mind is spinning. "Fuck!" I blurt as it suddenly becomes crystal clear that he used part of himself, meaning he is still connected to his sons.

"Ah, Elias got it."

Maverick let's out an aggravated grunt. "Elaborate."

"When we were kicked out of Hell, Lucifer could have killed Cain—should have killed him—but didn't," he explains.

The look on Maverick's face says he always wondered why that was, too.

Dorian goes on. "If he kills one of you, his sons, he's killing himself."

Aria is nodding. "Exactly."

Cain's forehead furrows. He gets it, and I already see the wheels turn behind his gaze as he processes the information.

"So, that's why he's never killed any of us, even though I swore to Hell he wanted to, and came fucking close some days—he couldn't take us out," Maverick states, excitement in his tone.

I can't believe it myself. Could we really have just found Lucifer's Achilles Heel?

"This explains so much," Cain murmurs to himself mostly. "Along with why he hated us all. He realized he'd weakened himself by making us."

Silence stills the air in the room, and I feel a sense of hope twisting in the pit of my gut. Hope that for the first time in too long, we've found something to our advantage.

Cain turns to the door and glances back at us all. "We're going to the Storm markets now."

CHAPTER FOUR

ARIA

The demons are glued to my side as we stroll up to an innocent looking dry-cleaners shop with a small black umbrella painted above the doorknob. The entrance to the magical Storm's markets.

Three of the demons, I should say. Maverick is still being held in the basement tied up.

I hate to leave him there, especially after he helped me when Sayah went rogue, but Cain, Dorian, and Elias aren't budging on this one. Not even an inch.

I mean, I can understand. He did have a knife to my throat. But he didn't blip me back to Hell when he clearly had the chance. And that has to count for something, right?

And he tore up Joseline's soul contract for no reason that I could see. Besides trying to gain our trust. *My* trust. Knowing she's free from it will help me sleep a bit easier, too.

Still, arguing is pointless against beings who've been around for hundreds of years. They've had much more time to perfect their stubbornness.

We just need to go to the markets, talk to the seer,

Miranda, and get back home, because we have a trip coming up. A trip that secretly scares me, but it is also a necessity. Should be simple enough, I hope.

The door chimes as Dorian holds it open for all of us, but on the other side, the powerful magic has transported us to what looks to be a cornfield in the middle of west bumble-fuck nowhere. As it always is when I'm confronted by the immense magic of this place, I halt in my tracks and stare. There have to be miles and miles of green stalks. In the distance, I can see the many tents and vendor tables that make up the markets.

Shit. Wrong day to wear a skirt and flats. This is what I get for trying to step out of my comfort zone on a regular, non-work day.

"Where in the world are we?" I ask. The door shuts behind us and becomes a random, floating object in the middle of the field. It reminds me of one of the surrealism paintings I saw during my yearly school trip to the museum.

"Looks like farmland as far as the eye can see. Maybe… Kansas?" Dorian replies. "The markets change on every visit."

"Have you ever even been to Kansas?" Elias asks, as we all walk toward the bustling marketplace, pushing tall stalks out of our way with each step. Elias purposefully pulls a handful back for him to walk through and then lets go, so they smack Dorian in the face.

He whacks them away, grunting. "Really? How mature of you."

Elias only snickers.

Cain's eyebrow raises, unamused, but he lets it go.

As we trudge past the many tables and weave in between supernatural patrons of all kinds, shapes, and sizes, we head to the very back where we know Miranda's tent is located. The sound of birds squawking catches my attention, and I drift off toward a booth with cages stacked high, all filled with small black birds. Are they pets?

That's when I see the sign above the vendor's table. *Messenger Birds.*

Hmm… Like the sparrow Joseline sent me, the one with the message of her leaving town?

"Hello, little lady," the kind-faced saleswoman says. "Near or far, if you have to send a message, these birds can do the job easy-peasy."

I don't even need to turn around to know Dorian, Elias, and Cain are approaching behind me. I can feel their nearness through our bond. Not sure how to describe it, but an overwhelming calm rushes over me knowing that they're nearby.

"How does it work?" I ask the woman behind the table. I'm certainly not a witch by any means. I can't conjure anything like Joseline can.

"Just whisper your message to them and the name of the person you want to receive it, and send them off. Of course, the more information the better. Like an address or town name, but I've seen these tiny birds manage it with only a name. Then poof, they're gone." She snaps her fingers for emphasis.

"Poof? What do you mean?"

"They aren't real birds, Aria," Elias explains. "Just a temporary spell meant to carry the message, and once their job is done, they disappear."

"Exactly." The woman nods. "No feeding or messy clean-up necessary."

I peer up at Cain, who's hovering at my side. As if reading my mind, he sighs and says, "You want to send something to your witch friend."

I nod. "I need to know how she's doing."

"I understand." He peeks up at the saleswoman. "We'll grab one on our way out."

"Thank you." I smile.

"Well then, let's get this over with. I don't like that snake being in our home by himself. Who knows if he's gotten out of those chains and is rubbing his balls all over our pillowcases," Dorian says, meaning Maverick, of course.

Elias gives him a look that says, "What the fuck is wrong with you?" but Dorian only shrugs.

"It's what I would do if I were him," he replies to the unasked question.

Elias grimaces. "I'm… going to throw all my sheets in the wash when we get home. For a completely unrelated reason."

He laughs, and together, we make our way toward Miranda's tent.

The first time I'd met her, she'd saved me from that brutish warlock after Cassiel knocked over his potions. But even with her kind gesture, something didn't sit quite right with me. It could've just been that she was a seer and knew things about me before we'd even met. Or maybe it was something else… I'm not sure.

Come to find out, she's also Dorian's ex.

Now, I know I shouldn't care. We all have a past. But for some reason, as we head for her tent made of brightly colored fabric, strung-up lights, and enchanted by magic, jealousy wiggles its way through me.

How will they act once they're in the same room? Will he remember their time together and want a second chance?

They are ridiculous thoughts—I know—but I can't help myself. Or the sickly feeling twisting my stomach.

Or the anger.

It surprises me how fast it surges forward, like the explosion of water after a dam is released. I imagine myself knocking into one of the floating lanterns that light up the inside of her place, and setting the entire thing of fire. With her inside.

The abruptness of my thoughts stun me. I may have wanted to knock someone out—or two—but never kill. Before my trip to Hell and my confrontation with Maverick, it had never even crossed my mind.

This isn't like me.

Is that because… it *isn't* me? Not really?

Sayah.

She's influencing me again.

A gentle hand brushes my arm, and when I glance up, Cain's there staring down at me with worry in his crystal-blue eyes. "Are you okay, Aria?"

I blink, forcing those murderous thoughts away. I just have to be aware of what she's doing to me, and keep my head leveled. Yeah, that's it. I can't let her take over again. She could end up killing someone. Like one of my demons. And I'll be damned if I let that happen. Shadow spirit or not.

In front of Miranda's tent, everyone stops and watches me closely. I realize I haven't answered Cain's question.

"Uh, yeah. I'm fine." I try to wave it away to really sell it being no big deal, but when Cain's eyes narrow, I know he's seeing right through me.

"If you feel like the shadow might rise again—"

"I'm *fine,*" I cut him off, a bit more forcefully than I would've liked. I clear my throat and try to regain myself. "I just want to get this over with. I'm a bit anxious about what's in that diary, you know?"

It's partly true, anyway.

It seems to have worked because Cain nods, pulls back

the tent's curtained opening, and gestures for me to step through.

As we all stroll into the enchanted circular space, we're shocked to see Miranda laying across the sitting area in the middle, made up of giant pillows and blankets and rugs. It's like she's been waiting for us to arrive. And maybe she has, being that she's a seer and all.

She stands and walks over to us with the grace of a cat, with that same confident aloofness that they give off, too. Without so much as acknowledging Dorian, Elias, or me, she strides directly up to Cain. As if he's the only other person in the room with her.

"Oh, Cain. Funny, I was just going to call you." A slow, lecherous grin spreads her lips. The way she looks at him, with hard determination captured in her dark eyes, makes anger weave through me again. But Cain's gaze is focused on everywhere but her, and I tell myself I'm just over-reacting.

"Call?" Dorian interjects.

She turns his way, unamused. "It's a joke, sweetheart."

"Not a very funny one," Elias grumbles. His voice sounds funny through his pinched nose.

"Don't think about it too hard. You might hurt your-self." Then Miranda puts all her attention back on Cain. Holding out her hand, she says, "The diary, please."

He pauses. No one had mentioned Lucifer's diary to her yet, of course.

"Do you want me to decipher it or not?" She waves her waiting hand impatiently. "Hand it over then."

Reaching into his jacket, he pulls out the small black leather book. "And you're sure you can translate it?" he asks.

"Let's hope so, for all your sakes."

"And before you ask about payment," Dorian begins, but doesn't get to finish.

"Payment? Oh, I'll just add it to your running tab." Eyes still locked on Cain, she throws him a wink while running a finger down the pages of the book. Suggestively.

Rage seizes my body. It paralyzes me for a moment. It's not Dorian she's after. It's Cain. And I don't know if that's worse. It's certainly not better.

She opens the book, licks her finger, and starts thumbing through the pages, murmuring to herself. "Hmm… It'll take me some time, but I'm sure I can get a chunk of it done. The important parts."

"Perfect. That's all we need," Dorian replies.

With a flick of her wrist she snaps the book shut. "Now, since we were talking about tabs and payment and what-not, I think it's time to discuss the terms?"

Dorian rolls his eyes. "You finally figured out what you want?"

She snaps her gaze his way, annoyance flaring behind it. "I've always known," she says sharply, "but good things come to those who wait. And now's the time to talk about it."

Cain's as rigid as a statue beside me. It's clear he hadn't expected this part of the conversation yet.

"What are your terms then?" he replies through clenched teeth.

"It's simple really." She turns away and starts walking around the circular room, swinging her hips and pushing past any of the brightly colored drapes in her way. Drawing it out.

Next to me, Cain vibrates with his repressed anger. His blue eyes begin to darken.

Once she gets fully across the room, she stops and turns. "I want Hell, of course."

Elias steps back, as if her words just struck him square in the chest. Dorians bursts out laughing, hysterically, and bends over, bracing himself on a nearby column. I don't know what to think. What does that even mean? She wants Hell. As in, she wants to own it? Rule? Surely she can't be serious.

Like a predator stalking its prey, Miranda never looks away from Cain as she makes her way back to us again. Completely ignoring me and everyone else, she strolls right up to him, presses her breasts against his chest, and tilts her chin up to look at him.

"I want to rule," she whispers, glancing at his mouth. "With you."

My hand shoots out before I can register it, clamping around her throat. The fury hits after, flooding me to the brim and making me squeeze so hard, her eyes bulge.

She stumbles back, and still holding her firmly, I step in front of Cain, watching the way she sputters and gasps for her next breath and loving every second of it. I've about had enough of her trying to make moves on him. Now she says she wants to rule Hell with him? I don't think so.

Cain's mine, bitch. Mine.

No one moves to stop me. Not even when Miranda claws at my arm to try and make me let go. Her long nails drag across my skin, leaving lines of red, some deep enough to draw blood, but I don't care. The stinging is *nothing* compared to the look of pure terror in her eyes.

Me. Little ol' me about to end her pathetic life.

Didn't see *that one coming, did you?*

"We… had a… deal," she manages to croak out.

"Fuck your deal," I snap back.

"She's right, though," Dorian pipes in from behind me. "A demon deal signed in blood. It's unbreakable."

"Can't… kill me…" Miranda wheezes.

"It's in the deal that we can't kill her," Dorian continues to explain.

"Well, I didn't agree to anything, so that doesn't apply to me." The hatred whirling inside me is untamable. Her face is beginning to turn blue, the veins in her eyes more prominent as I crush that snarky attitude right out of her.

"She's got a point there," Elias chimes in.

Perfect.

"Aria." It's Cain. Surprisingly, his voice is calm and it washes over me, easing the tension gripping my muscles. "Let her go."

Wait, he wants me not to kill her? But the contract—

I pause. There's no way he's actually going to give her what she wants, right? That he's going to rule Hell with her?

"Aria," he tries again, still gentle. "This isn't you. It's Sayah."

I glance at him over my shoulder and see the worry on his face. Looking back at Miranda and the desperate look in her eyes, I wonder if he's right this time. Is it really Sayah's darkness seeping into me, or is this my own rage, my own jealousy, finally set free? It feels like my own. It's too hard to tell anymore where Sayah ends and I begin...

And that thought alone has me releasing Miranda. She drops to the ground, clutching her throat and sucking in air.

When I feel Cain's hand rest between my shoulder blades, I jerk away and move towards Elias, near the tent's entrance, my lethal anger still buzzing inside me.

None of the demons move to comfort me again, and this time, I'm thankful. I just want to be left alone.

Looking grave, Cain turns back to Miranda, who's still rubbing her bruised throat and trying to regain her breath.

"Lucifer has the throne, so your side of the deal cannot be fulfilled," he states matter-of-factly.

"Yes, for now." Miranda's voice is scratchy when she replies. "But you have plans to overthrow him, do you not?"

"I may have wanted the throne at some point, but not anymore. It's more important that Lucifer is stripped of his power."

Slowly, and on wobbly legs, she raises to stand. "Ah, that may be true, but as his heir, that'll automatically make you next to wear the crown. And that's where my side of the deal comes in. I want to be at your side. As queen."

In my mind flash images of those red, pointed nails trailing down Cain's bare chest. The two of them wrapped in each other's arms, her head thrown back in ecstasy as he plows his cock into her, over and over. I can hear his grunts of pleasure in my ears.

Rage explodes within me again, driving me forward, wanting to sock her straight in that pretty little face of hers. But Elias's arm juts out, stopping me from moving any further.

"We're obviously not going to let that happen," Elias whispers, mostly to me, but Miranda hears it too because she replies quickly.

"You don't have much of a choice." She throws a glare my way. "That's my payment for helping you find this little wench and for translating Lucifer's diary. That's it."

Everyone looks at Cain, waiting for him to reject it. Lash out. Curse her off. Something. But instead, he grunts, "Very well," and spins on his heel to trudge toward the exit. When he passes me, he doesn't even glance my way, just throws the curtains back and disappears into the busy marketplace again.

I turn to Dorian and Elias. Both of them look just as

confused as I do. Before we leave, I glance at Miranda and find that she's grinning from ear to ear. Our eyes lock and I can see the spark of triumph behind them.

She thinks she's won. She thinks Cain's chosen her, and maybe he has.

But that doesn't mean I'm going to let him go. Not without a fight.

CHAPTER FIVE

CAIN

The ride home is quiet. Tense.

Questions hover in the cramped space between us, but as I suspect, no one is brave enough to speak them aloud. They're all wondering what I'm thinking. How am I going to get out of this one? Honestly, I'm not sure yet.

Miranda may have played innocent in the beginning, but she knew what she'd wanted from me from the start. She wants Lucifer's throne, and she sees being my queen as the only way to get it.

Problem is, I don't want it. Nor do I want anything to do with her.

I glance in the back seat where Aria, Dorian, and Elias are all squeezed in together. Instead of taking her usual spot in the middle, Aria's chosen the one end seat, as far away from me as possible. I suspect that's on purpose. Her irritation toward me is palpable. I saw the betrayal in her eyes when we left Miranda's tent. But I couldn't offer her an answer then. I couldn't give one to any of them. Especially in front of Miranda.

But I am going to figure this out. It's just one more thing to add to my long fucked-up list of things to remedy, but I refuse to be used in someone else's power play. I didn't let my father do it, and I'm certainly not going to let her, even with how clever she *thinks* she is with using our deals against us.

I'll have to speak to Aria once we get home and explain what's to come. After seeing Sayah almost make another appearance today in Storm's markets and how easily Aria almost killed Miranda, I'll have to be careful. She's incredibly fragile now, teetering on the thin edge of control, and the last thing I want to do is be the one to send her hurtling over that cliff and into the abyss.

When the Town Car pulls around our circle driveway and stops in front of the mansion's front door, Aria's the first to get out and march into the house, not even bothering to wait for any of us. As the rest of us watch her go, Dorian turns to me.

"She was kind of scary back there, don't you think?" he mutters, meaning when Aria almost choked the life out of Miranda before our eyes.

"Scary, but incredibly hot," Elias adds with a smirk. "Seeing her take charge like that, go all protective-mode..." He licks his lips, his thoughts clearly traveling somewhere dirty.

But he's not wrong. I was shocked to see her immense speed and strength at first, but then realizing she felt threatened by Miranda and refusing to let her have me—it sent shockwaves of desire through me.

I had to remind myself that it wasn't her, though. It's Sayah. And the shadow's ability to so easily manipulate Aria's thoughts and actions now is disturbing. I'm terrified we'll lose her completely to the monster, and I hate that I don't know how to spot it.

That's why we need Miranda to tell us what's in Lucifer's notes. It's the only thing we have to help us on this matter, so let the seer think she's getting what she wants. For now.

When we enter the house, I see the fluff of Cassiel's tail disappear down the hall toward the library, and if I were to guess, that's where Aria has gone. Either to the library or into the room to visit my brother.

Dorian places the messenger bird he bought for Aria on the way out of Storm's markets on a nearby table before heading upstairs.

"Where are you going?" Elias huffs.

"Shower. I don't know why, but every time I go to those markets, I feel like I have to scrub myself afterwards." He shivers for emphasis. "Filthy place."

"And I think you have some corn stalk in your hair," Elias says, pointing.

"What?" He runs his fingers through it multiple times to check, but of course, there's nothing there. When he realizes Elias is just fucking with him, he glares. "You little shit."

"I may be a lot of things, but *little* isn't one of them."

Shaking my head, I stride after Aria and Cassiel.

"Cain." Elias's call stops me, and I turn. "Are you planning on telling us what that was all about?"

Dorian leans over the banister, eager to hear my answer. But I don't have one for them right now.

"I need to talk to Aria first," I say instead. "Then I'll come find you and we'll discuss what happens next."

"With the Nightwalkers?" Elias asks.

"What about Maverick?" Dorian adds.

"*All* of it," I say through gritted teeth. "We'll discuss it all. But I need to get to Aria first."

Dorian continues up the stairs, while Elias heads for the

kitchen, probably for one of his many midday pre-meals before lunch.

Spinning back around, I head down the hall and pause once I get to the basement door. I'm about to open it to see if she's gone downstairs, when I feel the familiar vibrations of her soul through our link at the other end of the corridor.

She's in the library.

Inside, I find her sitting on the chaise lounge with a law book in hand. The sight of it makes me smile. She really wasted no time.

"You're not going to find anything in there," I say, and gesture to the regular law textbook. "Demon contracts are a lot more complicated than the ones humans sign."

Without looking up, she slams the book closed, gets up, and shoves it back on the shelf, all her movements stiff, jerky, and full of anger. Cassiel pops his head up from his place on the rug, watching as Aria scans the spines for something else to read, before stretching, yawning, and walking out.

"They don't make reference books about Hell dealings. Otherwise everyone would be able to find a way out of them."

Still, she doesn't respond or even look at me.

I move closer. "Aria…"

Nothing. She continues to pull out books and check their covers before putting them back.

I reach for her hand, but she yanks it away, dropping the book she'd been taking out, and whirls on me. "What?" she barks, fury flaming in her eyes.

"Have you heard anything I've said?"

"I have to do *something*," she bites back. "Someone does."

Her words stun me. "What do you mean?"

"I have to do something because you aren't."

"That's not true."

"You're just going to ride off on your black-winged stallion into the hellish sunset with her and never even think about me again."

Stallion? Sunset?

I almost laugh at the absurdity of it all, but when I see the real pain in her expression, I hold back.

As she reaches for another book on the shelf, I snatch her hand. I need to get her attention; I need to tell her how I feel about her. The truth.

When she tries to jerk it away again, I spin her and press it over her head. My body hovers over her, towering over her much smaller frame, and she lets out a little gasp in surprise.

"Let go of me," she says.

"No," I whisper. "I won't."

She grunts in annoyance and tries to tug herself free.

"You need to listen to me," I tell her more forcefully. She keeps squirming and tries to avoid my gaze. I hold her firm. "Aria, listen to me."

"No!"

I remember a time when she feared me. When I would make her quake with both terror and desire. Sometimes, the demon in me misses those days, but as she glares at me with fire in her eyes, the same kind of hunger I'd felt for her then rises within me with even more force. I enjoy the challenge. The push back. The resistance.

I like the game.

Because I always win.

My other hand grabs her by the chin, and I force her to look me in the eye. "Aria, I don't want Miranda."

At that, she stops resisting, and her body sags. The hurt

and betrayal she's been feeling really shine through as she peers up at me, and my heart aches. Does she really think I care nothing for her at all? Have I not made my feelings for her clear enough? I guess not.

This is all still so new to me. What I feel for Aria—what I confessed during the ritual—is something I thought demons could never feel. Something I thought *I* was incapable of feeling. Until she came into our lives.

"I don't want her," I repeat, just to make sure she hears the truth. Really hear it. "I have no desire to either rule Hell or have her as my queen. None."

She's quiet as the words sink in, but in her silence, I find myself rambling on.

"I want you, Aria. You. And only you. I don't know what else I have to do to—"

She kisses me, hard and fast, cutting off my words. I'm momentarily paralyzed as my mind catches up with what's happening, and in those milliseconds, she pushes up on her tiptoes and sweeps her tongue into my mouth to deepen the kiss.

Instinctually, my body presses her harder against the shelves, the need to have her more than this shooting through me like a lightning bolt. The hand that was holding her in place now snakes into her hair, tangling with her curls. I use it to wrench her head back.

Sucking in a sharp breath, her mouth opens and I capture her bottom lip between my teeth.

"Is that all you wanted to hear?" I breathe against her mouth. "That I want you?"

"And only me."

"It's true," I say. I press a kiss on her jaw. "Only you. Forever."

"Then show me."

A growl rumbles up my throat. That's what I want to hear. "Gladly."

Without wasting any more time, I reach up her skirt, find the seam of the nylon stockings between her legs, hook my finger in and yank. The material splits and tears easily down the middle.

No panties?

Perfect.

I'm not surprised to find her already wet and ready for me, and the demon in me loves it even more. Spreading her slick folds, I slip one finger inside her.

"Ahh…" She squirms against me, her mouth still hovering close to mine. Another finger in, and she's panting with need. I pump them into her fast, without remorse, knowing that she loves when I fuck her like this with my fingers. A little prelude of what's next.

And when she comes, I'm going to kiss her, taste her passion and drink down her ecstasy. Then, before she can even catch her breath, I'm going to drive myself into her. Over and over, until she's too weak to move and she's begging me to stop.

Still pressing her against the shelves, I feel her body tensing and her legs trembling, barely able to hold her up anymore.

"Come for me, Aria," I command. "Come for me, and then I'm going to fuck you so hard, you'll never have to question how I feel about you again."

With a small adjustment of my fingers, I find her sweet spot and she instantly comes undone in my arms. Screaming. Shaking. And I watch her lose herself to my touch, knowing deep down, this is what I want for all eternity. Her. No one else.

I withdraw from her and quickly undo my own pants.

She got her hands on them, rushing to pull them off. Seizing her by the thighs, her skirt bunches up and I lift her up to wrap those sexy legs around my waist.

"Cain," she begs, and as always, the sound has my control teetering. Liquid fire shoots through my veins as the demon rises, and my vision sharpens.

As her orgasm rages through her, I push into her tightness, grunting as her muscles clench around me.

Fucking hell, she feels so good.

With her back against the bookshelves, I drive my cock into her. A sweet mixture of pleasure and pain flashes across her face, and the books above us rattle in their place. I bury my face into her neck as she clutches the back of my dress shirt as if she's holding on for dear life. Maybe she is because I'm not slowing. I ram into her with so much force, the walls tremble and books rain down all around us.

I throw up an arm to protect her, and when her legs clamp around my hips, I know she's about to come again. Problem is, I can feel my own climax nearing, and if she reaches her peak, I surely will, too.

I slide myself out of her and set her feet on the ground, immediately winning myself a death glare from her.

I'm about to tell her not to worry—we're not done yet —but she grabs me roughly by the front of my shirt and jerks it down, taking me along with it.

Fuck. She's strong.

Somehow, I'm on my back, the fallen books digging uncomfortably into my spine, with her standing over me and a pleased grin on her face.

My heart pounds. This isn't like her first attempt in the Red Room. She's confident and so incredibly hot when she takes charge. My head's spinning with desire, but as I sit up and try to grab for her, she presses her foot into my chest and shoves me back down.

I may be in trouble. This woman has managed to get me, the first son of Lucifer, on my back. Literally and figuratively.

Emotionally as well.

Just then, she lowers herself on top of me and eases me inside her again. I grit my teeth. "Aria… Fuck…"

"My turn," she says, and I never thought two words could affect me so much. She begins to move up and down, sliding me in and out of her slickness and taking full control. Locking gazes with me, she picks up her pace.

I grip her hips, lifting my own in time to meet her thrust for thrust. The sounds of our bodies slapping together fills the room, and my entire body tightens. I'm not going to be able to hold back any longer if we keep this up.

She fists my shirt as she rides me, and I growl.

"Do you love me, Cain?" she rasps out as we move in perfect time together. She blinks down at me with those long, dark lashes that can hypnotize the strongest man.

"I do."

Like when I said it the first time, during the ritual, there's no hesitance or regret. Only truth. I can't deny it any longer. What I feel for her can't be anything else.

Aria is everything to me. And I'll do whatever it takes to have her by my side.

"I want to hear you say it," she says. "Say it."

My grip tightens on her, and we both speed up to a frantic pace. "I love you, Aria."

Throwing her head back, she screams as her climax sends her soaring. That delicious tingling shoots down my spine. Her muscles are tightening around me in all the right ways, and it's only seconds before I'm coming right along with her, unable to hold back anymore.

Breathing hard and with sweat slicking her brow, she collapses onto my chest. I'm full of so much relief and happiness, despite all the danger surrounding us, that I wrap my arms around her small frame and hold her there against me until everything calms.

We stay like that for a while, quiet and still, just listening to our rapid breaths until they return to a normal pattern.

Aria's voice is soft when she speaks again. "Cain?"

"Yes?"

"Why didn't you let me kill Miranda?" she asks. "It would've freed you from the contract."

Not really what I want to be talking about after some really good sex, but okay.

I sigh. "Because, my love, it wasn't you doing it. I was afraid that if I let you take her life, it'd be something you'd regret for the rest of yours."

"What if you're wrong, Cain? What if it was me all along? What if this rage and darkness I've been feeling isn't Sayah at all? What if it's actually me?"

"It's not. I know you, and that wasn't you."

She glances up at me, eyes big with concern as they search my face. "But do you really? Because I'm starting to think I don't even know myself."

I push myself up onto my elbows, and she pulls back to look at me.

"I do," I say, and brush a loose strand of hair behind her shoulder. "I'll figure another way out of Miranda's deal. I will. There's always a loophole in these contracts in the demon's favor. I just need to find it and exploit it."

Aria seems satisfied with that answer and leans into me again, causing me to lay down once more. She shifts to take the place against my side, settling under my arm, and I can't help but think how perfectly her body fits there.

"Cain?" she calls to me again, her hand resting over my heart.

I glance down at her and give her a small smile. "Yes, Aria."

"I… I love you, too."

CHAPTER SIX

MAVERICK

above me, the ceiling quakes, causing dirt and dust to shower down on me. I snort and shake out my hair, trying to get all of it out of my face and mouth.

I can hear Aria's cries and my brother's grunts as he fucks her brains out one floor above me, and a concoction of anger, jealousy, and hunger ravages through me.

Fuck Cain. He doesn't know how good he has it.

He's been on earth for a century, living it up, building an empire, completely free of Father's psychotic tendencies, when he was supposed to be banished. Punished.

Yet, my other brothers and I were in Hell, doing everything we could just to survive. It doesn't seem fair.

The old support beams above me rattle, the booming of their bodies banging against the wall becoming faster, their moans becoming louder, and I grit my teeth. That should be *me* fucking her. *Me.* I could tame that darkness within her, give her the kind of pleasure she craves. Something that hurts in the best possible way.

But will Cain ever accept me into the life he's made here? Will Aria? That is the ultimate question, now isn't it?

Glancing around the dark room, at the circle of fresh soil and salt around me, I'd say so far the answer to that is no.

I just needed to convince them that I'm willing to be in it for the long haul. *If* they'll have me.

Lucky for Cain, I hate Lucifer more than I hate him. And lucky for Aria, I don't hate her. Yet.

Tugging on my ties, the chains rattle. I yank them a little harder, but with the demon circle dampening my powers, there's no way I'll be able to break out of them. Or blip myself free.

But the downside to these traps is that they're very fragile. Just one little gush of wind or brush of the foot to break the circle…

I scoot myself down and stretch out my legs and arms as far as they can go. Shit. Even pointing my shoes, I'm still too short to reach the edge. Looks like this is about to get painful.

The sounds of sex on the floor above keep on.

Perfect. It'll drown out any noise I make down here.

At least my brother is good for something.

I keep stretching, my muscles straining, burning. But I clench my teeth, embracing the pain, and wait until I hear the audible pop of my shoulders dislocating.

"Fuck!" That shit hurts, but it does the trick. I'm able to slide down far enough for the toe of my shoe to brush away some of the circle's salt and dirt, and instantly, the pressure of the magic suppressing me eases.

I blink and reappear on my feet, the chains and ties off me.

My arms hang lifelessly at my side.

Damn. When was the last time I fed? I can't remember. Maybe when I'd drained that guy who'd been working for Cain, in the Missouri swamps.

That was a long fucking time ago.

That's going to slow down the healing process for sure.

Oh well. At least I'm free.

I stride to the door, but before I can step through, my brother's broad shoulders fill the frame, blocking me. I hadn't even heard his little fuck fest come to an end.

Icy gaze on me, he steps toward me, forcing me to shift backward, further into the room again.

"You're a skillful escape artist, I'll give you that," he says, expression as still as stone.

Out of all of us, it's amazing how much he looks like Father. In facial structure. In presence, down to his hair color. His demon. Both of them radiate dominance and power, command respect and authority, just by walking into a room. While I, being the last of my brothers to be pulled from Lucifer's soul, is almost his opposite. White hair, silver winged demon… The only thing we share is the sin that binds us. Greed—the need to always want *more* and never be satisfied with what we're given.

I look Cain over, noticing his wrinkled and untucked dress shirt with the top buttons missing and mussed hair. My chest pinches with jealousy.

"You didn't need to stop on my account," I say, gesturing to his disheveled state. "Sounded like you were having a hell of a good time up there."

His body tenses. Is he surprised I was able to hear them? Because I'm sure half of Vermont got an earful. They weren't exactly keeping it hush-hush.

"If you're planning on staying here, I suggest you get used to it," he replies.

Get used to it? I want to indulge.

"You're obsessed with her," I say, eyeing him.

Another step toward me. "I love her."

His words strike me like a blow, and I actually stumble backward, almost tripping over my own feet.

Unable to find my voice, I stare at him for a long moment, wondering if maybe I'd misheard him. But no. He'd said it. The "L" word. *Love.*

Hysterical laughter bubbles up my throat. I try to hold it back, but I can't help it; it explodes from me, and I laugh so hard I can't catch my breath. Soon, I'm coughing and hacking and wheezing all at the same time.

"I'm s-sorry, but did you say—" I manage between gasps.

His eyes narrow.

"You're joking!"

But there's not a hint of humor on his face.

I stop abruptly and stand. "You're not joking." Finally, the tugging and pulling of my body starting to heal itself starts. My fingers tingle as feeling returns to them. "But that's impossible."

"There may have been a time when it was, but not anymore," he says.

"But you're—I'm—we're—"

"Demons, yes."

"Lucifer's sons," I reply, my voice rising. "Pulled from his own soul. And we both know that bastard's incapable of feeling anything close to… *that.*"

"We aren't Father," he says, but then eyes me. "At least, I'm not."

"I'm most certainly not that psychopath."

"Which only furthers my point. Who's to say we can't have lives of our own? The way we want to live them. Love who we want…"

I lean back on my heels. I *still* can't believe what he's telling me. My brother had never shown interest in another person, let alone care for them.

Love? Forget it.

"Shit. That must've been some really good sex," I mumble. "Maybe I can take a spin next?"

He's in front of me in a flash, eyes black, veins lining his skin, and wings spread wide. What's left of his shirt hangs torn in half down his arms. He doesn't lay a hand on me though. Only stands over me, a threatening rumble in his throat.

"You stay the fuck away from her," he snarls. His voice is always deeper and thunderous in this state.

I meet his gaze head on. My own demon tries to rear up, not liking being challenged. "What are you going to do, Cain? Huh? Kill me? Go on, do it. Maybe you're more like Father than you think." But as my wings unfurl, pain ricochets through every muscle, paralyzing me, and I'm forced to reel them back in. I can't help it; my body trembles from weakness.

Dammit. I hate having to submit to him, but between the magical drain of the demon circle and my lack of souls recently, I have no other choice.

To my surprise, Cain eases back a little and his inky gaze searches me. "How long has it been since you've eaten?" he asks.

"Who cares?" I snap. More pain bites up my arms as things take their time realigning and connecting.

Stepping back, he opens his mouth to reply, but another voice interjects instead.

"What is this now?" It's Dorian, and he strolls into the room with his usual stupid, confident smirk on his face and wet hair. Like he'd just come from swimming or a shower. "Are we having a pissing contest among brothers? Oh! Maybe we're measuring dicks to see who is bigger?" He starts undoing his skin-tight pants.

"Fuck no. Keep that shit where it belongs," I say.

"You say that because you know I'd win."

"Yeah, yeah. We all know about incubi and the mess that's below the belt."

"It's a two for one special."

I don't even know what to say to that, so I leave it alone and glance at my brother again. He's shaking off his demon, and it snaps back fast and without a fight.

When his wings fold back in, he looks back at my dislocated shoulders and lifeless arms. "You realize you'll have to go back in the circle."

"And you realize that I'll find a way out again, right?" I reply. "I only stayed there as long as I did to show you all I'm obeying your rules and can be trusted."

"Yet you escaped," Cain says blandly.

"He escaped?" Dorian repeats, voice rising in disbelief. "How? The circle—"

"Apparently it wasn't drawn big enough," Cain finishes. He gestures to the spot where I was able to break the dirt with my shoe.

He glances between me and the circle, as if he can't believe I'd found a way out of it. "Well shit."

The sudden *blarrriingggggg* of a cellphone rings, and Cain pulls it out of his pocket, clicks the button, and puts it to his ear with blurring speed.

"Yes," he says into the receiver.

There's a muffled voice on the other end, not loud enough for me to make out. This is where having a hellhound's ear would be handy.

His expression never changes as he listens to the caller and only responds with "Mhm" and "I understand" and "Immediately" before pressing *end* and putting the phone away again.

"Well?" Dorian presses before I can. "What was that all about?"

"Our team has located another relic," he replies. I don't know how he does it, but his face is a mask of stone.

"Wait, isn't that a good thing? Haven't you been looking for the harp's pieces?" I ask.

"Yes, but after your stunt with one of the last ones we went to find, we have to be overly cautious."

Dorian blows out a breath. "You think this could be a set up?"

"From me?" I throw out.

Cain shakes his head. "From Lucifer."

I guess that's possible. He may not be able to get out of Hell easily, but he could always get one of our other brothers to set traps for him. He had recruited me.

"What's our next step then?" Dorian asks.

Cain's silent for a long moment, thinking.

"Elias, Aria, and I will go to Brazil to retrieve the relic," he instructs after some time. "Dorian, you'll stay here and make sure our house, our club, and our city is protected from those Nightwalkers. And from..." He glances my way. "Other unwelcomed guests."

Ouch. Low blow.

"And Nightwalkers are?" I clench and unclench my fists, biting back the pain that still lingers as the healing continues at a slower than normal rate.

"Vampires who're trying to encroach into our territory," my brother explains.

"Shit, you've been busy up here."

"You have no idea," Dorian mumbles, before swinging his attention back to Cain. "So, I have to stay here and babysit is what you're saying."

"I'm trusting you to stay behind."

He sighs. "Fine. I don't know why Elias gets to have all the fun."

As if summoned from thin air, Elias appears at the

door, completely naked, looking a bit frazzled for a hellhound.

Cain steps toward him. "What's wrong?"

Elias's tattoos and scars that mark up his torso are on full display, and blood matts his long hair. His skin ripples across his chest and his muscles bulge as he shakes off what's left of his hellhound form.

"Two more hellhounds stalking our property line," he huffs as he tries to catch his breath. "These fuckers gave me more of a chase."

I may not be able to stand Elias, but the hellhound is the best at what he does. There's a reason why he was moved up and commanding his own legion at an early age. He's a killing machine.

"Congratulations?" Dorian slow claps for him. "Did you come down here just to gloat?"

His head tilts as he tries to remember his purpose for barging in. "No, actually." He turns to Cain. "On my way back, I ran into someone else."

Everyone waits for him to finish.

"Viktor."

Dorian and Cain exchange confused looks.

"Isn't he supposed to be in hiding?" Dorian asks.

"He's in the foyer waiting for you." Elias nods toward Cain. "He wants to discuss the Nightwalker problem. Insists he can't just sit around and wait. He wants revenge."

"I don't blame him," Dorian replies. "So what now? What about the relic?"

Everyone looks to Cain for the final word.

Pulling back his shoulders, he addresses the room. "Everything still carries on as planned. Elias and I will stay here to handle the hellhounds and the vampire problems. Dorian, you and Aria will go to Brazil and follow the search team's directions to find the other part of Azrael's harp."

"I want to go," I pipe in. "I can help."

"Abso-fucking-lutely not," Elias answers before Cain can.

"Not a fucking chance," Dorian adds for good measure.

"I'm useful. I know the way Lucifer plots. If this is another trap, I'll be able to sniff it out before anyone else," I say.

Cain only stares at me, not saying a damn thing. It doesn't help that it's near impossible to guess what he's thinking. He's harder to figure out than Lucifer's book.

"I want a piece of this," I confess. "I want to live on this plane, make this city our own little slice of Hell. But mostly, I want to be free of Father once and for all." I'm hoping I can persuade him that I'm not a threat. At least, not anymore. "It's why I haven't just popped out of here. And you know I've had plenty of opportunities once I broke the circle. But I didn't."

Still, he says nothing. My insides tighten with worry. What if he rejects me? After everything I've done to him, his friends, and Aria, I wouldn't be surprised if he did.

"I stayed. Because this is where I want to be," I go on.

"Fine," he says suddenly.

"Wait, you want him to go?" Dorian croaks out, eyes wide with disbelief. "Why the fuck should *he* go anywhere besides pitched off a cliff."

"I get it. He's joking." Elias barks a laugh. "He's got to be joking."

But not a hint of humor can be found in Cain's expression.

"Cain…" Dorian starts cautiously. "I don't think this is a good idea."

Cain whirls on me suddenly, causing me to leap back.

Fire burns in his eyes. "This is your last and only chance to prove what you say is true, *Brother*." He emphasizes the last word on purpose. "Show us your allegiance and help retrieve the relic so we can get back to Hell and take down our father."

I nod, but inside, I'm buzzing with excitement. "Understood."

Get me the fuck out of this basement.

Then, he starts walking toward the door but stops and places a hand on Dorian's shoulder. "If he steps one inch out of line… kill him."

Dorian glances over at me and grins wide. "With pleasure."

CHAPTER SEVEN

ARIA

The snow cascades outside the Town Car. It's twilight and all the streetlights are on, almost giving the town a wonderland feel with the snow. Except, it's all an illusion. This world is run by supernatural creatures, and the things that go bump in the night are real. I should know—I'm living with three of them.

Three of us are headed to the airport, and I'm not sure any of us are ready for a mission in Brazil, in the Amazon Rainforest, but if one of the relics is there, well then, that's where we'll go.

Dorian sits between Maverick and I, his arm wrapped around my back. There's hardly been talk since we left home, so this is going to be an interesting trip.

"Have you been to the Amazon Rainforests before?" I ask them, mainly to break the silence.

Dorian shakes his head. "It'll be my first time. Though, I have always wanted to go there under different circumstances."

"Doesn't interest me," Maverick states. "There are piranhas and all kinds of shit that want to kill you."

"You're mistaking it for Australia," Dorian corrects him.

"Don't think so. There are insects in the Amazon that crawl up your dick and plant eggs in there."

Dorian stiffens against me, drawing his legs together. My mouth might have dropped open; and that's not something I'd expect from Maverick. Maybe he's a lot more spooked out about the trip than he first let on. Or he's been hanging out with Elias too long.

"Bullshit," Dorian barks.

Maverick shrugs. "I dare you to go for a swim in the water once we get there."

When no one answers, I giggle to myself. "Let's all plan to not go into the water, how does that sound?"

"You should be more worried about the anacondas," Dorian pipes up. "They're man eaters down there."

"Well, lucky for us, we're not men," Maverick answers.

I glance out the window as they continue their chest beating of what creatures they won't be afraid of. I suspect they'd both scream like a girl if they fell into the river.

A police car, its siren blaring, shoots right past us, and I press my face to the window to see what's going on up ahead.

Moments later as we race up the road, a lot of flashing red and blue sirens are clustered near the end of a residential street. It's too dark to fully make out what is going on.

Dorian leans against me, staring outside too. "What's going on?"

"No idea."

In a flash, something dark darts right across the street with the flashing cop cars. Fast enough that those on the road would have missed it.

"Did you see that? What was it?" I ask.

"Looked like a vamp to me," Dorian answers. "Freaking fanged bastards."

"Really? Could be a hellhound," Maverick interjects, his words covering me in chills.

"Why'd you have to say that?" I blurt.

Dorian growls and shoves him into his seat. "Seriously. If we encounter a hellhound, you are responsible for kicking its ass. It's your fault they're here anyway."

"I have no problem with that," he boasts.

Dorian has his phone out and is calling Cain by the looks of it. As the phone rings, he turns to Maverick. "Let's set ground rules for this trip. I'm in charge. You do anything to piss me off or hurt Aria, and I'll finish you. And you don't do anything without asking me permission."

"Dorian," Cain's voice is loud enough for us to hear. "What's wrong?"

"On the edge of downtown, something's gone on. I saw a vampire and the human authorities are involved."

He falls silent, listening, though I can't make out the murmur of Cain's voice.

"Sounds like a plan. Bye." Dorian hangs up, then tucks away his phone.

"What's he going to do?" I ask.

"Him and Ramos are going vampire tracking tonight, starting with that street back there."

Ah, the albino dhampir with the ninja skills. He'll definitely be good in a fight.

"Elias is still hunting down hellhounds on our property?" I ask, and he nods.

The car falls quiet once more, and I'm staring out the window, feeling strangely sad about leaving behind Cain and Elias. Especially after Cain and I confessed our love for each other. I understand why they stayed behind, but I wish they could have joined us as well.

When we turn off on the exit ramp toward the airport, my stomach clenches with excitement and nerves. I have no idea what to expect, and if our past experience of relic hunting is anything to go by, we're in for one hell of a ride.

———

The breeze swishes over my face and through my hair, the air fresh and crisp. We're in Brazil, on the Amazon River, and since we boarded the open vessel I've been hanging practically out from my seat, taking in the surroundings, in awe.

This tropical rainforest is how I might have pictured Eden. Lush green trees and plants, so densely packed together along the river's edges that there is no way of seeing what lays beyond. It explains why there are so many howler monkeys swinging in the branches, unleashing loud whooping barking sounds. It's the only way to move about in this place.

"Everything wants to kill you out here," the boat charter guy had told us. Even traveling with two demons, we agreed not to go off by ourselves and take any chances.

The murky water ripples as we carve our way across the river. The longer we are out here, the longer I'm certain that I don't want to spend too much time in this wilderness.

I turn in my seat to find Maverick and Dorian sitting at the back of the charter boat, talking almost normally. I can only imagine they have quite a history, having both grown up in Hell. Despite missing Elias, it makes more sense that he's not here, or else Maverick would already be pitched into the river. Or out of the airplane.

I completely adore the big hellhound, but his short temper can be problematic in such situations.

I shuffle out of my seat and make my way past the two rows of seats and flop down next to Dorian, our legs touching. We're all wearing long pants and boots to avoid creepy crawlies.

"You guys talking about going for a skinny dip later on?" I glance to the murky water and back at them, laughing.

Neither of them jump at the chance, but only give me a deadpan look.

"I'm only kidding," I say. "How much farther?"

Maverick tells me, "It might be a while."

It should be easy, I keep telling myself. We disembark wherever Dorian gave the driver instructions based on Cain's lead, and I just have to track down the relic, right? Except, we've been on this boat for over two hours, and I have yet to see a break in the thick woodland and foliage to allow anyone to penetrate it.

I lounge back in the seat, Dorian stretches out his arm behind me, and I enjoy the sun beating down on us. There is no cover on the boat, just a few rows of seats and the captain at the front, steering us amid the serpentine channel. And it's just us in the boat. Guess it's not tourist season.

By midday, I lean forward and look across to Dorian and Maverick, both lounging in the seats, their eyes shut, sunbathing like lizards.

"Hey, this is taking a long time, don't you think? What if it takes us just as long to find the relic? I don't fancy spending a night out here, unless there's a hidden five-star hotel behind all this tangled forest."

Dorian pries one eye open. "We aren't spending the night here. It'll be alright." His arm around my middle shuffles me toward him, pressing our sides together. He's scorching hot. It's too much and I'm on my feet, going to the supply of drinks and snacks in the cooler. I grab two bottles of water and toss them at the guys. Dorian catches both, as Maverick hasn't even stirred.

Does he miss Hell so much that being in the sun has rendered him into a sloth?

When Dorian shoves the bottle at him, he groans and straightens in his seat. I guzzle down half my bottle, then grab some of the premade sandwiches, figuring I might as well eat to keep occupied.

On my last bite, the boat starts taking a sharp turn right, and I sway in my seat. We're following the curve of the river, then careening down an adjacent waterway that takes us off the beaten track… or water track I should say.

It's a narrower passage, the trees hanging lower over us, the sun faded.

I glance around at how close the branches are, to the point that I can reach out to touch them, which I resist. I've seen the movie *Anaconda* where they are on a boat like this in the Amazon, and let's just say that beast decides to make the people his meals.

Geez, I've let the guys get into my head.

When we slow down, I raise my head and see that we're pulling into a muddy bank where the forest opens up to a track, a hidden doorway like we're in Narnia.

Nerves dance in my stomach.

"This is it," Maverick calls out as if he's finally woken up.

I'm grabbing my backpack and stuffing a few more bottles of water and snacks into there, figuring it might be a gift in case we meet any locals. The charter guy had told us that a small indigenous tribe lives out in this part of the woods, so I figure I can use food as a bargaining tool if needed.

Once the boat pulls up as close as possible, the driver,

an older man with deeply sun-tanned skin and pitch-black hair, looks our way.

"Two hours," he says, showing us two fingers in case we didn't understand his words. "I will return in two hours; don't be late."

I want to ask him about traveling at nighttime across the river, which unsettles me, but I keep it to myself. Instead, I let Dorian usher me to the edge. He climbs out first, hoping into ankle-deep water, while I'm frantically threading my arms through the backpack.

"I'll carry you," he tells me, and I don't waste a moment, but climb over the edge of the vessel. He swoops me into his arms. We cross the water quickly and the splash of water behind me confirms Maverick is right on our heels.

My feet hit the soft soil, and I feel a heavy heat across my back as if the forest itself is exhaling.

Almost instantly, the three of us are standing by the water's edge, watching the boat glide away, the man apparently scheduled to pick up a group of trekkers from farther down the river and take them to another point.

Once he's out of sight, we all turn to the forest. And it's overwhelming. Everything is enormous, crowded, and there are so many strange noises that I can't tell if it's coming from bugs, birds, or monkeys. Maybe something worse.

"Okay, where to?" Maverick looks at me.

"Now, Aria does her thing," Dorian says, his hand sliding across on my lower back. "We have two hours. So we stay on the track, and we move fast."

Maverick's gaze falls on me. "Aria's...thing?"

Dorian presses his lips together, instantly regretting letting it slip.

Oh well. It's not like him knowing is going to change

anything. If he's truly on our side, then great. And if not, Lucifer wants me anyway, so it doesn't matter.

"I can sense magical objects," I begin, glancing Dorian's way to see if he'll stop me. He doesn't. "Through my toe."

Maverick blinks, as if waiting for something more, but when I don't go on, he bursts out laughing. He clutches his chest, head thrown back, his body shaking from the force of it.

"Okay, okay. It's not *that* funny," I say.

He doesn't stop, and my annoyance grows.

"Hey!" I smack him in the shoulder, and only then does he start to settle down.

Wiping tears from his eyes—yes, actual tears—he says, "Fuck, that was a good one. Hilarious!"

"She's not joking," Dorian pipes in with a straight face.

Maverick glances between us, disbelief still on his face. "I'm sorry but what? You're trying to tell me that your…*toe*…lets you track relics?"

"The darker the magic latched onto them, the better," I reply.

"This is absurd."

"It's how we've been able to find the other harp relics so far," Dorian explains. "It's quite a nifty trick."

"Wow, okay then." Maverick rubs his forehead. "So that's why we brought her on this trip."

My eyes widen. "You thought I shouldn't come?"

"To the wild Amazon? Honestly, no."

Well, that stings, but if I am being honest, this wouldn't be the first place I'd pick to vacation to.

"Can we just start moving?" Dorian smacks his neck. "I'm already getting eaten alive by mosquitos."

"What a wuss." Maverick shakes his head.

I nudge them both forward. "Let's be focused. No bitch fighting."

We make our way into the woods, following the worn track. They close in behind me. Shrubs and greenery spill over into our path, while the ground is littered with dried leaves. I'm scanning the ground to avoid stepping on a snake, while looking around for anything to drop out of the trees.

But I need to calm the hell down before I go into a panic attack as my head swings in every direction, and my breaths are racing.

Sweat drips down my back, and I pull my hair up into a ponytail with the elastic from around my wrist.

We're tracking for a decent half an hour, when the tune of a soft song finds me.

I pause, and Dorian runs right into my back. "Sorry, babe."

"Do you hear that?" I ask, turning on the spot, determining the direction of the sound.

Both of them have their heads raised. "A panther's cry perhaps?" Maverick suggests.

"No, it's a song, almost like a lullaby. You know, the kind made by those wind-up jewelry boxes. It sounds exactly like that."

It's coming from my right, and when I turn in that direction, the song seems to grow louder. Something feather-soft curls in my chest, and suddenly, I'm cutting right across the deluge of plants, stomping on vegetation, needing to find the source of the music.

Someone snatches my arm, strong fingers pausing me in my track. I turn to face a worried Maverick.

"No leaving the path." He tugs me back out of the jungle, and I shake my head, clearing it of the music that seems to haunt me, to call me.

"I think it's the relic," I say, but neither Dorian nor Maverick are forcing me to go chase it down.

"We follow the track and see if it gets stronger as we keep going," Dorian instructs.

Of course, I know they're right, but for a moment there, the determination to go to the song overcame me. Just as it had when I tracked the first relic in the basement of the demons' mansion. If all goes well, we can find it fast and be out of this rainforest.

I scratch my arm for the hundredth time, convinced bugs are eating me alive.

We keep on moving, the shadows growing murkier, the heat intense, and the strangest sounds come out of this forest. Except, my attention homes in on the music that lures me forward with fast steps.

We step around a gigantic tree that has to be a few hundred years old and emerge into an open area free of greenery. The ground is well worn, and further ahead the land opens up to reveal a cluster of homes made of flimsy wood. They sit on stilts, taking them off the ground a decent three feet, the roofs pointed and made of dried leaves and what looks like straw.

"Whoa, we found the tribe," Maverick states, brushing right past me and going in first.

Fine by me. If he wants to be the first to be potentially attacked by trespassing into a tribe's home, then he can be my guest.

Except the stillness sends a shiver up my spine.

"Where is everyone?" I ask Dorian.

"Maybe they abandoned the place."

"Why?"

Dorian takes my hand in his, and he guides me in behind Maverick.

There are no people.

No movement.

Except the music, it's stronger here, and with it a slight

tingle starts at the tip of my toe. "I feel it," I admit. "The relic is close. Let's find it so we get out of here, as it's creepy as hell with no one around."

Unease consumes me with each step, shadows shifting in the woods circling the tribe village.

A sudden blurry figure flashes in my peripheral vision, and I'm not the only one who sees it, as all three of us twist in its direction. All that's left is a rustling of shrubs and palm-like plants, as if someone had indeed burst right past them.

My heart is thundering wondering what it could be.

When a brutal howling sound echoes around us, I flinch. It's quickly followed by more howls, all so savage sounding, like they're declaring war. And we are the enemy.

"Shit, what is that?" I murmur.

Dorian and Maverick close in around me, their backs to me, each scanning the village for anything.

My heart thunders in my chest, and I twist around on the spot, trying to find something, see something. "Are we being hunted?"

Another flash of movement, directly across the open field. And that time the image is clear... a dark tanned man in black shorts, which tells me they have definitely been in contact with people before, is running at full tilt across the land, gripping a long spear over his shoulder.

And just like that, he vanishes into the woods.

"Okay, that was strange right?" I ask.

"Must be a tradition to scare away newcomers," Maverick says. "We need to look as unthreatening as possible."

"Not like we have any weapons on us," I say.

"Shhh," Dorian interrupts.

The music is louder here, my toe's still vibrating, so we

are in the right place. All we need now is to overcome the fearful locals.

"You, shh," Maverick bickers back, and I would roll my eyes if we weren't in danger. Well, that guy had been carrying a weapon, and to them, we entered their territory.

"Let's make an offering to show them we come in peace? My sandwiches."

Dorian and Maverick both scoff at my suggestion in unison.

"Wow, you two have suddenly turned into jerks. What are your ideas?"

But when a sudden explosion of howls comes again, I lift my head to the dozen tribespeople bursting out of the forest.

A small cry slips past my lips, and I'm recoiling.

Terror clings to my lungs. I'm struggling to breathe.

The locals are rushing toward us with weapons ready, except that's when I notice others are running toward one another and clash into a brawl. They're fighting amongst themselves.

Of course, the worst-case scenario comes to mind. Half the group wants us dead and the other doesn't? Please don't let them be cannibals. I don't even know if they exist in this region, but right now I'm too terrified to think straight.

"We fight them," Maverick says, pushing the sleeves of his shirt up.

"No, you can't hurt them. We're the intruders." I'm determined to not be the reason a tribe in the rainforest is eliminated.

I grab the back of his shirt and wrench him backward with me, Dorian by my side.

"She's right. Don't be such a dick, Maverick. You're good at running away, so that's what we do."

Maverick swings toward Dorian, both of them standing toe-to-toe, nostrils flaring, the testosterone off the charts.

But we are in the middle of a battle and men with long spears are coming our way. I can't help but wonder if those sharp tips are dipped in poison.

"Run," I bellow, and turn to run out of there, the buffoons can deal with their own crap if they want to have an argument in the middle of a battle.

But they are on my heels just as quick, breathing heavily.

I can't think where to go, but when I swing back down the track we'd come, it's blocked by two men with spears arguing with one another. Instinct has me swinging in the opposite direction, shoving my way into the shrubland, darting past branches and lofty trees, plants tearing at my pants, but I don't stop, not while the tribesmen are howling with anger right behind us.

CHAPTER EIGHT

ELIAS

With Viktor's unexpected visit to our house, Cain took the evening to discuss the Night-walkers at Purgatory with him. He even brought Ramos for back up, just in case more vamps crashed into the club and wreaked havoc again. And, you know, since I'm busy with my own shit.

I've been left to guard our home. While we wait for Dorian, Maverick, and Aria to return from their trip, I'm responsible for keeping our property hellhound free. Like cockroaches, they're relentless. They'll keep coming until they get their claim. So I'm on pest control duty 24/7. Even been sleeping outside. When I can sleep at all, that is.

I don't mind, though. I was missing the fun of the hunt and chase, and now I got that in spades.

As I trot along the lake's edge, the blood from the last hellhound I'd mangled still damp in my fur, a touch of sulfur rides the passing breeze, and I swing my head in that direction.

Another one. Has to be.

I'm off and sprinting north, through the dense forest

and muddy terrain. It's the dead of winter and the freezing temperatures can't touch me through my thick black fur, but it still nips at my nose. I think of the days when I was still a youngling, taking commands from another, and running all across this plane to find damned souls and bring them back to Hell. It's how I'd originally met Serena. Being a crossroads demon, she was always on Earth to make deals with unsuspecting humans.

Most supernaturals were wise enough to stay away from her kind, but humans? They were easy targets, especially when they got desperate enough. And finding the most pathetic and needy ones was her specialty.

I guess you could say I could've fallen into that category, too. She had played me for a sap. A love-sick puppy.

Like every time I remember Serena's betrayal, my blood runs hot and rage consumes me. Not just for what she did, but for my own stupidity. I speed up my pace, chasing down the scent all hell-beings leave when they first pop into this world, wanting to tear into something. To release these feelings. To taste blood.

I'm closing in, and to my surprise, the creature isn't running away or charging toward me, like most will do once hearing me coming. And I made sure to be noisy on purpose—I like the chase—but from the lack of sound or change in scent, it seems like the hound is staying put. Just waiting for me.

He wants a stand off? Fine. Doesn't bother me any. The cocky ones are usually the ones to die the fastest, and it's not like he can hide from me and try a sneak attack. I've already pinned his location.

He's a sitting duck.

Spotting a shadow in between trees, I leap through the brush and land on the other side, in the middle of a small clearing. And what stands before me isn't a hellhound.

Hell, it isn't even a man. It's a woman.

And not just any woman, either.

Blonde hair styled in an asymmetrical bob, piercing green eyes, leather motorcycle jacket, torn jeans, and a smirk that says, *Yep, it's me…*

Serena?

Speak of the motherfucking devil.

She gives me a little wave. "Hello again, Elias."

It's been so long since I've seen her, I've almost forgotten how smooth and enticing her voice is.

I recall my hound, pushing him back so my human form can step forward. He tries to protest, not ready to be caged, but I can't talk to her in this state. I give him another firm nudge, and he relents, and within seconds, I'm standing on two legs again, with the bitter cold biting into my bare skin.

I stand there for a moment, completely dumbstruck with what to say or do. I haven't seen her in a hundred years—since that night she ripped my heart out and betrayed us. The hound in me is confused, too. With the ritual's bond still linking us, it's not sure whether to kill or sit.

When I finally find my voice again, I decide to just go with the obvious. "What the fuck are you doing here?"

Her gaze roams me over from head to toe, and her green eyes spark when they linger on my groin. I take a step back.

"Believe it or not, I came to check on you," she says, and crosses her arms. "Hell's been buzzing about you three again. Seems you've found something Lucifer deems interesting."

The name "Lucifer" on her lips has my jaw clenching. Of course she would know all about him and his *interests*. She's been working as one of his lackeys to gain his favor.

"Get away from here," I snap. "This is my territory."

She rolls her eyes. "Hounds and their *territory*. What did you do? Pee on all the trees?"

I clench my jaw so hard, pain shoots through my temples.

"So…What have you been doing up here?" she asks. "Missing me?"

"Quite the opposite," I reply.

"Oh, Elias. Don't be like that." She walks over and places a hand on my cheek. I don't know why, but I let her. And when she smiles tenderly at me, my heart begins to race again, like it used to whenever I'd see her. After all this time, after all she's done, there's still a part of me that cares about her.

And I hate it.

Something cold flashes behind her gaze, despite the warm smile lifting her lips. "You've always been such a good boy for me, Elias. So loyal. Loving. Obedient."

I huff. "You've described a dog. A pet."

"And maybe you were like a pet to me," she says with false sweetness. "Maybe I just wanted something to train, something to follow me around."

"I loved you." My entire body is trembling now with the conflicting needs, to either rip her to shreds or fall apart at her feet, warring through me. Her betrayal destroyed me, left a gaping hole in my heart.

Her hand drops from my face. "That was your mistake. Demons aren't capable of love."

I snarl. "Yes they are. We love fiercely. Dangerously. Brutally. With fangs, fur, wings, and claws. With all the darkness in our souls."

"Are you a poet now?" She laughs, and the sound that once brought me joy now grates on my nerves. "You've grown soft, Elias!"

"Fuck you."

"Don't tell me you really believe in that garbage."

"I did." But then Aria's beautiful face rises in my mind, and warmth spreads through me, drowning out some of the pain. "I still do."

"Then you are a fool."

Rage rockets through me, and my beast rears up. Throwing my head back, I roar so loud, the trees quake and nesting birds launch themselves into the air. Her heart is as black as Lucifer's. Why hadn't I seen it sooner? She's incapable of feeling anything besides her own thirst for power.

Serena doesn't even flinch, which only angers me more.

"You won't hurt me. I know you won't," she says smugly.

"Are you sure about that? A lot has changed in the last hundred years." Which is more than true. A lot has changed just within these last few months. Ever since Aria came into our lives.

With a growl rumbling in my chest, I take a giant step toward her. That makes her shift back, and there's actual fear in her eyes. As a crossroads demon, she doesn't have any outstanding powers like incubus or the sin demons do. If I wanted to, I could kill her on this plane. Easily.

And right now, I want to.

"This is your last warning. Leave. Now."

She doesn't move.

Man, this woman is really testing my limits.

I take another threatening step.

She shrinks back. "Fine, I'll go," she says, holding up her hands in surrender. "I think that was enough time anyway."

I lean back onto my heels and stare at her in confusion. "Enough time? For what?"

A howl tears through the night, and icy cold dread

shoots down my spine. That's just not any wolf's howl. It's from my kind. A hellhound.

And it's coming from a mile southeast of here. From the mansion.

Shit.

That's why Serena is here. To distract me long enough to let the hounds reach our home.

Glancing one last time at the woman I once loved, I find her grinning broadly, pleased with herself. But as much as I want to slash that smile off her face, I'm off and running back the way I came, changing into my animal again mid-stride, and then picking up speed once all four paws hit the dirt.

CAIN

In the basement of Purgatory, in one of the meeting rooms, I sit at the long table with Ramos to my right and Viktor taking the seat at the far end. Charlotte's here, too, sitting on the master vampire's lap, and I'd be lying if I said seeing them together doesn't affect me. The way she looks at him with such admiration and love, with her arms wrapped around his neck and her head on his shoulder makes me miss my Aria fiercely. I wish I could have joined her on the trip, but these Nightwalkers are getting too bold for my liking.

"I want to thank you again for keeping my Char safe while I was…indisposed," Viktor says, with his thick accent. "I don't want them alive a second longer, knowing what they did to her."

Of course, after bringing Viktor here and reuniting him with Charlotte, he was furious when he discovered what the Nightwalkers had done to her while he was gone. It had made him even more determined to slaughter them all. And I didn't blame him. If anyone had done that to Aria... well, I wouldn't sleep a wink until I ripped every single one of those bloodsuckers' hearts out with my bare hands.

Love has definitely made me even more crazed. And I wasn't exactly sane to start with.

"I understand," I say. "Charlotte has been with us for a long time. She's like family to us."

"Do you have a plan? Stephan has infiltrated my clan. Turned some of my most loyal men against me. There's no one to trust anymore."

"Stephan is turning everyone and anyone he can to increase his numbers, but as you and I both know, young vamps can only do so much. They're clumsy, sloppy, weak. He has the soldiers but not the army."

Viktor nods.

"We were able to extract some information from the vampires we found in the Queen Anne Townhomes. That's how we discovered who was behind this mess, so my assumption is that these baby vamps aren't exactly loyal to their master yet. If we capture one, we may be able to extract information that could be useful to us," I go on, and glance at Ramos. He's no stranger to our interrogation... practices, having participated in many of them himself. "If we find out where his nest is, or even where they're storing this new drug, Hush, then we can rally our allies and get ready for a full-on attack."

"No survivors," Viktor says, and slams his fist onto the table, making the thing rattle.

"Exactly."

Ramos stands, ready to go. Viktor lets Charlotte down and is raising to his feet when I hold out a hand to stop him.

"We don't want Stephan to know you're still alive," I tell

him. "It may be wiser for you to stay here, enjoy your time with Charlotte. Ramos and I will do the hunting."

His gaze flicks Charlotte's way and a smirk lifts his lips. She winks at him.

"But you will be bringing the vamp here, yes?" he asks.

It doesn't take a genius to know what he's implying. He wants in on the action, and that's something I have no problem allowing.

"For the messy part? Yes."

Darkness slides behind his eyes, and his fangs push past his top lip. "Perfect."

***

Tracking down and capturing one of the Nightwalker vamps is easier than expected. After Dorian's call on their way to the airport, all we had to do was follow the sirens. Ramos and I were able to pick one off in the industrial part of town, right before the highway exit ramp. A man in his mid forties who was scoping the area for new customers.

We dropped him off at Purgatory, and Ramos made him "comfortable" in the basement. Before I left, I told Ramos to do what he must to get him to talk, maybe even invite Viktor to get a few jabs in. As long as they kept him alive, I didn't care much what they did. But with Ramos's more...unique skills, I had no doubt we would be getting an answer fairly soon.

Exhausted, I have Holmes drive me home. As I walk through the front door, I check my phone for any calls or messages, but the screen is blank.

I'm not sure what I expected. Maybe a text from Dorian saying, "Oops. Had to off your brother. Didn't even make it to the airport."

And honestly, I wouldn't be surprised.

Laughing to myself, I look up and stop dead at what's before me. The carpet is torn to shreds, mud and blood paint the walls and floors, and deep scratches mark up the staircase. The entry table—which we had *just* replaced—is splintered in pieces again, the messenger bird's cage we'd bought Aria at the marketplace crushed and empty.

It looks like there's been a wild animal running amok through here. Maybe two.

My stomach tightens into a knot, but before I can call to Elias, he suddenly appears at the top of the second landing, covered in blood and completely naked.

"What happened here?" I snap, glancing into the parlor to see the couches torn up and the books all ripped apart, too. Fuck me. No one better have touched my office.

Elias hurdles himself over the railing, falls the two floors, and hits the ground in a crouch. When he straightens, I see worry etched deep on his brow. Something obviously happened while I was gone.

"Hellhounds," he growls. All the blood, scratches, and wreckage make sense now. "They tore up the entire place. Our rooms. The parlor. The dining room."

"My office?"

"I haven't gotten a chance to see the total damage yet, but so far it looks pretty bad."

It sure does. Especially from where I'm standing. "They must've been looking for Aria."

"Or the relics," he points out, which I hadn't even considered. It's a pretty good assumption though, and more than likely a right one, since Lucifer doesn't want us back in Hell. Send his hounds to bring Aria and the relics back to him.

"Thank fuck Aria wasn't here," he goes on. "That could've been really bad."

I don't even want to think about it. "And the hounds?"

"Dead. All of them."

"How many?"

"Four."

"Four?" Anger prickles up and down my arms. How the fuck did four hellhounds get into our home? It was Elias's job to keep them away. What the hell has he been doing all this time? Hunting rabbits? "And where were you?"

"A mile up north chasing…" He glances away. "…something else."

What is that supposed to mean?

"Cut the crap, Elias. How did four hellhounds get into this house?"

He runs a hand over his face and lets out an exasperated sigh. "Serena," he mutters on the exhale, and I'm unsure I've actually heard him right.

"I'm sorry, but did you say Serena?"

He nods. "The one and only. Yep. She popped up north of here, near our property line, and used the opportunity to distract me so that Lucifer's four mutts could sneak in here and trash the place."

Looks like her loyalties have remained the same. She's still one of Lucifer's groupies. I doubt she ever cared about Elias at all.

"You said you were chasing her… Please don't tell me you fucked her," I say. He may have said he learned his lesson when it came to her, but I don't know. He had fallen for her lies hard before.

He blanches. "What? No!"

"Good."

"I did almost kill her, though."

"I wish you had." I scan the foyer again, taking in all the damage. All our furniture, the walls, stairs, decor… All of it is going to have to be either fixed or replaced. Sighing, I rub the place between my brows where a terrible migraine is brewing. "Please tell me they didn't touch the relics."

"That was the first thing I checked. Still safe in your room."

Relief washes over me. At least there's that.

"And where's the lynx?" I ask, thinking how devastated Aria would be if anything else happened to him.

"Cassiel? Good question. He didn't come out to help when the hounds were here. I just assumed he was hiding under a bed somewhere, like a coward."

"If he's hurt…" I start but Elias is already nodding, understanding where I'm going with this.

"It'll break Aria's heart."

"Exactly."

A crash sounds down the hallway, near the rear of the mansion, and my heart drops. Elias and I stare at each other, the same thought passing between us.

More hellhounds.

Another loud thud, this time like something heavy falling over. A chair?

Not waiting a second more, we rush down the corridor, toward the loud sounds of destruction. We burst into the library to see not a hellhound but Cassiel balancing his massive body on the end of the chaise, surrounded by upturned tables and broken glass. He swats the air where a small black bird circles, just out of reach. The messenger bird.

"Are you shitting me?" Elias snorts. "He's just a giant pussy cat."

He walks over, and when the bird swoops low, he snatches it out of the air with one hand. Cassiel growls at him, and he snarls back, flashing sharp canines. Gingerly, he passes me the bird, which I hold in my enclosed hands. Its wings beat against my palms.

Even though the thing isn't real, the magic is fragile enough to snuff out with the slightest pressure of my closed fists. I think about how bad things could've been today—how close we could've been to losing Aria or the relics only because we glanced away for a millisecond.

There's too much at stake now. Too much riding on us succeeding in this. Not just for us, but for every soul out there.

If Lucifer succeeds in his plan to take down Heaven, well then, he could flex his muscles—one little squeeze of his hands—and all of earth, every human, every supernatural, would be at his mercy.

Crushed.

A day like this one could never happen again. No more slip ups. Because the next one could very well be our last.

CHAPTER NINE

ARIA

I'm running crazily through the Amazon Rainforest, panic squeezing my lungs.

Strong arms grab me around my waist and I'm off my feet in seconds.

I cry out, batting away the hands gripping me, when a familiar voice floats in my ears. "Slow down, Aria." Maverick's breath is warm on my neck, his hold protective. "We've lost the tribe. They're no longer chasing us."

Gasping for air, I twist my head around to find that he's correct. Dorian is behind him, glancing back the way we came too, but we're alone. We are standing in the middle of the rainforest, practically swallowed by the greenery.

Maverick lowers me to my feet, but his arm remains tightly looped around my waist, holding me close.

"Okay, we need to regroup," I say. "What the hell just happened? Did anyone else notice that they were fighting among themselves as well? Perhaps we walked in on a tribe argument?"

"More like a war," Dorian adds. "Those spears are meant to kill."

"Maybe we should have fought them," Maverick says.

"Bad idea," I say. "We need to get back into the village without being attacked to retrieve the relic. It's in there, so attacking them is the opposite of what we need right now." Though, truth be told, the idea of just charging in there and taking the relic hums in the back of my mind too.

"What if they know what we came for?" Dorian asks.

"You're being paranoid," Maverick barks back. "They want Aria for themselves. Did you see any signs of females?"

I want to argue with them, but part of me starts to wonder if both of them are right. I don't even have the logic to reason why, but it feels right. Like these tribespeople are against us somehow.

"Okay, so what's the plan then? We sneak in and track it down?" I'm talking fast, my gaze swinging left and right. I know I'm buzzing on adrenaline, I feel it humming in my veins. I also don't feel completely right, as if something's twisted in my mind and I can't see beyond it. I keep praying it isn't Sayah, except, it feels different and I can't work it out.

"How are we going to do that?" Dorian asks. "They are everywhere and now we've lost our element of surprise."

"Have you gotten sloppy in your hunting since leaving Hell?" Maverick taunts.

"Fuck off. I'll run circles around you."

I rub my temples as the two go at it again, their fuses so short, anything sets them off. I get it, as I feel that way too, like I want to scream. And the realization comes to me fast that there's another element at play here that's influencing us.

Instead, I take a deep inhale, pushing aside the storm inside me, and place a hand on each of the guys' arms.

"Enough. Don't you feel it? Something's in the air. It

makes us all angry and paranoid. It has to be what's affecting the tribesmen as well."

They look at me, neither responding right away, like my words take a bit to filter through the fog in their thoughts.

Dorian nods first and reaches over to take my hand in his. "I think you're right. We gotta stay focused."

Maverick's heaving for breath, his gaze on where Dorian holds me, where his thumb strokes the inside of my wrist.

"I know what this is," Maverick mutters. "You just want Aria for yourself and want to separate us, don't you?" He shoves a hand into Dorian's chest, sending him back a few steps.

Before I can even find the strength to put him in his place, Dorian releases me and leaps at Maverick. They both hit the ground and are rolling around like madmen, punching and fighting.

"Seriously, are you idiots? There are snakes, venomous spiders, fire ants, and so much more crawling all over the place. Get the hell up."

Not that they are listening to me, and I'm convinced at this rate, we will end up spending the night in the woods, then we'll die after being swarmed by all the deadly insects in this place. And eaten alive.

I find a stick on the ground and grab it before poking the two guys in the back and legs, who seem to be on a different level of existence. I huff with frustration, then pull out a bottle of water from my backpack and splash it all over them.

Their growls and attention swing my way, that has done the trick.

"Can you two stop fucking around and focus for two seconds?"

I feel the sting of my shoulder blades burrowing into my muscles at how tense they're making me. Realization resigning in their eyes, the duo climb to their feet, brushing off the debris from their clothes and hair. The blood from their split lips and cuts from their punches will heal soon enough I guess, but I don't care right now as I'm seconds from hitting them myself.

"We are not the enemy," I implore them.

They nod in unison, when I catch movement over Maverick's shoulder.

My heart nearly stops at the sight of the world's biggest centipede crawling up and over his shoulder, and holy shit, it's long and fat. I'm sure I've read these things are venomous and eat snakes.

"Maverick, whatever you do, don't move," I say.

Dorian rears back from him instantly, and of course Maverick does the opposite.

He's shifting around, moving. "What is it?"

The centipede is scrambling down his chest, making its way between the buttons of his shirt. Maverick might have screeched as he flicked the thing, which then comes flying towards Dorian and I.

I scream and throw myself out of the way, while Dorian catches the thing like he's superman and tosses it into the woods. He shakes his head at us. "Babies."

"I wasn't scared," Maverick says, trying to look over his shoulders for more bugs, turning on the spot like a dog attempting to catch his tail.

"Well, I sure as heck was. New rule. Anyone gets a creature on them, don't freaking fling it at me, understand?"

We're all just standing there, I'm flustered as fuck, but I need to calm down.

"Let's set a plan," Dorian begins, his voice semi-normal, and please let it remain that way. "We go in calmly, maybe offer them your sandwiches, and I will use my mojo to reassure them we are safe. As I do that, you and Maverick go and collect the relic."

I nod because I don't see how else we can do this.

"Alright, I'm ready for this. How much time do we have until the boat comes back?" Maverick asks.

Dorian pulls out my phone and gasps. "Shit, forty minutes. How the hell did we lose so much time?"

"We gotta do this fast then," I say.

"And please, fight the urge to be paranoid and fight," I instruct them, to which they both agree, though proof will be in the pudding I guess.

We make our way back through the dense woodland, and I have no idea how we came so far and hadn't been bitten by something. Now that we're moving closer to the path, everything catches my attention, from the bright green snake curled up in a branch, the tarantula with a bird in its mouth, the bugs…I have never seen so many insects in my life. I'm surprised anyone can live here.

Dorian pauses as we reach the edge of the track, and farther down to our right lays the opening into the village. Unlike last time, the dozen men are now standing around, arguing in a language I don't understand, two are beating each other up.

"Hand over the sandwiches and water," Dorian orders. "Once I've got their attention, you two sneak around the back and do your thing."

"Deal," Maverick confirms, and he's eyes are on me with a ravenous look that sort of scares and turns me on. Why is he so weird sometimes?

Dorian grabs hold of the offerings and he takes off toward the village in a split second. Upon reaching the flat land, he slows and puts his hands in the air, with the food in his grip, I guess trying to look as harmless as possible.

Which might be hard, considering the locals are lucky if they reach his chest in height, and are nowhere near as broad as him.

They turn on him, their spears pointed, but he doesn't flinch or back away. Instead, he talks to them. It's too far to hear them, but part of me swears he's speaking a combination of English and Portuguese. I lean forward, needing to hear his words, know what he's saying. For all I know, he could be ratting us out, telling them exactly where we are, so he can grab the relic first and look like the hero in all of this.

Maverick's in my ear, his hands on my waist, distracting me. "You ready to do this?" he whispers.

I turn my head to meet his gaze, and there's something almost obsessive in his eyes, like he's been waiting for the moment to have me all to himself. Of course, I might be imagining it all, as I still feel the heated call of the relic, the faint hum of the song, all while thoughts of paranoia swarm my mind like gnats.

It's almost like I'm suffocating on these overwhelming feelings.

Maverick grabs my hand, and we run in a roundabout trek around the village to avoid being seen. I can't even think about the fact that we're moving so quickly through a forest filled with all kinds of creatures, and I'm pretty certain this is the wrong thing to do.

I mean, sure Maverick doesn't care since he's a demon and things out there can't kill him, even if he did freak out over a centipede.

Branches swipe across my face, my hair caught in the plants we shove past, and I'm getting tangled in vines. Maverick is having none of it and like a knight in shining armor, is ripping at the plants attempting to wrap themselves around me.

"Do you want me to carry you?" he asks, sincerely.

While I entertained the notion, I doubt that would help our cause in moving swiftly, or from having things touch me. That is impossible.

"I'm fine," I whisper. "Let's just move quickly."

Maverick is next to me as we make haste.

"This jungle reminds me of the hunting grounds back home. It's fuming hot, plants and vines everywhere, and filled with monsters. Cain and I would go hunting there long ago," he whispers.

I never got the impression from Cain that he did much with his brothers, but then again, they've been around for an insane amount of time, so it would make sense that they had.

"What happened between you two?" I ask quietly as we push past the foliage.

"Time. Hell drama. Lucifer. Thing about my father is that he's a jealous bastard. When any of his sons got along, he saw it as a threat and drove them apart with lies. Because, you see, if any of us grew close, it might mean we could conspire against him."

"He's a psychopath." Just hearing the stories made me loathe Lucifer even more, which is hard considering I already want to see him dead.

"And so much more," Maverick answers.

Trampling onward, we soon find ourselves in the woods facing the rear of the huts. With no one in sight, Maverick and I move out silently, and sprint across the open ground to hide behind one of the homes. Our backs press to the huts, my heart pounding in my ears. His side presses so close to mine that I feel the heat he radiates like a furnace.

The hum of the song from earlier grows in volume in

my ears. My toe is also buzzing uncontrollably in my boot. "The relic is near."

From our position, Dorian's voice reaches us from where he stands in the main village area.

"I am like a god," he says to the locals, in English this time. "The gods you pray to, that is me."

I roll my eyes while Maverick makes a fake choking sound. He leans in, whispering, "I just want to go out there and knock him flat to the ground. Then we'll see who the god is."

"Don't you dare," I hiss, snatching his arm, though I can't deny that hearing Dorian bragging does have my hackles rising.

Focus on the relic, I repeat to myself.

Maverick nods, except I don't believe him.

Not wasting another moment, I drag him around the curve of the hut we're near. I peer out from the corner and find the tribesmen all looking up at Dorian as if believing his words. There are no other people around.

Where are the women and children?

I can't make out what Dorian is saying, but a man with facial markings stands before him, his hand weaving up and down as if describing a wave or a snake or hell knows what. Then he points to the sky. They are still talking about gods is my bet, maybe challenging Dorian.

Maverick is pressed up against me, his growl rolling through his chest, vibrating against my back. When I look at him over my shoulder, his eyes are locked on Dorian and the men. He's like a territorial wolf, ready to attack his prey.

"What's the bet, he's going to sell us out? I think it's just us two from here," he whispers. "We get the relic and leave him behind."

For a moment, I consider his words, when I catch myself, and scold myself for even thinking of such a thing.

"Shut the hell up and pull yourself together." I swear, we need as much distance from this relic as possible because it's the only reason to explain why I feel like I've got a split personality all of a sudden, except for the fact that we have to find it first and take it with us back home.

Maverick's hands are on my ass and he squeezes it. I flinch and turn, before shoving a hand to his throat. "What the hell are you doing?" I hiss.

But his eyes are milky, and he's not himself. Just like back in the woods, he's losing his mind fast.

Crap. I shove him to the back of the hut, and then slap him hard across the face. Yeah a bit over the top, but hell, I can't have him go haywire. "Pull your shit together."

Fire burns in his eyes, and next thing I know, he's throwing himself at me, and our mouths clash. It's explosive and scorching and so fucking hot that I forget myself. That hungry, devious side of me screams for him, to bring him over to my side, so if Dorian does turn against him, we are stronger together. I kiss him back with desperation, loving the way he tastes, the way he holds me like nothing can tear us apart.

Desire sparks within me, an arousal I've desperately held for Maverick whether I want to admit it or not, I crave him insanely.

I want this…I want him…I want him to have all of me.

He groans against me, his body pinning me to the back of the hut, his erection between us. His hands are on my breasts, squeezing, and he swallows my moans. I wrap a leg around his hip, practically climbing him like a tree, every inch of me begging him to claim me this very moment.

I whimper as his hand slides between my thighs, teasing

me as he slowly drags his fingers over my aching pussy, only the fabric of my pants between us.

"Fuck," he growls in my mouth. "I'm going to taste you."

There's a sudden explosion of Dorian's laughter in the distance that breaks us apart, and we're both gasping for air.

Maverick's eyes cut toward the front of the hut where Dorian is still bragging. He snarls, fury morphing his expression, and before I can even clear the fog from my head and remind myself we're derailing and failing badly, he darts between two homes, directly for Dorian.

"Shit!"

CHAPTER TEN

ARIA

'm gasping for air myself, stumbling to find my footing after Maverick's kiss…it left me completely destroyed. And as dumb as it sounds, I want more.

Except, my head isn't right, and I fear I'm being delusional.

Maverick and Dorian are falling apart around me, and I'm not doing any better. We're all going to kill each other, I feel it, and that's if the natives don't do it first.

"Focus, Aria. What are you here for, again?" I'm rocking on my feet. "Relic. Hell, we need to find the relic in this village, except, we are in so much trouble."

The sound of Maverick's voice booms along with Dorians from in front of the huts, but I can't make out their words.

So, I choose to leave them behind and move quickly while I have a fraction of my brain in working order. The sting of rejection that he left me, that he will now partner up with Dorian against me flares, but I fight the jealousy, the paranoia.

Focus. Focus. Focus.

My buzzing toe brings me to a hut right at the end of the village. The building is larger than the others, with a pointier roof.

I hurry up the creaky steps that resemble a small ladder to reach the front porch, when I notice none of the men are even remotely looking my way. I do catch Maverick and Dorian in an argument, their hands thrown in the air, their chests puffed out. Seriously, I can't even try to make sense of anything when my insides feel twisted like I've been morphed into a pretzel.

The doorway to the hut is dark and covered by hanging strips of long grass.

I know this is the right place. My toe is going berserk, the song wailing in my ears, and on the inside my chest is on fire.

With soft steps, I part the grass doorway, then slide inside. That's all this hut is, just one huge room. There are close to twenty people in here already, all women and children by the looks of it, but they are on their knees and bowing forward, murmuring things I don't comprehend. They are all facing the front of the room, seeming to be worshipping a small, golden statue positioned on a wooden pedestal.

I blink through the darkness, waiting for my eyes to adjust from the bright light outside to see things clearer.

Without a shadow of doubt, I know instantly that the golden object they are worshipping is the relic. It doesn't take an expert to work out that thing is affecting these people. To the point that they consider it godly.

Sticking to the wall, I inch forward to get a better view of the item, my pulse racing.

How the heck do I get that thing out of here, anyway? I doubt they'll let me skip away with their god under my arm. Maybe I ought to bring Dorian in here so he can claim to be their god instead. While I had mocked him, it may not be such a bad idea.

On the bright side, the more I shuffle up in slow motion, the clearer the object comes into view. I'm staring at a golden snake coiled in on itself with its diamond-shaped head sticking out from the middle with the brightest emerald eyes. It's beautiful for sure. Where in the world did these people find the relic anyway?

I shift to turn around, when the floorboard creaks under me.

Panic freezes me on the spot, and everyone's head snaps up, their eyes on me. I might just pass out. Their looks are confused, and who could blame them? They are praying and just found a completely strange, city person in their place of worship.

"Hi," I say stupidly, while awkwardly waving my hand.

But my chance to make a bigger fool of myself is stolen by the sudden explosive sound of shouting coming from outside. I flinch in my boots, and even the women and children are up on their feet, scrambling to the door, pouring outside in a flash flood.

I'm swaying on my feet, my gaze swinging from them exiting to the relic they've left completely abandoned. Every inch of me is trembling, but there's no time to waste. I run across the room and grab the golden snake, which is the size of a small chihuahua, and won't fit in any of my pockets, but holy shit, it weighs a ton. It must be made of pure gold because my arms are about to break off.

Shuffling off my bag from my shoulders, I unzip it and shove the snake in there, except when I drop it in, it falls all the way through the base, tearing a hole in the fabric of my bag.

Plonk.

The relic hits the floorboards.

Oh, fuck off!

I'm seething with anger. Seeing I have nothing of real value in the bag, I dump it and pick up the statue then glance around, but there's nothing else in the room for me to use to carry it. I dart right outside onto the wooden veranda. All the women and children are down in the center of the village with the men, and they're surrounding something…

I step to the end of the veranda and I gasp at the sight.

Dorian and Maverick are each tied up to a thick branch at their backs, and the men are building a mountain of broken branches at their feet. They're going to burn them? Why the fuck are they just staying there, shouting at each other, still arguing?

Carefully, I step down the ladder while juggling the golden snake that keeps threatening to slip out of my grasp.

I have half a mind to just leave them behind because for all I know, they tried to tell the locals about me stealing the relic which caused them to be tied up in the first place.

The snake hums in my arms in tune with the lullaby in my ear, while the fire of paranoia bubbles in my chest.

Leave them, that's what I should do.

A sudden loud honk blares in the distance, and the familiar sound cuts through my thoughts.

The boat. Oh, shit.

The charter guy has returned, and there is no way in the world that I am being left behind in this place to go mad.

I rush right past the cluster of people seeming to cheer their newly captured victims. Once I'm closer to the path that brought us to the village and against my better judgment, I unleash a loud whistle, gaining everyone's attention.

Seconds are all it takes and all eyes are on me.

The tribesmen instantly see what's in my arms and swing in my direction, their spears pointed at me, promising death.

"Pare," I call out, one of only two words I know in Portugese. One being stop, and the other is cócegas, meaning tickle, and that isn't going to work now, is it. Joseline had taught me a few of the words she'd learned from taking language at school and those were all that stuck with me.

Raising the golden snake over my head as if to show I'll throw it and break it, I realize what a terrible mistake that is. My arms are trembling horribly.

"Pare," I yell again, the tribespeople pausing while the women and children have fallen to their knees in my direction praying to the snake. My heart goes out to these poor people, fooled by the magic of this object. Just like Dorian and Maverick, seemingly made to forget that they are freaking demons and mere rope can't hold them captive.

They are both looking at me strangely, like they are trying to work out what I'm doing.

"The boat is here, free yourself or I'm leaving without you," I yell at them.

As if my words actually ring some common sense in their relic-influenced brains, they writhe and thrust against their restraints. They break out of them like the Hulk, and those around them back away. Smart move.

"Please, we need to leave now," I insist, already recoiling, but the few tribal men in front of me haven't taken their attention off the snake in my hands. I lower it because my muscles are screaming and cradle it against my chest instead.

Dorian is shaking his head, and I see the same battle across Maverick's face.

"Focus," I call out. "We got the relic, and we need to go."

When one of the spear-wielding men turns to Dorian, screaming for him to get back, he moves as swiftly as the wind, snatching the weapon from the man's grip and snapping it in half over his knee.

And well, let's just say, that has the rest of the men swinging in his direction with aggressive stances and war cries on their lips.

But when another honk of the boat comes, panic digs its claws into me.

"Run," Maverick says. "Get to the boat, and don't you dare leave without us."

I spin on my heels and clumsily run down the dirt track through the woods the way we came. The relic is a bitch to carry, but when I glance back, there are half a dozen women chasing after me, their grassy dresses flap in every direction, revealing they are completely naked underneath.

Except, it's their panic-stricken expressions that worry me. They'll do anything to get back their god, so I run faster. The way back seems so much farther than I remember, and it feels like I'm running forever.

My lungs burn, my arms are on fire, and my heart is drumming.

The boat soon comes into view, and he's already starting to pull away from the shore.

"Wait!" I scream. "Please wait, I'm here. We're coming."

The driver's head turns in my direction, and he must see the mob on my heels as his eyes widen to the size of orbs.

Everything in me is thrumming, the shudder in my chest unstoppable.

Our boat driver has hopped out of the boat and is coming right toward me, grasping a gun. Next thing, he points it into the sky and shoots.

The sound is ear-piercing, my ears ringing louder than the relics' song. I hunch forward and dart right past him, taking a look behind me.

Those chasing me have ceased chasing me, but they aren't retreating. They are staring at me taking what they believe belongs to them. I hate doing this, the pain painted on their face leaves me feeling like shit. But this relic isn't their god, or anyone's, and if left with them, how long before they turn on one another?

Once I reach the water's edge, I spot Dorian and Maverick sprinting toward us so fast, the women barely notice them zipping past. They're by my side in seconds, and our driver is rushing to the boat.

"Get in," he yells at us. "I don't know what you did, but I don't want to kill anyone today."

I gasp for air, breaths see-sawing in and out of my chest. My gaze swings from Maverick to Dorian. "What do we do? This relic seems to have a large radius. We can't take this back through the city or even on the boat for long before it starts influencing the driver."

"Cover it with soil," Maverick suggests. "The earth should safeguard its power, even if for a bit."

"How can you be sure?" I ask, doing exactly what he says regardless. The soil from the water is muddy, and I use it to frantically coat as much mud on the snake as possible, covering its eyes, and in that exact moment, a sense of heaviness slips off my shoulders.

"Do you feel that?" I say, glancing up at the men.

"It's done." Maverick tears off his shirt, revealing a sculpted chest that has me staring at him a bit too long, and he wraps the relic in it.

Dorian snatches me into his arms and I'm on the boat in seconds. We all are, standing there, filthy, breathing heavily, and terror leaching through me at how badly that could have really turned out. The tribespeople crowd near to watch us leave, and I wish them all the best to find happiness once more from the demonic relic that only brought chaos to their doorsteps.

"I'm not even going to ask," the driver says, steering us out of the tight channel and onto the main Amazon River, back the way we'd come.

"Best you don't," Dorian says.

The three of us are sitting in the back seat, and I'm stunned at what we just went through. "For the next relic, I vote Elias and Cain go to fetch it without us," I suggest.

"Fuck yes," Maverick answers. "I still can't make sense of the things I was feeling back there, you know. I mean, to be honest, they're still lingering in the back of my head like a cobweb of that angry, possessive sensation, but I completely lost control in the village."

"Yes, you both did."

Maverick arches an eyebrow, his hair unruly and dirt covers his cheeks. "Says the girl who kissed me like she might rip off my clothes despite the danger."

My mouth drops open. "Excuse me, you attacked me."

"Wait up," Dorian says, his voice deepening. "You two kissed while I was trying to save our asses? And since when is there kissing going on between you?" His hands are on me, and he tugs me against him possessively, which I completely adore.

Maverick bursts out laughing. "Is that the time you were telling everyone you were a god?"

I can't hold it back and I'm giggling at him. "That part was hilarious, not to mention both of you letting yourselves get tied up like roast chickens. What the hell did you two do?"

Dorian cuts Maverick a sharp look. "This idiot levitated himself off the ground."

"I had them convinced until you lunged at me."

I'm still laughing, collapsed back into the seat, enjoying the cool breeze, never wanting to do that again. Maybe I'm laughing so much because of the serious danger we were in. "You two lost control big time."

"No one is to ever talk about what happened here, deal?" Dorian asks, his wrists still raw and pink from where he'd been tied up.

"Deal," Maverick states, and now both of them are glaring my way.

"Elias would love to hear how you both almost became kebabs."

When their glares only intensify, I huff. "Chill out, I won't say a word. I swear it."

"Good," Dorian says. "Now, I have an important question for you."

"Yeah, and what's that?" I ask.

"Who's the better kisser between us? It's me isn't it?"

Maverick barks out a forceful laugh, and it seems the relic isn't fully out of their system.

"That's something I'll never tell." I'd rather tease them and not cause competition because, before I know it, this will filter back to Elias and he will demand it's him. That's what happens when dealing with so many egos.

I laugh and kick back, smiling, because for the past two hours, it felt as though I'd been run through a meat grinder, and now I just want to catch my breath. And if these two don't stop staring at me like I'm some kind of candy, I might very well have to announce that I pick neither as my ideal kisser.

CHAPTER ELEVEN

ARIA

The cab driver comes to a quick halt halfway down the driveway of our mansion. There are half a dozen trucks parked in front of us, and then there are men in brown uniforms everywhere carrying boxes and furniture into the house. Is that a couch?

"What's going on?" I lean forward from the back seat. "Did Cain and Elias decide to move out while we were gone?"

Maverick laughs. "I wouldn't put it past them."

"They wouldn't." I'm already climbing out of the cab, worry burrowing through me. I hurry across the snow-covered grounds, the cold biting into my flesh, mostly because I left my coat in the cab. But I need to know what is going on, to make sure Cain and Elias are alright.

I rush up the front steps and Elias pulls open the door at the same time that I reach for the handle.

"Aria!" His eyes widen, and he's got me in his arms before I can even say hi. I'm wrapped in his strong arms, our mouths finding each other. The kiss is hungry but short as he has me on my feet in seconds. "We had no idea you were back already. No one contacted us. How did it go?"

"Yeah, Dorian's phone went dead back in Brazil, and it's not like Maverick or I have one, but the mission was a success." I grin. "But is there something we should know?" I glance at the trucks behind me. Add to that, the hallway is barren of furniture, the walls sport gaps in them, and someone is plastering and filling as we speak. "Was there a war in here?"

"Excuse me," a man says from behind me, and Elias takes my hands, drawing me out of the doorway. Two workmen shuffle through the double doors carrying a bed.

"Close to it," Elias says. "We've had a hellhound incident. Fucking furballs broke in and destroyed the place, searching for you or the relics. Probably both."

"Shit! Did you and Cain get injured?"

He shakes his head. "Boss man is in his office setting things up after the hounds tore it apart. He's pissed. But I told him it's the perfect chance to redecorate the mansion with new furniture." He's talking fast...the nervous kind. The attack rattled him whether he tries to put on a brave face or not. We definitely need to trade war stories once we settle down.

But my head is too blurred to think logically, when my thoughts fly to what would have happened if I'd been here at the time of the attack. Then panic strikes.

"Crap! Cassiel? Please tell me he's okay?"

"He's in your room, little rabbit. Slept during the whole ordeal and not a whisker was harmed."

I'm already darting up the stairs to my room, needing to see him for myself. Passing more furniture deliverers, I sprint right into my room to find it empty. Everything is gone.

Except for Cassiel, who sits on his belly in the middle of

the room, his tail swishing from side to side, his eyes glued on the small cage with the magical messenger bird Cain had bought for me from the Storm markets.

I dart over to him and loop my arms around his neck, but he doesn't even look my way. "Did you even miss me?" I kiss the top of his head and pull back on my heels, scratching his back, which he loves. "It seems I missed quite the craziness here. But I'm super glad you, Cain, and Elias are all safe. That's what matters."

"Fascinating. The cat comes before me?" Cain's deep voice says from the doorway behind me.

A smile curls my lips, and my heart is in my throat. I'm on my feet, flying in his direction. I crash into him and he's stumbling back into the hallway, not expecting me to come at him so fast. He's got me in his arms, my legs curled around his waist, and we're kissing. I feel dirty at how quickly I jump him, when a workman can walk in on us at any moment. But in truth, I couldn't care less when I've been desperate to be back home with my men.

Cain's hands are on my ass, squeezing.

"I've missed you," I whisper against his lips as he turns around and has me pinned to the wall, pressing into me with his hard body.

I whimper when his finger slides to the fire between my legs, his forehead against mine, and his breathing heavy. "I want to strip you down now, spread your legs, and fuck you."

His breath is on my face, and I'm moaning against him, a shiver of excitement racing over my body.

He gently kisses me again, finding my tongue and sucking on it. I rub my hips against his erection pressing between my thighs, gasping with pleasure.

His teeth nibble on my lower lip, pulling it, the intensity in his eyes overcome with desire. "You make me so hard," he growls, pushing his hips against me, the hunger in his eyes deepening.

I wrap my arms around his neck. "So, what are you going to do about it?" I tease, when he slides a hand down between our bodies and pushes under the band of my jeans and underwear.

He grins wickedly, and I moan as he slides two fingers into me, curling them to find that exact spot that drives me insane.

"Oh, hell." My hips rock to meet his thrusts, our kisses wild and chaotic, matching the racing adrenaline bursting inside me.

"Is this what you had in mind?" he growls, and captures my lips again while he keeps fingering me ferociously.

I shiver against him, completely falling apart at his touch, writhing as he drags his mouth down to my neck where he licks me. "I love how you taste, how you smell. I never want you gone from me again for so long. Never."

His movements are aggressive, fast, and I'm drowning in arousal. I'm clawing his shoulders to hold on as I've lost all ability to control my body. Cain owns me, he does as he pleases, and I just moan, losing grip on reality.

Rocking back and forth on his fingers, his teeth find the sweet flesh just above my collarbone, and the moment he bites down, I scream from the orgasm that tears through me.

Cain never ceases his fingering, his biting, until I beg for mercy.

His eyes are completely black when he looks up at me, and I see that he lost himself too, and I fucking love that about him. With a blink, his eyes are back to normal, then he takes his hand out of my pants.

"I'm guessing you missed me too?" I laugh and get to my feet, my knees wobbly at first.

"You have no idea."

Only then do I realize we've had an unexpected observer.

One of the delivery men stood at the end of the hall near the staircase, his mouth and eyes wide open, and the box he was carrying lay discarded by his feet.

"Leave," Cain growls at the man, who flinches and scrambles down the steps. Then he turns to me. "I never asked. How did the trip go?"

"We got the relic is all that matters, and Dorian thinks it's the intestines since it resembles a snake."

He's nodding, smiling with that perfect grin. "Should I ask what that means?"

"Best you don't."

His phone rings from his pocket, drawing his attention from me, and I want to toss the thing out the window. I've missed him and Elias like crazy and I want nothing more than to be in their arms.

Cain collects the phone and looks at the screen, his brow pinching. "I've got to take this. I'll be back though. I want to hear everything." He hurries down the hallway and downstairs, and I enter my room where I find Cassiel, still obsessed with the bird. My breaths are still racing from how intense things got there, but I'm not surprised in the slightest. My relationship with the demons in my life has taken on a life of its own.

When a knock comes at the door, I'm greeted by two delivery guys carrying what looks like my new bed. I know instantly that I need to get out of their way.

"I'll let you guys set up, I'm heading out," I tell them, then rush over to collect the small cage with the bird. Cassiel instantly rushes after me, sniffing at the little black sparrow. I don't stop until we're in the backyard. I sit on the porch steps and stare out into the woods in the distance. Cassiel plonks down beside me while I cradle the cage in my lap.

The little creature looks real with the little chirps it makes, even its eyes move about, and seeing the house is chaotic, this is the perfect time to use this spell.

I open the cage and collect the sparrow into my hand. It doesn't fight me, and at my touch, it feels feathery but soft on the inside, like if I squished it too much, my fingers would go right through it.

Cassiel props his chin on my shoulder, intrigued by the bird way too much. I take a deep breath, and say, "I have no idea if this is going to work, but I'm gonna try. Hey Joseline, it's me Aria. Great news, Maverick has canceled your contract, so your soul is free, girl. No demon owns you. Anyway, I miss you terribly, and please—"

The bird flinches in my grasp, and it's twitching in my hand, so I unfurl my fingers. Then it flutters its wings wide and takes off. Cassiel lunges after it, but I snap my arms around his neck, and hold him back. "Nope, that's not for you."

Guess there is a limit on the length of the message. I lift my neck and watch the little thing disappear into the distance. Cassiel plonks back down next to me, both of us bathing in the sunlight, and I wish I could hear Joseline's voice and make sure she's doing alright.

DORIAN

Cain caught me up on the shit that had gone down in the mansion over the last few days, leaving me furious. We're dealing with enough shit from Lucifer without having these bastard vampires causing havoc in our town.

In hindsight, we should have spilled their blood the moment we got a whiff of their intrusion on our territory. But we fucked up and let the opportunity slip as we dealt with more pressing issues—Hellhounds, Sayah, not losing Aria.

So, now I stroll right into Purgatory at Cain's command to get intel out of the vamp with my incubus power. Ramos and Viktor hadn't had much success it seems, and I have no doubt those two excel at torture, which tells me these bloodsuckers are more afraid of upsetting their new master vampire, Stephan. Cain told me to do this fast, so that's the plan.

The club is quiet during the day, but still operates for business clientele who love to share a drink and lap dance over their lunch breaks.

I amble my way down into the basement of Purgatory to find a vamp half slumped over in the iron chair he's tied to.

On my approach, his head snaps up, fangs bared. The fucker is bruised and bleeding, one eye closed shut from how puffy it is. I feel no remorse for this ass. He looks like he could be in his forties in human years, short dark hair, huge bent nose, and lips that are all cracked. He's on the thinner side, but when it comes to vampires size doesn't matter as much, as they are all fucking strong. The undead seem to have that ability in natural abundance.

He hisses at my approach, writhing and fighting the chains restraining his arms and legs.

"I have a feeling you're going to tell me everything I ask," I tell him.

He huffs and spits out blood on the concrete floor between us. "Try your hardest. You're not going to scare me, so save your breath. It won't last once we take over Glenside and everyone in it."

I walk around him, circling him, knowing this will be so easy…too easy, and really I'm not beyond having some fun. I hate anyone who threatens me or those close to me. And right now I'm just pissed that I'm wasting my time with this prick instead of being back at the mansion with Aria.

Circling around him once more, I slap a hand to the top of his head and fist his hair, wrenching his head back. He stares at me upside down, and that's when I unfurl the demonic magic that makes me who I really am.

His eyes widen as he takes in the dark horns that curve out from the top of my head, at the intricate tattoos weaving across my flesh, but I see his attention homes in on the blue runes in my skin that awaken my incubus power.

"How you feeling?" I ask, grinning.

"What the fuck are you, man?"

I grab the knife from my belt and place the blade against his neck. No words are needed because the terror on his face is all I need. The knife bites into his flesh as I swipe it across his throat, just deep enough that it bleeds him, but not enough to kill him. Not yet anyway.

He bucks in the seat, thrusting against my hold on his head. I release his head, then move to stand in front of him. Blood drips from his neck and onto his clothes, and he's hissing at me, the cold-blooded monster showing its true form.

Crouching down, I flick the blade in my hand. "Demons don't need weapons to kill, did you know that? We do well enough ourselves, though it's messy. Flesh torn, bones snapped, all while you're alive. That's the thing about us, we love to watch the terror in our victims' eyes."

I don't give him a chance to respond, but jam the blade

right in that sensitive spot between his thigh and groin. I smile as I draw it back, blood spurting everywhere.

His screams bleed into the darkness around us and I close my eyes, bathing in them. There's something almost soothing about terrified screams. While I preferred not to get my hands dirty back in Hell, I never passed up the chance to make the worst of the worst suffer. That's the thing about Hell…many feed on fear, and the sweet, sickly sensation that slithers over me from this vamp brings back memories of ancient times. Of the blood, massacres, the battles, the fun we'd have. From a young age, Cain and I hunted, and once we brought Elias into our pack, he took it to a brand-new level of torment.

I won't deny, I do miss some of those old days. But now, I take pleasure in slow torture, which fits with seeking information.

When his screams are stifled and morph into sobs, I close in and grab his tongue from his mouth, a disgusting pale thing, then I grab the knife again.

He whimpers, his eyes drowning in terror, and when the stink of piss hits me, I look down to see he's wet his pants.

Fuck.

He's trying to say something, so I release that slimy thing he calls a tongue and wipe my hand down my pants.

I stare him in the eyes, and I call on my persuasion ability when I talk to him, needing him to open up before he bleeds out too much and becomes hysterical, like vamps have been known to do.

"You will tell me everything I need to know." I push out with my power, letting it coat my words.

"I'll talk." He's nodding his head like one of those bobbing dolls, his face streaked with blood and tears.

"Of course you will. What the hell is Stephan up to?"

He's whimpering, and it's pathetic really, how much I see him fighting my ability. Except he's never going to win.

I point the bloodied tip of the blade to his groin and press down, just in case he forgets who's in charge here. I don't give a shit what big bad monster you are, no man wants his cock hacked and sliced, even if it grows back.

"Don't make me ask again."

He's shaking terribly, and starts mumbling, "C-Cookies."

"Come again?" Seriously, he fucks with me and I'm finishing him now.

"T-The abandoned cookie factory down t-town." He's practically convulsing, fighting himself to shut the hell up. This is so much fun.

"What about it?"

"Hush. It's where Stephan keeps the Hush."

The drug that the news has been talking about with humans overdosing and dying, and I've heard similar stories of supernaturals.

"Why?" I press him.

"Money," he yells. "For fuck's sake, I've told you everything."

I somehow doubt that.

"Try again," I growl, tired of this game, and heavy power seeps from my words.

He falls silent in response and looks at me like he's gone comatose, then he speaks. "H-He's gonna kill you all and those who don't die from Hush will be turned."

I'm on my feet and wipe my blade on the shoulder of his shirt before tucking it into the back of my belt. So, Stephan's making himself an army, while building his wealth, and then like any dictator, he'll spread his takeover across the country, the world. It's what I would do too, if I was a sadistic bastard. But those days are way behind me.

"Y-You gonna let me go now?" He's shaking, bleeding worse, and I'm tired of looking at his damn face.

"Sure, I'll give you the freedom you seek." I undo the chains keeping him locked to the chair, and rip them off his ankles, but leave his hands tied behind his back. "Now, you're going to be a good boy, aren't you?"

He is desperately nodding, and doesn't even move to run.

I grab him by the hair and drag him up the stairs. He's stumbling behind me, crying out. Thing is, while he's in my influence, he stands no chance to think for himself.

The few customers in the club glance our way, including Antonio from the bar, but this is a rather regular image seen in Purgatory. Us taking out the trash. I rip open the doors into the foyer and then the main door.

The vamp is backpedaling now. He's screaming for help, but no one's coming to his aid.

I heave him forward and kick him right into direct sunlight.

He howls instantly, and rushes back toward us, but I slam the door shut in his face. And my last image of him is his body already disintegrating into ash. Seconds later, I reopen the door to a small pile of dust on our doorstep.

Well, that definitely feels better. One vamp down, dozens to go.

CHAPTER TWELVE

MAVERICK

I stand at the edge of my room, staring down the crudely painted target I made and hung up on the opposite wall to practice on. Well, I say *my* room loosely. Since when we'd come back from Brazil, I'd found Cain had set up a single bed and dresser for me in the basement room they'd locked me up in.

How sweet of my brother, right?

It was hardly close to the extravagance I lived in back in Hell, but it would do. Besides, I didn't mind the dark and damp, almost dungeon-like atmosphere. I've slept in worse.

Retrieving the intestine relic has granted me other liberties, such as allowing me my daggers, so I've been passing the time sharpening them and brushing up on my combat skills, just in case they're needed in the final show-down with Lucifer.

Or anyone else who feels like testing me.

With only a quick glance at the target, I throw one of them with a flick of my wrist. It sails across the room and its blade embeds perfectly in the bull's-eye.

I laugh to myself. It's almost *too* easy.

Closing my eyes, I chuck the other dagger. The door creaks open the same time I hear the thud of the blade making contact with the target, and I look up to see Aria's head peering inside, staring at my dagger only inches away from her face with complete and utter terror.

Slowly, she pushes the door open more, her cheeks deathly pale and her hands trembling. "That was a little too close for comfort," she says, and swallows when she glances at the daggers again. She's wearing a white sweater that swoops down one shoulder and exposes the creamy skin of her collarbone and cleavage. The tight black leggings may not reveal any flesh, but I can make out every curve of her tantalizing body. Her thighs. Her ass.

Even though there's no secrecy to her—I've seen her naked, after all—my muscles tighten at the potential of getting a look at it all again.

I walk over, getting close enough to brush by her, and rip the daggers out of the wood. Just the brief contact with her sends my pulse skipping. It's unnerving and invigorating at the same time. I never thought anyone could affect me this way, especially a female.

"I wasn't expecting any visitors," I say, strolling across the room again and taking my position like before.

She quickly moves away from the target, closer to my bed. "I can go…if you want."

"No." The word flies from my mouth faster than my brain can realize it, and I quickly clear my throat and regather myself. My grip on the blades' handles tightens. "I'm not doing much anyway. Just practicing my way around a knife or two."

She glances back at the wooden plank, marked up with all my past throws. Mostly in the middle circle. "I can see that," she replies. "I was almost your new target."

"Believe me. If I wanted to hit you, I would have. I never miss."

She eyes me. "Right…"

"Is there a reason you're down here?" Holding up each blade, I pretend to examine their edges, running my thumb along them to test for sharpness until the pinch of pain and the swell of blood on my skin gives me the answer.

"Can you teach me?"

Her question throws me off kilter. "Uh, excuse me?"

"Can you teach me," she repeats a bit louder, "you know, to use a weapon like you."

Interesting…

Definitely not what I expect from her, but I am learning quickly that Aria is full of surprises. And this one I rather like.

I run my bleeding thumb over my bottom lip and then chase it with my tongue. Her gaze watches my every move with intrigue. Studying me.

I confuse her.

Excite her.

Good.

I want to do all that to her, plus so much more.

I want to test her limits.

Fuck her.

Taste her need.

Hurt her in the best kind of ways.

But as much as I long to explore those things, there's one big problem blocking my way.

My brother. Cain.

He's obviously smitten with her, and I'd heard his threat to leave her alone loud and clear. If I ever want to escape Lucifer's tyranny and make my own little piece of Hell on earth, then I need to stay on his good side. Gain his trust. Follow his rules.

And playing around with Aria clearly isn't going to gain me any of those things.

But boy, would it be fun.

"You want to learn how to fight?" I ask her, wondering what her true motives could be. She's so small, young. If it weren't for her shadow, she wouldn't be able to defend herself much.

Maybe that's the point.

She nods. "Whenever we're attacked, I have to run or watch from the sidelines as the guys take the lead, and I'm tired of it. I don't want to be rescued anymore. I don't want to be scared—" She stops abruptly and clamps her mouth shut. I suspect she's just revealed something to me she wished she hadn't, and when a blush kisses her cheeks, that guess is confirmed.

"Being afraid isn't a weakness, Aria," I say. "All emotions can be harnessed, learned from and used to your advantage."

"How do you know that?"

"It's my business to know," I reply.

"Oh, that's right. You can manipulate emotions."

"I wouldn't say manipulate. That sounds like I'm doing something wrong. I simply amplify or repress the ones that are already there."

She rolls her eyes. "Same thing."

"I don't think so."

"Whatever helps you sleep at night, Maverick," she says.

Arguing with her is pointless, so I turn and place my daggers on the dresser.

"Look, let's try this again." Aria begins and comes up behind me. "Please show me how to defend myself. You're the only one who can."

I don't know why, but hearing her say the word "please" has desire stirring. Fuck, what I would do to hear her begging to taste my cock while on her knees. To wrap one of my brother's stupid ties around her neck and use it to force myself so far down her throat that she chokes and gags but still can't get enough.

I shake the poisonous thoughts from latching onto me. Tragically, I have to be good. At least until Lucifer is defeated and the power shifts to us. Then I can say fuck Cain and do whatever I want.

But that isn't now.

"Ask one of your demons upstairs," I bite out. "I'm sure Cain would show you if you asked."

Aria glances away. "He'll never let me touch a weapon. Let alone fight with one," she murmurs. "He's too afraid I'll break."

I huff a laugh at that.

"Besides, I don't think I've ever seen Cain, Dorian, or Elias using a weapon before. Just you."

Also true. My brothers—well, most demons—use their brute strength or abilities when facing down an opponent. Weapons are seen as a sign of weakness. But not to me. I fight smarter, not harder. Living with six older sin demon brothers and one crazy as fuck father has taught me that.

I see no shame in using my daggers. I see strategy.

This may be a way for me to spend more time with her. Not break any rules, technically, but annoy my brother in the process.

Snatching my daggers again, I turn around with a smirk. "You know what? I think that may be able to be arranged."

She grins at me and bounces on her toes. "Okay, what's first?"

I answer by pushing one of my dagger's handle into her hand.

Gripping it loosely, she pales. "Uh…Shouldn't we start

without the daggers first? Maybe work on stance or balance or something?"

"My brother's paranoia's gotten into your head I see." I laugh. "If you're going to be learning to fight from me, then that's just what we're going to do. Learn while fighting."

"Can't I get hurt?"

"Of course you can. Either of us can. That's half the fun." I hold up my dagger and point the tip at her. Hesitantly, she mimics me, but I can already see her hand quivering. Despite her obvious fear, she holds her chin up as she faces me down.

Oh boy. I'm going to enjoy this.

I lurch forward and swing my blade, causing her to leap back with a squeal. I come at her again, jabbing right, but she dances out of the way.

"Are you *trying* to kill me?" she gasps as I slice the air, trying to catch a piece of pretty unmarked flesh.

"Not kill. Only maim a little."

Backpedaling, she continues to dodge my attacks. Her back slams against the wooden target, and when she realizes she's trapped herself, panic flashes across her face. "Maverick!"

I aim for her shoulder, adjust my grip on the handle, and stab out. She drops at the last minute and the sharp tip embeds into the wood instead.

"You can't run forever," I say, as she hurries under my arm. Grunting, I rip out the dagger, spin, and something silver flashes before my eyes.

I feel the burning sting on my cheek before my brain can register what's happened. Aria's holding up her blade and red glistens on the edge. Blood.

My blood.

My fingers fly to my cheek, and when I pull back, they're covered in blood, too.

Shit. She's drawn first blood.

Shocked and slightly amused, I look up at her to find that she's smiling. There's a devilish gleam in her eye, too. The same one I'd seen when we'd faced off in front of Lucifer, and again the night Sayah took over.

It may be the shadow creature's influence this time; it may not be. There's no way to really know. But one thing's for sure, seeing that familiar darkness slide behind her gaze, the one I can recognize in myself, it makes my cock hard as a rock.

"You like to see me bleed, don't you?" I ask her, my voice deepening as my arousal grows. "You want to make me hurt?"

At first, she hesitates. But then, her gaze slides to the dagger with my blood dripping down it's blade and a pleased smirk lifts her lips.

Oh, yes...

Lunging toward me, she swipes at me again, her movements increasing in speed tenfold. I dash to the side, and lash out with my own, but she twists and throws out her weapon to meet mine. Our daggers clash.

"You lied to me," she says, sliding the knife up and down mine. It makes an ear-splitting sound ring out, and chills race up and down my spine. It's as if she knows what she's doing to me. Teasing me. Pushing the boundaries of my control.

"You made me trust you." Her dark eyes are locked on mine. "Put your ring on my finger."

"Don't forget I dragged you to Hell," I tack on.

She stomps on my foot with her heel, and pain bounces through me. I grunt, but I see her next attack coming, so when she swipes at me again, I shift and find my opening. This time, my weapon finds skin.

She stumbles back, bumping into the dresser, more

shocked than anything. It's just a small cut, nothing seri-ous, but her dagger drops from her hand and she peers down at the delicate crimson line across her right breast.

My mouth parches at the sight of it, and suddenly it's all I can focus on. All I can think about.

She's breathing rapidly, and with every rise and fall of her chest, my heart pumps a little faster. I'm moving closer to her before I know it, sliding my hand behind her back, and pulling her body against mine. She doesn't fight me at all. Doesn't even say a word as I dip my head and run my tongue across the curve of her breast, along the cut, and tasting salt and copper.

Still, she doesn't stop me.

It's so easy to become enveloped in her intoxicating scent. This close to her, I can see the sheen of sweat gleaming on her skin. Her pulse thumping in her neck, her throat as she tries desperately to swallow.

Fucking hell, I want more of her.

As I lift my head, our eyes meet again, and I find hers hooded with the same lustful hunger I feel. In that instant, she grabs the sides of my face and crushes her mouth against mine.

There's no saving me now. I'm drowning in her very essence, unable to come up for air. She kisses me fiercely, her fingers raking up into my hair and tugging me closer as our tongues wrestle for dominance.

During the madness, she pulls my bottom lip between her teeth and bites down hard. Blood coats my tongue, but it only seems to fuel the raging fire within her and the kiss grows more wild.

My one hand glides up her back, grabs a fistful of her hair, and yanks her head back. She cries out, but not in pain. And when I run my tongue up the curve of her throat, that cry turns to a delicious moan that sets me on edge.

"This is going to hurt," I warn her, my voice husky with my own deranged need.

"Doesn't everything with you?" she snarls back, and I yank her head back again to prove it true.

When she glances down at me, there's conflict warring over her face—she wants to hate me; she thinks this is wrong, but she can't stop herself. Deep down, she's loving it.

Just like me.

And I…I need *more.*

This may be a mistake, but I'm too far gone now. Suddenly, I don't care about any of Cain's warnings or threats. I'm going to fuck Aria. I'm going to make it hurt. I'm going to help her release some of those darker desires she's kept buried. To hell with the consequences.

Taking my dagger, I draw another thin cut across her collarbone—just slicing through the surface of her skin. She hisses as she draws in a sharp breath, but like before, I trace it with my tongue then nip the end with my teeth.

Her hand finds the hard bulge of my cock through my pants and rubs me through the material. I clench my jaw.

Yes. More.

I make another small nick on her shoulder and press my mouth against it, sucking and swirling my tongue along the wound.

Her body trembles against my lips. "Ah…Maverick…"

I usually like to take my time when it comes to sex. Draw out the pleasure as much as I can, but hearing my name on her lips like that makes me want to rip off my pants and those leggings she's wearing and plunge into her with no remorse. Until those moans turn into full-on screams and we're both riding on that thin edge of ecstasy and torment.

And that's just what I am going to do.

When I reach for my fly, the sound of footsteps echo down the hall. I hesitate.

As if waking from a trance, Aria abruptly puts her palms against my chest and shoves me back just as the door to my room swings open.

CHAPTER THIRTEEN

ELIAS

"*W*hat the fuck!" In seconds, I take in the scene before me.

Aria looks startled, blood seeping from the cuts on her shoulder and collarbone, her white sweater torn and stained red. Her eyes are wide in that doe-in-headlights kind of way a victim freezes when they are terrified.

Maverick stands near her, blood drops on his lips and at the corner of his mouth.

The air is thick with the scent of arousal, and that cuts me to the bone. All I can picture in my mind is Maverick forcing himself on Aria, hurting her like the beast he is. I see her face now, twisted and terrified, her screams covered by his hand.

I'm shaking, absolutely livid that he took advantage of her like that.

Fire burns through me, my anger like kerosine.

A howl tears from my throat, and I curl my hands into fits, eyeing Maverick warily. Everything inside me roars, the blade of guilt spearing into my heart that I didn't find them earlier, before he hurt her.

His mouth is moving, as is Aria's, but I don't hear a thing. My heart is thumping in my ear, my mouth-watering for his blood. I need to hear his cries.

I fly at Maverick and bowl into him.

He hits the floor hard with me on top of him, and I'm seething as I slam fist after fist into his face for daring to hurt my little rabbit.

The bastard fights back, of course he does, but I barely register the punches he delivers, not when my speed is unmatched by him.

The sounds of screams coming behind me are followed by Aria grabbing at my shirt and trying to pull me back.

I grunt, needing to finish this asshole first. He never should have come to our home. Fuck, Cain knows better, except he has a soft spot he refuses to admit. And it's going to get Aria killed.

My jaws clenches as I pummel into Maverick and growl in his face. He catches me under the chin with a sharp jab, giving him just enough time to shove his fists into my chest, sending me back.

The slippery prick rolls rapidly out from under me, and Aria is there in my face, shoving a hand into my shoulder.

"Stop!" she's bellowing in my face, her eyes watery, while the rush of my heart hammers in my ears louder.

The fuck! "You care for this monster who attacked you?" Maybe I had it wrong, and the slimy bastard didn't just attack her. No, he tricked her into believing he cared, into some made up shit to get into her pants.

Next thing I know, a heavy weight crashes into my back, and his razor sharp fangs pierce into the back of my shoulder.

"You sonofabitch," I shout, and twist around with enhanced hellhound speed, but the thing is, Maverick might not be as big as me but he's a sin demon. Those asses are just as powerful, just as strong, and that means they come complete with ammunition. For Maverick, it's fangs, horns, and spiny wings.

I shove him off me, and he stumbles backward a few steps.

He's heaving for breath, blood streaked across his cheek and chin, dripping onto his shirt. Everything about seeing him this way makes me beyond happy. But what I find interesting is that he isn't running away like he normally does. He's standing toe-to-toe with me, and ready to fight.

Maybe he isn't the weasel I'd always seen him as.

Aria's yelling at us to stop, but when I see the grin on Maverick's face, enjoying the fact he got a rouse out of me, I lose the sliver of calm that found me.

"You are nothing but ego, dog-boy," he drawls.

Before I can say anything, I'm flying across the room at him and slam him into the wall, then headbutt him, needing to wipe the stupid grin off his face.

"You were saying," I snarl in his face.

Except, Aria is there, slapping and punching us both to stop. "Get out of here," I yell. "Before he attacks you again."

Maverick, the snake he is, clips his bony fist right into my nose in that same moment. Stars dance in my vision, the pain is a bitch, and blood drips over my lips and chin. He's fucking broken it. The world spins for a second. I stumble backward, shaking my head, but that isn't going to work.

Aria's pushing her hands against Maverick's chest, trying to shove him out of the room, and maybe the dick-head should listen to her. I reach up and snap my broken nose back into place, my eyes watering from the fucking pain. But it subsides just as quickly, and I wipe the dripping blood.

"It's time you left, Aria," I tell her. "This is something I should have done a long time ago."

She whips around to face me, fury narrowing her gaze, her small hands balled up. "Will you get your damn head out of your ass, both of you, and fucking stop!"

"He's going to be sorry for touching you, for tricking you, trying to rape you."

She stills, staring utterly surprised. "What are you talking about? You think I'm that stupid? That I'd let him trick me?"

"He's done it before!"

She stills, staring at me in disbelief.

Maverick wipes the blood from the open gash across his brow. "Maybe we should start again?" he suggests. And I fucking hate him for sounding so calm when I'm shaking with anger, with confusion.

Aria lets out a sound of pure frustration, throwing her arms into the air. "Why must everything be a fight with demons? He was..." She pauses and glances over to Maverick. "Teaching me how to fight."

My head swims with her words, trying to make sense of what she just said.

Then a wave of rejection flares over me. I turn toward her and take her hand in mine. "Why didn't you come to me? I would teach you anything you want, little rabbit. I've been a warrior my entire life."

She doesn't respond right away, but I still smell arousal in the air. There's no denying that, if she is telling the truth, what I'm smelling is her willing attraction toward him. Is that why she asked him for training tips? It had nothing to do with who's the strongest warrior, but an excuse to get closer to him. What the hell happened in Brazil to make her want more of Maverick?

What am I missing?

"So, the cuts on your shoulder and…?" My gaze dips to the one that slides down beneath her collarbone, blood staining the fabric of her white sweater.

"Fighting wounds," Maverick answers and steps past us, standing behind Aria, like somehow he's now her protector. Over my dead body.

Aria glances over to the floor near the door, where a blade rests. She goes to collect it. "I've got hellhounds on my heels, and I love that you all protect me, but I need to be able to defend myself better, too. I can't always rely on you four to be around."

Four. So she counts Maverick in the mix now?

I reach a hand out to her. "Let's go get your cuts cleaned and bandaged."

There's no hesitation in her taking my hand, but when she looks over to Maverick, jealousy claws through me. I accepted long ago that Cain and Dorian will share her, but I'm struggling with Maverick, considering I still don't trust the bastard. But I'm left curious…what does she see in him that I'm missing?

Unexchanged words float between them, then she lowers her head and we walk out of Maverick's room. I shut the door, locking it behind us.

She rips her hand from me once we leave the basement and are upstairs in the hallway. She turns on me, clearly pissed at me. "Do you really think I'm that stupid?"

"It's not you I don't trust," I tell her truthfully.

"Then at least have faith knowing that I wouldn't risk myself by going to see Maverick if I thought him dangerous."

I bite my tongue, knowing I shouldn't say anything, but keeping quiet has never been my strong point. "Like I said, it's not your judgment I question, little rabbit. You seem to forget who Maverick really is. He's the demon who sold out Cain to Lucifer, who lied to you about being an angel, who kidnapped you and took you into Hell. How can you be sure this isn't another game? The asshole has been around for too fucking long, has experienced so much. So don't you think it's strange he is suddenly the good guy?"

She stiffens in front of me, the fury on her face reddening her cheeks. "And what about you? And Cain and Dorian? None of you started out *good*." She air-quotes the word 'good' with her hands. "But you changed, so why can't Maverick?"

I understand her frustration. Hell, it bleeds into my veins. "Because it took us centuries to get to this stage. Not overnight."

The angry expression doesn't leave her face, but only then do I notice her hands shaking by her side. Just as quick, her face pales, and a different kind of terror encases her. I know the look instantly, and she looks at me with a pleading desperation.

"Sayah," she breathes the name, and I rush to her, collecting her in my arms in a panic.

I don't waste a second and rush with her outside into the cold. It's the first thing that comes to mind…to cool her down, to help calm the anger she's feeling, which would be fueled with heat.

She trembles terribly when I set her down in the yard covered in perfect white snow.

"Deep breaths," I tell her. "You're in charge, Aria."

She's nodding but scrunching up her nose as she shuts her eyes—clearly her battle is within her. And I realize now how careful we need to be about setting off Aria's emotions as they seem to be a trigger for Sayah to gain control. Or is it that she feeds off them, giving her strength to emerge?

I swear under my breath for being so fucking stupid

and not shutting my big fat mouth about her and Maverick. For pushing her when that's the last thing she needs.

I've got her in my arms, holding her closer, her body tense as hell.

"Listen to my voice, Aria," I say. "Focus on staying strong because you are in charge of your body, and not Sayah."

Her eyes flip open, and I stare at the war waging behind them, the tragedy, the ache, the darkness. There's so much to Aria we still don't understand, and I hate that it makes her vulnerable, that it leaves us on the sideline when I want nothing more than to reach into there and rip Sayah to shreds.

Her lip curls into a sneer, and my heart plummets that she might be losing the battle. Panic has me throwing Aria over my shoulder and rushing her into the house, directly to Cain's room where he'd had her in his bed. Last I remembered, there were ropes still in the room. I had to tie her down just in case… Something I should have done initially, but alarm bells have a way of fogging my brain when all I care about is helping Aria.

I burst open Cain's bedroom with a kick and rush inside as Aria's voice calls me, "Elias, please put me down."

Cautious, I eye the coiled rope near the window, so I move to the side of the bed near it and set her down there.

I'm still gripping her arms, and stare into her eyes, needing to see for myself it's not Sayah. Eyes are the window into someone's soul, and that's one thing Sayah can't hide from us when she takes over Aria. Well, not to mention her going psycho and wanting us dead. It's not my first rodeo show.

Aria flops down on the bed, sitting there gasping for breath like she's run a marathon. It's like I can physically see the tension bleeding out of her as color returns to her cheeks.

"I don't know how long I can keep doing this," she whispers, her voice still shaky, and her hand holds onto my arm tightly.

I draw her into my arms, her cheek pressed to my chest, and I never want to let her go. The urge to keep her with me forever is unbearable.

It's only when the floorboards creak in the hallway that I look up to find Cain standing in the doorway of his bedroom, his eyebrow arching, wondering why we're in his bedroom no doubt.

Aria shifts around to look at Cain, but she doesn't move from my arms.

Cain is quick to lower his attention to the cuts on her shoulder and around her collarbone, the blood staining her sweater.

"What happened?" He steps inside quickly.

"Had a scare with Sayah almost showing up," she says. "I don't think it's going to stop, or that I can keep holding her at bay. She is getting so much stronger."

"Is the screaming match downstairs what led to Sayah coming out?"

I nod once, and it's clear Cain is clued up on most of what led us to this point. The rest I'll fill him in later.

Silence falls between us, and Cain stands close now, reaching over to wipe his thumb over the blood smear from her jawline. Trepidation deepens his expression and furrows his brow.

"We can't wait around for an answer anymore," he says. "This is getting worse."

Aria shakes in my arms, and I want nothing more than to press her against me, to make her forget the crap following her.

"What do you suggest?" I ask.

"Maybe this is a good time to go and visit your mother, Aria, and see if she knows anything more about Sayah. Something we've missed," Cain suggests.

She tenses in my embrace and untangles herself from my arms. "Wait, you know where my mother is?"

He nods, and something crosses his face as he realizes he's revealed a secret he's been keeping from her. Shit, this isn't going to go well.

Clearing his throat, he says, "I managed to track down the residential home for the mentally unstable where she's being kept."

I'm holding still, knowing Aria well enough to understand this news won't go down well with her. It's why I didn't agree with Cain in holding back information from her.

She's staring at him, her eyes glistening, but when I reach out to her, her body is tightening up. Those aren't happy tears. "How long have you known?" Her voice is deep and her shoulders bunch up.

"A short while. The time hasn't been right for me to tell you with everything going on."

She's trembling. I collect her into my arms again. "Let's all keep calm," I say, directly staring at Cain, who understands my concern instantly, as she exhales loudly. But she shoves against me and pushes herself to her feet, confronting Cain head on.

"A...while?" she repeats. "Why the hell didn't you tell me this earlier?"

Cain stiffens, his lips thinning, but I watch the war raging behind his eyes—not wanting to hurt Aria while defending his actions. "Would it have made any difference? At the time, we didn't consider Sayah a danger, and things have now escalated fast."

"Yes, it makes a difference to me," she snaps back. "You don't own me! And you have no right to keep such information from me. Do you know how long I've wanted to find my mother?" Her voice trembles, and my chest tightens.

I hold back the urge to correct her that in fact she does belong to us now. We're locked in from our blood ritual for eternity, but that's not going to help anyone. Except make her as pissed at me. And I sort of like the notion of him being in her bad graces. More for me.

"Aria, please. My decisions are never made with the intention to hurt you. Quite the opposite." He stretches out a hand to her, but she doesn't take it.

"What else are you holding from me?" she demands.

He exhales loudly, his nostrils flaring. "I found her name. Victoria Dawson."

Aria falls quiet and wipes her tears with the back of her hand. The hurt on her face kills me, and it feels like she's going to burst into inconsolable crying any moment now, and I want to throttle Cain for doing this to her.

"I-I c-can't believe you," she stutters. "All this time, I could have gone and seen her, but you let me believe she was lost to me. How could you do that?"

He steps toward her. "Aria—"

"Don't," she growls. The darkness in her tone has me shooting to my feet. My thoughts fly to Sayah making an appearance any second now.

The same resolve must have crossed Cain's mind, as he lowers his arm and doesn't push her. His eyes darken as he watches her though, expecting the worst. He's not the kind that takes defeat well, but he knows the danger simmering inside Aria.

"Maybe it's time we went and visited your mom," I suggest, to defuse the situation.

Silence.

She finally twists around to face me, her cheeks red, her eyes brimming with tears. "Yes please. Just us two, okay?"

"Of course, little rabbit." This time, when I pull her close, she melts against me.

My gaze locks with Cain's, and there's fire in his eyes. Without a word, he storms out of the room. Well, that went to hell.

ELIAS

I finally get to go on one of these trips with Aria alone, and where are we going? A mental hospital in Illinois.

Quaint.

Oh, it's to visit her mother—the mother who abandoned her and sent an evil shadow creature to kill her father.

Romantic, right?

And that's the shadow that's attached to her soul and who's trying to take her over.

Perfect.

As our Uber driver parks in front of Clover Hill Mental Wellness Center, I grunt and shift uncomfortably in the front seat. Since I don't drive and Aria can't, Dorian made sure to arrange a service to pick us up at the airport.

How do I know it was Dorian who did it and not Cain?

It's a mini cooper that picked us up.

The entire hour and a half ride, my knees were smashed against the windshield, and my back aches terribly. So, the moment we're parked, I throw the door open and un-pretzel myself to get out. The entire car teeters and groans as I do, and I silently curse Dorian. He's going to pay for this one.

After stretching my back until it cracks, I open Aria's door and help her out of the back seat. I can feel the driver staring at me the entire time, probably wondering how I'd managed to fit my massive self into such a small car. Honestly, I don't even have an answer to that one.

"Give us an hour or so," I tell him.

"No problem, chief," he says with a nod, and speeds off to circle the lot for a spot to park.

Chief? Okay. Weird. But I've definitely been called worse.

As we step up to the glass front doors to the psychiatric hospital, Aria grows tense beside me. It doesn't take the bond between us to know she's panicking on the inside about this meeting. And I don't blame her.

"She's just a woman," I whisper, as she stares unmoving at the doors. "Practically a stranger."

She glances up at me, worry etched into her beautiful face. "I know…" But her voice cracks, some of her fear leaking through.

I slip my hand over hers. "I'll be with you the entire time."

A small smile flickers across her lips, and she nods once. I walk over to the intercom with Aria at my side and press the call button. The speaker crackles and a high-pitched female voice answers.

"Yes?"

"Er—hi." I stare into the camera lens pointed my way. "We're here to see a Victoria Dawson?"

"You're visiting her?" She sounds surprised. Guess mommy dearest doesn't get visitors often.

"I'm her daughter..." Aria pipes up next to me, and pushes onto her tiptoes to get into the camera's frame.

Only the crackling of the speaker answers for a while.

I'm about to ask if she's still there, when the loud buzzer sounds, then there's a click of the door opening. I push the door for her and we walk inside to a waiting room with a few chairs, large double doors, and a visitor's window where a woman in a white nurse's uniform is waiting for us.

Aria strolls up to it first.

"You're here to see Dawson?" the nurse asks her.

"Y-Yes. I think so." Aria's voice shakes with an abundance of nerves.

"Do you have any ID?"

The window is on the short side, so I bend down so the nurse can see me. Instantly, her eyes grow wide and she steps back. It's the typical initial reaction I get from most humans, so I'm used to it. "I believe someone called for us ahead of time. Cain. He should have sorted everything out for us."

And by "sorted out," I really mean he donated a large sum of money to the facility if they let me and Aria in, no questions asked.

Aria snorts at the mention of Cain's name, unimpressed and still ticked off at him for not telling her about her mother sooner. Maybe it's because he finally seemed to have a breakthrough with her only to have this happen, but I feel a bit bad for him. He's only doing what he thinks is best for her, even if it's a bit skewed.

Another one of the nurses hurries out from the back and shoves the other to the side. "Yes, yes!" She shoos her coworker away, leans closer to the window, and lowers her voice. "You can come right through to the back. She's on the third floor. Room 310."

Perfect. I love when things are this easy.

She presses a button on the desk and a loud buzzer sounds again. The large mechanical doors swing open for us and we go through. Before us is a set of elevators, and when I push the button to go up, Aria starts to rock on her feet.

"Still nervous?" I ask her as we both watch the numbers on top of the elevators count down to the ground floor. The right one dings and, once the doors roll open, we step inside.

"Yeah, but mostly still furious at Cain for hiding this from me for so long." She jams the third floor button with a scowl. "I could've been here months ago. Asked her about myself or my dad or—whatever—instead of wasting all this time wondering. Searching. Worrying."

We start to ascend, and although she's not looking at me and staring straight ahead, I can see her anger reflected against the metal elevator doors.

Man, Cain really fucked up.

When I get that ominous tingle through the magical link between us, I also suspect Sayah has something to do with her rage at him as well. She seems to like amplifying all Aria's emotions—that's when it's the easiest for her to take over, or so it seems.

"You know…he probably thought you didn't want to know any more about your mother. That's why he kept it from you," I try to reason out, trying to think like Cain does. "He did say you were pretty upset about finding out you were abandoned during your trip to the closed-down hospital. Maybe he didn't want to upset you more."

Her head whips my way and anger flares in her eyes. "Are you defending him?" She snaps the question at me like a whip.

"Defending? No, I wouldn't say that. I'm just trying to understand."

"He should've told me," she says and crosses her arms. "I'm beyond tired of the lies, the coverups. But what else am I supposed to expect from a demon?"

Well, shit. That's a punch below the belt.

The elevator dings again as we reach our floor. Once the doors open, we're greeted by a long hallway with more metal doors and sterile white walls.

Not very homey of a place, is it?

We walk in silence, passing a nurses' station and a few empty gurney beds lined up against the wall. The entire place is way too cold and reeks of alcohol, urine, and latex. Eventually, we come to a door labeled 310. Aria stops dead in her tracks, the anger she felt before quickly draining out and leaving only the heavy worry, fear, and uncertainty she'd felt before.

She rubs the backs of her arms and glances over at me again. "Elias?"

"Hm?"

"I-I don't even know what I'm going to say. We're meeting each other for the first time. She won't even recognize me."

"You can start with hi, I would think," I say with a short laugh.

"This isn't funny."

"What did you want me to say? That you should walk in there and start with, 'Hey ma! It's me, Aria. That's right. The daughter you latched an evil dark entity to? Sound familiar?' Is that what you want from me?"

She swallows roughly. "I feel so sick…like I need to throw up."

I turn to her and grab both her shoulders, forcing her to face me. "Aria, listen to me. The pressure you feel, you're putting on yourself. This woman may be your mother by blood, but blood doesn't determine family. Look at Cain, Dorian, and me. Not real brothers, but I trust them with my life."

She nods weakly.

"Victoria Dawson can only get to you if you let her," I go on. "And you shouldn't let her. She's just another person —someone that might be able to offer you the closure you need."

Aria presses her lips into a thin line, and I can see pending tears gathering in her eyes, but she manages to hold them at bay. I can't stand to see her torn up like this.

"If you really don't want to do this…"

"I do," she answers quickly, but when she reaches for the door, she pauses. "You won't leave me, right?"

"I'll be with you the entire time."

"Okay." Then, taking a deep breath, she grabs the handle and pulls the door open.

ARIA

The first thing I notice is how quiet and still the room is. No sounds. No movement. Not even from the bed where the woman who's supposed to be my mom lays.

I focus on her face, how pale she is, with sunken cheeks and gray greasy hair. It's hard to see any similarities between us when she looks so sickly and aged. She definitely doesn't look like she has the strength to summon an evil entity, or like the psycho bitch my father described. But a lot of time had passed since then, and like Elias had said, she is a stranger.

When Elias's hand presses into my lower back, I realize I haven't moved from the doorway. I step further inside.

Still, my mother doesn't move. It barely looks like she's breathing.

I glance over my shoulder at Elias.

"She must be heavily sedated," he whispers. "I'm not sure we'll be getting any information out of her."

I think he's right. It looks like this trip was for nothing.

Defeated, I shuffle back to the door.

"Is it time for my medication again?" a frail voice calls out.

I freeze on the spot, my breath catching in my lungs.

"Nurse?"

Elias grabs my shoulders and helps me turn around. My mother is pushing herself up in the bed, skinny arms quaking, and licking her dry lips. When her gaze dances over me, it doesn't hesitate. Only passes over me. And why wouldn't it? She wouldn't recognize me. I was a newborn when she'd dropped me off at the hospital and left forever.

I don't know what I was expecting, but my heart pounds frantically against my ribs.

Then she sees the massive, brooding man behind me and she frowns. "I won't fight this time," she says. "Please don't restrain me. I won't fight."

Restrain?

They'd actually tie her down?

My heart aches and I'm not sure why. I shouldn't have any feelings for this woman.

"We're not nurses." Elias speaks while I'm still finding my voice. "We're just here to ask you a couple of questions."

She blinks in confusion.

Elias steps in front of me to take the lead. He makes

sure to keep his voice calm and gentle. "Around eighteen years ago, your husband was killed—"

"Not my husband," she shoots back. Her stare turns cold. "Thank god I never married that lying, cheating bastard."

Take aback by her intense reaction, Elias glances at me. But I'm lost for words. Not being married isn't a big thing —people have babies out of wedlock all the time. But what strikes me the most is how quick her anger is. Plus, what she's said is eerily similar to what Liam had told me, too.

"The world's a better place with him gone," she says. Her entire body is shaking, her hatred for the man pouring through her. "But he deserved more for what he did to me."

I peer around Elias. "What did he do?"

Victoria looks at me. "Unspeakable things. Horrible things…" Her voice breaks, and she glances away as if the memories are too painful for her to remember. "He was a monster."

Something in her wounded expression, the way her shoulders curl forward, and the pain lacing her voice all resonate with me. I'd been through my share of fucked-up shit in the foster care homes I stayed in. Foster siblings or caretakers who were too handsy or had sick fetishes taking advantage of scared little girls. And I recognize the look of a broken woman in her, along with the fierce anger that arises with it.

Could my father have lied?

He is in Hell after all…

But Sayah admitted to killing him, so what gives?

The only way I'm going to get the information I need is to ask for it.

I draw in a deep breath. "You…had a daughter? Is that true?"

She hesitates, and the lines around her mouth deepen

as she frowns. "I did," she says. "The most beautiful baby girl."

Of course, I know the answer to this question, but I have to ask it anyway. "What happened to her?"

Her gaze dances between Elias and me. Unsure. "I…had to give her up for adoption."

It hurts even when she says it, and tears begin to prickle in my eyes.

Elias steps forward to take the reins of the conversation again. And right now especially, I'm so thankful for him. "Was it because of Liam Cross?" he asks. "Did he make you?"

She shakes her head meekly. "No, not him. But it wasn't safe."

"What do you mean?" he presses.

She stops suddenly and bites the side of her cheek.

"You can tell us," Elias goes on gently. "We're here to help you."

Still, she looks over us with uncertainty and distrust. And I don't blame her. But there has to be a reason she ended up in this place. And that Sayah came into my life. I need to know more.

"Where did you say you're from?" she asks.

Oh shit. We hadn't even thought up a good lie to explain why we were here asking her such personal things. What are we even going to say?

But, as smooth as butter, Elias rolls out his lie. "We're part of the board of directors," he says without so much as a second's delay. "Some patients have been selected as improved or rehabilitated enough to return to everyday society, and you were one of the few chosen. We just need you to answer some basic questions to the best of your knowledge, so we can make our decision. Can you do that for us?"

I stare at him, stunned. Quick thinking and spinning lies? Those are things I expect of Cain. Even Dorian. But Elias? Guess he's been hanging out with the other two a little too long. They're starting to rub off on him.

The lie seems to work, though, because Victoria sniffs once and nods. "Okay, but this is going to sound crazy." She looks at the door behind us.

"Trust us. Nothing is too crazy," he assures her.

Again, she glances past us at the door, as if she's expecting someone to come bursting in at any moment. When no one does, she goes on, voice low. "As I said before, Liam was an asshole. He abused me. Beat me badly. The only reason we had a kid was because he forced himself on me one night when he was piss-drunk. I would fight him sometimes, but he was too strong, you know? And the beatings that came after were always worse if I tried to defend myself. So, most times, I just...let it happen."

My throat dries.

No wonder my father is in Hell.

"He wanted me to terminate, but I refused. Even though the pregnancy was a bit of a shock, I wanted to be a mom. And I knew I could do it without him. But when I refused to get rid of the baby, things got more scary. *He* got more scary. Outbursts and stalking. Stole from me. Planted drugs in my apartment, you name it. Anything he could do to make my life miserable. I needed a way to protect myself and my daughter. The law obviously wasn't helping me any. He had a buddy on the police force, and I swear he was helping him out behind the scenes so I became desperate...

"One night, after work, I knew Liam would've set up some chaos waiting for me at home, so to delay it a little longer, I stopped in this antique bookstore. I was close to my due date and my anxiety was through the roof. But I stumbled across this old book about occult magic. Dark stuff. Scary stuff. But there was a spell to 'rid you of your earthly demons' and, like I said…I was desperate."

"You performed a spell?" I say, listening intently and hanging on her every word.

She huffs a laugh. "Sounds crazy right? I told you it would."

Elias gestures for her to continue. She does.

"That night, I performed the spell. At least, I think I did. The book was so old, a lot of the words were faded and hard to read. I did what I thought it said, and as expected, nothing came from it. At least not that night. I ended up having my baby girl two days later. For once in my life, I was happy. Truly, truly happy." Tears glisten in her eyes, and my chest clenches. I'd been so wrong to think she'd never wanted me. So, so, wrong.

"With Liam, happy moments never last long, and the day I came home with Aria, he was there waiting for me. He attacked me." Her voice begins to rise as the words tumble out of her mouth in a rush, and her body shakes. "He tried ripping her out of my arms and punched me in the face, broke my nose and fractured my eye socket. I blacked out. I must've. I don't remember much else except that when I came to, I was laying on the ground with Aria next to me, screaming. And this massive black shadow was hovering over Liam's dead body."

Shadow.

As if being summoned, Sayah stirs inside me. I feel her slithering around my mind, like she's waking from a deep sleep. Her icy cold influence washes over me, covering me in goosebumps.

"Elias…" I breathe as panic crawls up my throat.

His head whips my way, and whatever he sees has his

eyes widening in fear. He seizes me by the arm and jerks me towards him, but it can't stop the darkness sliding out of me, making my shadow grow along the tile floor and change size and shape.

Victoria scrambles back in bed, her face contorted in absolute terror. Her screams fill my ears, but Sayah is already lifting off the ground and filling the small space of the room.

Sayah, no! Come back!

My pleas go unanswered. She continues to stretch and grow, her ruby-red eyes shining my mother's way. Is she going to try and kill her, too?

Rushed footsteps come from outside the door, and it is thrown open. In a blink, Sayah zips back into me as four female nurses in white uniforms hurry to Victoria's bedside. She thrashes, pointing at me, and screams while the nurses struggle to hold her down. One holds a needle, one I'm sure is full with some kind of sedative.

"We gotta go." Elias is shoving me out the door and into the hallway. More nurses run past us to get into the room. We use the chaos as our cover and slip down the emergency staircase to the first floor. By the time we get to the large metal doors, Elias is practically carrying me. He dashes us out of the building and through the parking lot. The waiting mini cooper's engine starts up and Elias heads towards it.

Sayah spins inside me, restless. Wanting out. Even when Elias places me in the back of the car, I can feel the frigidness of her touch grabbing onto me and starting to pull me down.

"Elias…" I gasp. Head whirling, my vision darkens, and I try desperately to stay afloat.

"Hold out a little longer, okay?" he says, and shoves his massive body into the front seat.

"What's going on?" the driver asks, picking up on his urgency. "Is she sick?"

"Hotel. Now." Elias growls like the half animal he is, making the guy—a human—yelp in fear. The cooper's wheels peel out as we speed out of the parking lot and onto the main road.

CHAPTER FIFTEEN

MAVERICK

If there's one thing I hate about my brother Cain…well in truth there are plenty of things but one to focus on now, it's that when he wants you locked up, he does a fucking fine job of it. Back in Hell, he'd do Father's dirty work and sometimes that involved securing one of us sin demons until Lucifer was ready to deal with us. Cain would use anything he found around, be it vines or a curse. Whatever got the job done, right?

I grab the handle to the basement door and tug. It opens a sliver only. "Oh, fuck you!" I wrench on the thing, but it's like trying to haul a wagon of fat-ass hellhounds. I glance out into the hallway through the thin gap and find a line of salt and earth running along the floor, and it's clear it's the spell keeping me locked down here. "Fucking ass." Of course Cain would make it impossible for me to break out this time. Crouching down, I take a deep inhale and blow a long breath, hoping to dislodge the salt and soil.

Nothing.

No chance of breaking the line from my distance.

Shit!

The huge cat in the house comes to mind and how he could scuff the dirt to release me. I have no idea if he'll come like a dog, but I'm not beyond trying anything right now.

I give a low whistle. "Here, kitty kitty. Got a treat for you." Okay, that sounds creepy, but I don't stop.

After fifteen minutes of calling, the familiar click-clacking sound of nails hit the floors. Around the corner, the lynx appears, and it approaches, sniffing.

"That's right, come closer, kitty." I make small kissy sounds, as I hear cats seem to respond well to them.

Sniffing the line of salt and soil, the cat stops, not far from the door, then lifts its head at me. "Now come closer," I say with the sweetest voice I can find. "Drag those huge fluffy paws over the line."

Instead, the thing looks at me as if understanding what I'm up to. And as quickly as he came, he turns and pads his way out of here.

"Wait, no, come back, you stupid cat!" I growl under my breath, and it vanishes around the corner. "Fine," I yell out. "Go choke on a furball."

Huffing, I turn back to the basement and resume my pacing.

The thing is, I didn't leave one prison in Hell to come to another on earth.

I drop onto the bed and groan. Apparently, helping my brother equates to locking me back up like a dog. Even that furball gets treated better than me.

Of course, sitting around doing nothing has my thoughts drifting to Aria. She's constantly on my mind, and I can picture her standing in front of me. Five-foot-five, long black hair, pouty tempting lips, and huge vulnerable eyes that scream 'I need saving.' She may not know it, but that look drives men nuts, and just like my brother and those two idiots who follow him around, it's close to impossible to resist such a beauty. Now, add on to that her toned legs, a curvy ass, and perky breasts, and I'm drowning in her presence.

I need to taste her, bite her, draw blood. Fuck, the distance between us is infuriating. But my cock is hard just thinking of her. The taste of her blood and skin is still on my tongue, her intoxicating scent in my nostrils. I've been aching for release since we came together, and I need her.

My fly is down before I can even think straight, and my cock jerks to attention at the thought of her.

My hand wraps around my dick and I palm the thick, heavy flesh as I tilt my head back. I pump it slowly up and down at first, my eyes closed as I imagine it's Aria's mouth. I'm so fucking hyped, so wired, that my heart bangs in my chest from the blood diving south.

Working faster, I picture Aria with that gorgeous body naked, her determination to play my blood games ripe as she grips a blade. In a quick swipe of her flesh above her breasts, she stares at me, and I take all of her in. The drops of blood rolling down her tits, following the perfect curve of them, and how delicately they drip from her gorgeous little erect nipples.

"Fuck," I groan, pumping faster.

Lines of blood run down her body, the red so striking against her pale flesh. They follow the sexy-as-hell curves and find her sweet pussy.

My body twitches. I'm restless, starved for her. I can still hear her moaning and gasping when I licked her wounds.

Each breath I take comes out ragged and my pulse pounds as I picture her climbing onto me, straddling my lap like the good girl she is. I draw in a deep breath and still smell her, that honeyed, mouth-watering scent that is all her.

I grunt with pleasure as I imagine her sitting down on me, my cock plunging into her wet pussy, and the cries she'd make already drive me to insanity. I jerk my dick faster, and I'm reaching the point of no return.

In my head, I hear her screaming out her orgasm, panting as I never stop fucking her.

I'm growling deeply, stroking harder, doing a shit imitation of how Aria would feel. Every muscle in my body tense and builds as my own orgasm bursts through me. My cock stiffens in my hand, my balls tightening as ropes of cum spew from the head. I groan, wanting to spill into her, fill her, the climax rocking through me for what feels like eternity. My dick keeps pumping out ropes of thick cum that spill down my hand as I keep thinking of her.

Finally, when I'm finished, I'm breathing heavy, free of the arousal over Aria that refuses to let up. But for how long? I wipe myself up with one of the bed's pillows and chuck it onto the floor.

Even after spilling my seed, her face remains pinned to the forefront of my mind, those striking dark eyes, her wicked grin like she knows the effect she has over me.

"Fuck," I mutter to myself. "What am I doing?" I'm now starting to better understand why my brother is so addicted to Aria. She's a storm that bursts into your life and once she's got a hold of you, fuck... She'll have no mercy on your heart.

CAIN

While Elias and Aria are away in Illinois, Dorian and I decide to follow our captive Nightwalker's lead and head over to the older part of the city.

Choosing an old cookie factory isn't the most stereotypical place for a vampire hideaway, but that's the point, isn't it? Choose a place that's the least expected. And in this case, the vamps picked an abandoned building that once made Aunt Ida's famous snickerdoodle cookies.

The moment we step out of Dorian's Ferrari and step into the dark lot, we're hit with the tantalizing scents of sugar, cinnamon, and ginger. Along with some more unpleasant ones, like gasoline and sitting water. The factory is a massive square building with almost every window broken and boarded up, and graffiti decorating the walls. Among the scribbled spray-painted nonsense is the mark of the Nightwalkers—an upside-down triangle with a cross in it—painted small just above one of the loading dock garage doors in the back.

"This is definitely the place," Dorian says, when he spots the symbol as well. "Are we sure we even want to wait for Viktor to do this thing?"

"I made him a promise I'd let him get the revenge he craves. Especially for what they did to Charlotte."

He sighs. "You're right. If it were Aria, I'd want a piece of that vengeance pie, too."

Aria…Just her name stirs emotions in me that I'm still having a hard time sorting out. I love her. Fiercely. And the intensity of it worries me. My list of enemies is vast and deadly beyond imagination. As proven time and time again, my love could kill her.

And I can't forget how pissed she is at me for not telling

her about her mother. The pain in her eyes. As if I'd betrayed her. It's been eating at me since they left.

I want her back. Plain and simple. But I know how much this trip means to her. She needs the closure, so I'll finish our little problem with the Nightwalkers and welcome the distraction for now. Then, when she gets back, I'll have to find a way to mend my mistake. Flowers or chocolate…or whatever it is women of this realm like.

I'll have to ask Dorian.

"Let's just hope Viktor gets here sooner rather than later. I don't trust your brother in our house alone." He peeks at me to see if I've been listening, which I haven't. He snorts and slaps a hand on my shoulder to shake me out of my thoughts. "Cain, come on, relax. Loosen up some. We're about to get our hands dirty. Rip some vampire heads off. You love this stuff."

Normally he's right. I do. But there's too much shit going on in our lives for me to truly enjoy it like I used to. I just want it over with to move on to the next thing; I just want Aria safe. From everything.

If that means from me, too, so be it.

"She'll get over it," Dorian goes on. "You did it to protect her."

"Every time I try to protect her, I end up hurting her anyway, it seems."

"Women are complicated creatures. It doesn't help that Aria's even more so than most." He offers me a sympathetic smile, and in that moment, I'm thankful to have him by my side through all this chaos. He's proven to be a good ally and an even better friend. A brother to me—a *true* one. Unlike whatever creature resides in our basement at the moment.

Behind Dorian, the shadows shift, drawing my attention.

Noticing my change, Dorian spins around just as Viktor strides out of the darkness. As if he's walked out of the pages of an old-style romance novel, he's wearing a flowy white cotton shirt that's open wide at the neck and tight black pants. His dark hair is even slicked back, but there's murder in his eyes. He wants blood to be spilled tonight. And lots of it.

"About time you showed up," Dorian says and waves him over.

Ignoring his quip, Viktor examines the run-down factory. "We're sure this is where the Nightwalkers are hiding?"

"Their nest? No—" I begin, which makes him scowl.

"Then why the fuck are we here?"

"From what I got out of the vamp we had in lockdown, this is where they're storing their Hush. This is where the money is coming in and out of," Dorian explains, but by the look on Viktor's face, he's not happy with that answer either.

"I don't care about drugs or money," he snaps. "I want Stephan's head."

I nod, making sure to keep my voice low. "And we understand that. But one of the reasons his gang has been able to expand rapidly like it has is because of the money backing them up." It's something I learned quickly after coming onto this plane. Money equals power; it is a simple concept to see, and that would be anyone's focus when trying to rule over a city. Increase the money flow coming in. "Kink the pipe, stop the water flow, cripple the town."

Tilting his head, Viktor stares at me in confusion.

"Here, let me help you out." Dorian chuckles. "Cain likes to speak in tongues sometimes. He means to say that by taking away their money, we'll be weakening them from the inside."

"But—"

"You want to slaughter them all. We know," Dorian cuts him off.

"Believe us. This will help get rid of the Nightwalkers completely. Just dethroning Stephan will only do so much. His followers can keep up his work without him," I explain.

Viktor considers my words for a while. Then, with his tense muscles easing, he says. "Like cutting off the head of a hydra. Only to have more grow in its place."

Now he got it. Metaphor and all. "That's right."

"Besides, any Nightwalkers inside we'll let you have."

He agrees, even if he doesn't like the less bloody plan.

"Don't worry," I say. "This is only the first step."

"I trust you," he replies and dips his chin Dorian's way. "Even for demons, you've always been fair to me and my coven."

"Your alliance is one we need and appreciate." I glance back at the loading dock and the door with the painted symbol above it. Then Dorian and I lock eyes. He's thinking the same thing I am. It's time to get this night moving before we draw too much attention to ourselves.

We walk to the door, which has a heavy padlock on the latch. Easy enough to break, so I grab and wrench it. It pops off. As I chuck it to the side, Dorian takes the lever and lifts the garage door slowly. The rusty metal whines loudly against the silence, and if anyone is hiding out inside, they'd know to come running.

To our surprise, no one comes running as we step inside. Oddly enough, we're greeted with only more stillness.

"Are you sure this is the place?" Viktor asks in an impatient whisper.

"Dorian's gift never fails," I reply as I scan the large open warehouse. Besides us, the only things occupying the space are abandoned confectionery machines, sacks upon sacks of sugar and flour, and boxes stacked with Aunt Ida's cookie logo. "This is where the vampire's Hush should be."

"And you'd think there'd be some of the fuckers guarding the place," Dorian chimes in as he circles the places. "But there's not an undead soul here."

He's right. This Stephan bastard has some balls. That, or he isn't afraid of us, and that only enrages me more.

But no one is as furious as Viktor. Throwing his head back, he roars, spit flying and eyes turning a bloodshot red. He throws himself at the boxes and starts tearing through them. Cookies fly in all directions. Then he shoves over one of the large mixing machines, the massive weight of it shaking the ground.

"He's on a rampage," Dorian says as he comes to my side. "Should we stop him?"

I shake my head. "It's not the bloodshed we promised him yet, but Stephan will know we were here either way. It's better if we leave him an important message."

"Got it. Then I'll let him have his fun."

We watch as Viktor destroys everything in his path and shouts at the emptiness.

"I won't rest until every one of you are nothing more than ash in the wind!" he yells, seizes a hundred-pound sack of sugar, and chucks it across the room like it weighs nothing. He reaches for another. "STEPHAN, YOU COWARD! FACE ME YOURSELF!"

This time, when he chucks the bag, it tears midair, spilling a purple crystalized substance all over the floor.

He stops.

That definitely doesn't look like any cookie ingredients to me.

Walking over, Dorian crouches and touches the stuff. He examines it between his fingers. "I know we're still new when it comes to most earthly things, but I've never seen purple sugar before."

"Me neither." I glance over at Viktor. He's temper tantrum proved more helpful than we thought.

"Looks like we've found their Hush." He rises to stand again. "Now what?"

There's a sharp sound and a burst of cold air. Water splashes across my face, and I look up to see Viktor hanging from the rafters, holding a broken pipe. Water gushes out of it all over the sacks of hidden drugs, soaking it all. As the Hush rapidly dissolves, a river of purple flows toward the center floor drain in the middle of the factory.

Pounds of drugs, all washed away.

Thousands, possibly millions of dollars, gone.

We wanted to get Stephan's attention.

There's no doubt he'll be listening now.

CHAPTER SIXTEEN

ARIA

I wake up to a weight pressing into my chest. My lungs struggle to suck in enough oxygen, and my head whirls.

What the heck happened?

It's hard to remember through the stabbing pains in my chest and the fogginess in my brain, so instead, I take in the room where I am.

I'm in a large bed, covered in white linens. Like a hospital or a hotel. No, not a hospital. The mattress and pillows are too comfortable to be from a hospital. A hotel then. Yeah, that sounds right. There's a dresser in front of me with a flatscreen television and mirror, a lamp, and a small eating nook with a table and two chairs.

Once I see my reflection staring back at me in the mirror, I quickly avert my eyes. I'm a hot mess. Hair sticking out of my ponytail, eyeliner smudged across my cheeks, lips dried and pale.

Gah! I look like I've been out of it for hours.

Movement through the closed balcony doors catches my eye, and Elias's gruff voice slips through the cracks.

Not enough for me to make out the words, but from his urgency and annoyed, frantic movements, I'm guessing he's talking about me. And more than likely, to Cain.

The memory of the mental hospital and everything that happened with my mother starts to come back into focus. I've learned a lot on this trip.

For one, my dad was a lying bastard. He was the one who had made my mother's life a living hell and then wanted to get rid of me before I was even born. She'd only been trying to protect me and, out of desperation, sought out dark magic to do it. Apparently, Sayah attaching herself to me had been a complete fluke. An accident. Sayah had done what my mother had asked and killed Liam, but what she'd seen left her mentally unstable and in the hospital.

Am I any closer to knowing what Sayah is and how to stop her?

No.

But I do know the reason she's around. And that I wasn't completely unloved and unwanted like I thought I was. That makes a world of difference. To me, at least. My mother had loved me so much, she was willing to do anything to keep us safe. Things just hadn't turned out the way she'd hoped they would.

The creak of the balcony doors opening steals back my attention, and when I look up, Elias is trudging back into the room. When he sees me awake, he stops and a smile breaks across his face.

"Rise and shine, sleeping beauty," he says.

I kick off the blankets and scoot to the edge of the bed. "Who were you talking to out there?"

"Cain."

Knew it.

"I had to tell him about everything that happened. He's a bit worried about you."

Again, I'm not surprised. But right now I'm still peeved at him for not telling me about my mother. If I'd known sooner, I could've made this trip, asked my questions, and gotten some closure a lot earlier than now.

He wants to protect me? From what?

I'm starting to wonder if he's just afraid of losing me. Which is stupid. He's given me chances to go—I've had plenty of opportunities—and I've stayed. I'm in way too deep with these demons. I care too much. I'd even dare to say I...*love* them.

"We're all a bit worried about you," Elias confesses, running a hand through his long hair. "Back in the Uber, I thought—" He stops himself and glances away.

Guilt tumbles inside me. Elias can be a big brute and fearless, so whenever he shows these moments of sweetness, it strikes me right through the heart.

I walk over and place my hand on his thick upper arm. "What's happening with Sayah scares the shit out of me, too. But right now, I'm okay."

He glances down at me, worry creasing his brow.

"I hope you're not beating yourself up about it. Nothing about this is your fault."

He heaves a big sigh. "I've made it my life to serve, fight, and protect the ones I love. But when the enemy isn't... well, *here* here, I don't know what to do. How am I supposed to protect you from yourself?"

"That's a good question. One I don't have an answer for," I say.

Turning, he strides back out to the balcony and leans over the metal railing. The sun presses against him, and when the breeze picks up, it blows through his hair and kicks up the white curtains.

I bite my bottom lip and wonder if it's best to follow him or give him his space. When things get tough for Elias, or he gets too much in his head, he goes for a run through the forest. Or a hunt. But in a hotel, in the middle of a city, there's not many places for him to go to unwind. Besides out on the balcony.

After a few seconds, I decide to join him and slowly come up to his side. Placing my elbows against the metal, I lean over like he is and draw in lungfuls of cold, wet air. It must've rained while I was asleep because the streets and sidewalks below are littered with puddles

We stay like that for a while, looking out and not speaking at all. Just watching cars zoom by five stories below us.

"You know…" I begin, peeking over at him.

His brows rise. "Hmm?"

"I'm pretty sure you made that poor Uber driver wet his pants before," I say with a chuckle. "The way you screamed at him to get driving."

He shrugs but a smile teases his lips. "That's okay. I'll leave him a good review."

"I think he deserves it. A big tip maybe, too."

"Probably right." There's a soft buzzing sound, and Elias pulls out his cellphone from the pocket of his sweats. He frowns.

"Cain again?" I ask.

"Yeah, he's booked us an earlier flight home."

"And you're upset? I thought you'd be jumping to get out of the city and back to the woods."

"You're right. I am," he begins, gaze stretching out to the noisy streets again. "But I was hoping for more time away with you."

I hesitate as tingles spread all over my body. I know *exactly* what he means. My heart seems to know, too, because it thumps faster with excitement and anticipation.

Swallowing, I reply, "Well, how much time do we have?"

He glances at his phone again for the time before putting it away. "A little more than three hours."

"Ah."

"Not nearly enough time for all the things I want to do to you."

Every part of me tightens at his words, and my mind instantly jumps to a very unholy, unclean place. With Elias, I know the possibilities are endless, but one thing's for certain. We're going to be exhausted, sore, and gasping for breath by the end of it.

My favorite.

Even though my throat is drying at the thoughts running rampant through my mind, I put on my best calm and coy act and blink up at him. "And what did you have in mind?"

To my surprise, he drops to the ground and flips over so that his shoulders are pressed against the railing's bars and his long legs are spread out. This massive hunk of a man is half-sprawled out across the balcony floor. Confused, I only stare at him.

"First, I'm going to need you to do me a favor, little rabbit," he says with that devilish gleam in his amber eyes.

"Oh? And what's that?"

"I'm going to need you to sit that delicious pussy over here. On my face."

His dirty words and cocky attitude light a fire in me, and when he tacks on one of his famous animalistic growls, I almost turn to mush on the spot. I'm not even sure I'm breathing anymore, let alone thinking straight, and he hasn't even laid a finger on me yet.

"Well?"

It's tempting… And would be a hell of a lot of fun, but before I can do anything, a car honk blares in the distance, reminding me that we're very exposed up here. Anyone walking by or in a neighboring building could see.

"Let's move this inside," I say and walk towards the open doors. But Elias snatches my wrist and pulls me back to him.

"No. Here. Now."

"But everyone can see—"

"And?" he snaps. "Do I look like I give a fuck?"

He grabs my thighs and tugs my leg over him. I'm still wearing my dress from my visit to my mom, so when he shimmies himself lower, his face is right where it needs to be to make his request a reality. The grip he has on my legs strengthens, and when he peers up at me, he looks like a starving man now confronted with a feast.

Like he's going to devour me.

I tremble.

He seizes the hem of my dress and wrenches it up, exposing all of me to the city around us. "Now come here." I don't move; don't need to. He yanks me forward, perfectly positioning himself between my legs, and leaving me to do nothing but grip the railing for dear life as his fingers pull aside my thong and his tongue dives into my heat.

No warning. No more sexy talk. Just him lapping at my sex like he can't get enough.

Suddenly, I don't care who can see us. I'm lost in the pleasure sweeping through me, of his rough hands digging into my ass cheeks as he makes a feast of me. When his masterful tongue stops its rampage and concentrates on my clit, my vision fogs. Bolts of electricity shoot through every nerve ending, and it isn't long before I'm panting, my hands clutching the railing for dear life as my muscles tighten in the most delicious way.

My orgasm slams into me, turning my legs to jelly, but Elias isn't letting up. Instead, as he licks my all too sensitive nub, he spreads my ass, runs a finger along my slit, up my backside, and presses against the tight little hole back there.

I tense automatically, but with more teasing flicks and sucks on my clit, I'm soon relaxing and pressing myself against his finger.

He growls against me, sending vibrations through my core. My hips begin to move on their own, grinding against his mouth. Loving the sounds coming from him. He's enjoying this as much as I am, and that only manages to turn me on even more.

Another finger pushes into my back entrance, but the shock of it is soon replaced by the mounting pleasure as I increase my speed.

I'm not even sure he can breathe okay down there with how aggressively I'm riding his face, but at the moment, I don't care. The climax I'm chasing is explosive, and I'm too close to stop now.

His fingers move slowly, pumping in and out of my ass, and the sensations clashing inside me are too much. This time, when I reach my peak, I cry out, and then quickly bite my lip to hold it in. Don't need someone calling the cops because there's a woman screaming on the fifth floor.

Elias's hold on me shifts back to my hips and he lowers me onto his lap, where he's already yanked down his sweats and pulled himself free. The hard silky length of him rubs up against my sex, the heat of him burning me up from the inside out. From his tongue and my intense need for him, I'm already dripping wet.

"There's just something about fucking you with a dress

on," he says, his voice heavy with desire. "It drives me fucking crazy."

"Easy access." I slide onto him easily and groan as his full length buries itself deep inside.

His eyes shine a little brighter when he stares at me. "Exactly."

Elias is no little man in any way, especially when it comes to his cock. The sheer size of him should hurt me, but he's always so careful when he moves, so particular with how he holds me and positions himself, that having sex with him is never anything less than mind-blowing.

And this time's no different.

He never lets go of my hips, but instead, uses his hold to take full control of the pace and how deep and shallow he thrusts. He's testing me. Making sure I can handle him before going full force, and I dig my nails into his shoulders and arch my back to give him my answer.

That's all he needs. With another growl vibrating in his throat, he pounds into me and hits my inner wall each time. It hurts, but in the good kind of way that has my eyes rolling back and me whimpering for more. When he kisses me, his tongue is as relentless and aggressive as it had been on me before, and I'm drowning in the feeling of him all around me. Inside me. Overwhelming me. Controlling me. Dominating me.

I love every fucking minute of it.

"Fuck, Aria," he gasps between strokes. "I can't get enough of you."

"Good thing you don't have to try."

Something passes over his face, a hesitance and a question lingering behind his eyes, but before I can ask about it, he lifts me off him, puts me on my feet before getting up himself. Then, he spins me around and pushes my stomach up against the chilly metal of the balcony's railing.

My gaze zeros in on the city street below and my stomach somersaults at just how high we are. "Uh…Elias?"

When I glance over my shoulder at him, he's spitting into his hand and lathering up his cock with it, pumping it over and over in his fist. The gesture should disgust me, but for some reason, it only excites me more. Heat prickles along my skin.

"What-what are you doing?" I rasp.

"What does it look like I'm doing? I'm going to take that sweet ass of yours."

His words make me squirm.

He presses one hand into my lower back, forcing me to lean over the railing even more, and my heart pounds with a mixture of lust and fear. One false move and I'll tumble over this thing. To my death.

"Elias…" I call to him again. I'm not so sure about this.

He captures my gaze with his. "Do you trust me?" he asks.

That's a silly question.

"Yes, but—"

"Then shush." He grabs my wrist and jerks it behind me enough to make me yelp in surprise. With my dress already pushed up to my waist, I feel his cock running up and down my ass crack as if asking for permission.

"You're going to have to bend over more, or this is going to hurt," he whispers.

"But if I lean over any more…"

"You won't fall," he assures me. "Don't worry."

That's easy for him to say. He's not the one dangling over a balcony right now, facing a huge drop.

Still, I do as he says and lean over a little more.

His tip pushes into my tightness, and I suck in a sharp breath at the spike of pain that always comes in the beginning. Slowly, carefully, he goes deeper, and the initial pain is replaced by nothing but sweet, sweet bliss.

"Oh yeah," he practically howls. If no one had heard us yet, there's no doubt they have now. "That's what I'm fucking talking about."

He throws his head back and closes his eyes. With one hand still holding my wrist behind my back and the other spreading my butt cheek to help him fit, he begins to draw in and out of me. Gently at first, like always, to test my comfort.

But slow and steady rarely does it for me, so when my own need to kick things up a notch takes over, I reach between my legs, find his balls, and begin to massage them. His entire body tightens.

"Aria." There's a warning in his tone.

"Fuck me, Elias. I'm not risking my life here for nothing."

He chuckles softly. "I love a woman who knows what she wants." He readjusts himself behind me, pressing his chest against my back, and grabbing my breasts. Then, he rams into me so hard, I scream.

"Is that what you want?" His voice rumbles by my ear. He thrusts into me again, hard, and again I cry out. "Me to fuck you like this? This hard?"

Fuck. His filthy mouth paired with the rough and risky sex is driving me wild.

Another merciless thrust, one that steals my next breath away.

"Huh? What was that? I can't hear you, little rabbit."

He slams into me again.

"Y-Yes! Yes! Just like that." I can barely get the words out, but by some miracle, I do. Thank god his arm is around me, otherwise I might collapse from the sheer intensity of the pleasure spinning through me.

"Would you like more?" he asks. His hot breath spills down my neck, causing goosebumps to rise.

I nod, and with that, Elias pulls back slightly. He spits again, but this time, he rubs his wet fingers up and down my ass before inserting himself again. The whole thing makes me feel dirty and sexy and horny at the same time.

When I look over my shoulder again, he's smirking wickedly at me.

"Hold on," is all he says before plummeting into me. Over and over. Each time going deeper until I'm sure I've managed to fit all of him inside me somehow. Colors explode before my eyes, and I'm gripping the railing so tight, my knuckles turn white.

He fucks my ass with no remorse now, and with each thrust, the bolts holding the metal bars together groan and whine from his forcefulness.

There's a familiar pressure building, and I know if he keeps this up, I'm going to come for a third time. I just don't know if my body—or this balcony's railing—can take it.

Guess we're going to find out because within milliseconds, I come undone. Another scream rips from my throat, but I'm quickly silenced by Elias's hand as it clamps over my mouth. I yell into his palm instead, everything shattering into a million pieces, and he crashes into me a few more times before every muscle of his tightens and relaxes in a final release.

Together, we lower ourselves onto the cold floor, me cradled in his lap and his arms coming around me to hold me close. We sit in silence for a while, just listening to the booms of our racing hearts, our stagnant breathing, and the loud noises of the city going on all around us.

Finally, when I find a way to string more than a few

thoughts together, I lick my dry lips and say, "So, do you think anyone saw us?"

He peers down at me with brows furrowed. "Absolutely. And whoever didn't *see* us certainly *heard* us."

I slap him in the chest, and he kisses the top of my head.

"It's okay, little rabbit. We gave them quite a show. One to be jealous of."

At one time, I would've been embarrassed at what we'd just did, but now...now it doesn't bother me at all.

When I look up at him again, I see that same hesitance as before wrinkling his forehead. Something's on his mind. Something more than just the heart-stopping sex we just had. But he's struggling to tell me.

"What is it, Elias?" I ask him, a bit worried about the answer. If it's bothering him this much, it can't be good, right?

"Hmm? What do you mean?"

"There's something you've been wanting to say to me. I can see it in your eyes."

He stares at me, mouth agape, shocked I've figured him out. But he doesn't deny it. Instead, he sighs and presses me tighter against him. "The other day...I heard you talking to Cain."

Not exactly sure where he's going with this, I wait for him to continue.

"Did he really tell you he loved you?"

Oh.

Shit.

"Uh, yeah. He did."

"Did you say it back?"

I pause. "Yes, I did."

He glances away for a long moment, his thoughts drifting.

Now I'm even more curious. "Is that a problem?"

"What?" He shakes his head. "No, no. I'm just surprised is all."

"Surprised?"

"Yeah. I never thought Cain was capable of any feelings like that. Especially not love."

Where is he going with this? "Do you think he lied to me or something?"

"No! Shit." He runs a hand over his face. "I'm really fucking this up."

"Why don't you just come out and say it then. I'm not sure what this has to do with Cain at all."

"It doesn't," he replies. "Not really."

"Then tell me, Elias. Tell me."

He pales. It's the first time I've ever seen him so confused and weak. And by what? Knowing Cain and I said I love you to each other? I don't understand.

His gaze searches my face, but I don't know what he's looking for.

"Elias…" I begin and touch his cheek. He leans into my palm "What's going on?"

He draws in a deep breath. "I asked about Cain because, well, I'm pretty sure I love you too."

I let his confession sink in. Let the truth seep into the emptiness I've carried so long in my heart and fill up the holes. Like when Cain told me the same thing, my chest warms and I'm overcome with happiness. So much so that tears prickle the corners of my eyes.

Aria, the orphan who grew up having no one, now has two demons to love forever. It's no fairytale, by any means, but it's more than I could've asked for.

I realize then that I haven't said anything, and Elias is watching me intently, hanging on by a thread for my response. And of course he would, after what his bitch of an ex put him through. No wonder he was terrified to tell me.

To ease his fears, I tilt my head up and press my mouth against his for a sweeter than usual kiss.

When I pull away, I meet his golden hellhound eyes and say the words I feel in my very soul and the ones I know he's been dying to hear. "I love you, Elias."

Elated, he jumps to stand, pulling me up with him. He kisses me again, and the passion he puts behind it makes my head whirl. When he finally lets me go, I become aware of the wetness trailing down my legs from all the seed he'd spilled inside me.

"You sure know how to make a mess," I say lightheartedly. "I need a shower."

He laughs. "I don't know. I kind of like seeing you covered in me. It marks you as mine."

I roll my eyes. That's an animal for you.

He slides an arm under my knees and scoops me up like a bride ready to cross the threshold after her wedding day.

"What in the world are you doing?"

"You wanted a shower, didn't you, little rabbit?" He grins.

"Well, yeah but I didn't think I needed company."

"Saves water that way." There's a mischievous gleam in his eye as he carries me into the hotel room and heads for the shower. "And besides, we still have about two hours and ten minutes to go before our flight. We can get clean and we'll still have plenty of time to…"

My pulse speeds up.

Oh boy. When it comes to Elias, it looks like this little rabbit is going to have to turn into the Energizer Bunny.

CHAPTER SEVENTEEN

MAVERICK

I'm not sure how much time has passed in this void they call a basement. Ten minutes. Ten hours. Ten years.

When a scuffing sound comes from the far corner of the room, I jerk my attention in that direction.

A figure stands in the shadows, green eyes glowing, and I know instantly who it is.

"What do you want, Nix?" I growl.

He steps out of the dark, his brows narrowing, and he's staring at me with a grin. He's taking in the dingy room, wrinkling his nose while strolling closer. The tee he's wearing is at least two sizes too small and it pulls taut across his chest and biceps, not to mention riding up his stomach. As always, he's in jeans. His arms up to his elbows are painted in blood, droplets hitting to the floor on his way toward me.

"You escaped a blood bath?" I ask, well aware that his sudden arrival must have been impromptu.

He pauses in front of me, then sniffs the air and glances at the door I left ajar. His lips curl upward at the edges, and fuck, his smugness pisses me off. He knows instantly that I'm trapped down here. That's the thing about my brother, Nix. Despite being the sin demon of lust, he notices every tiny little thing.

"What'd you do to piss off Cain?" he asks, circling the room. After my little stint with Aria, Cain was pissed. Hell knows what that green-eyed hellhound told him, but I didn't give a fuck when what blossomed between Aria and I can't be undone. The wicked spark I discovered within her awoke the beast in me, and now I will make her mine. The complication of the other three men in her life should be a fun obstacle to deal with. The way I see it, this can go a couple of ways. They accept I am not leaving her, or I take her for myself. A decision that still hangs heavily on my mind, seeing I don't have anywhere to take her without Cain on my heels. For now, anyway.

I shrug. "When isn't Cain in a pissy mood?"

He laughs. "Man, Hell sucks worse than before with you gone."

"What's Father said?"

"He's quiet. Really quiet, and you know when he gets like that, it's fucking bad. Overheard him talking to Torryn how you'll pay for betraying him."

Maybe I should be scared, but how much more terrified can I get when I've been living with the devil my entire life? He's been torturing me endlessly, so the distance we have between us is a vacation for me. "He threatens to kill everyone," I say. "And is Torryn the new favorite son now? Guess with Father's crappy mood, why not talk to the demon of Wrath, both of them can be constantly seething anyway."

"You laugh, but this is different, brother. He knows things you've done, and Lucifer will not be played."

I lick my lips as my thoughts swing to the diary I stole

from him. Of course he'd know, and of course he'd suspect me. I knew that the moment I grabbed it and tucked it under my shirt. A sick feeling rises through me, except I can't change what's done. Cain's been tossed out of Hell for betraying Father, and he's made a life for himself out here. So I can too.

Nix steps back and glances at the door of the basement then back at me. "I could help you get out. What do I get for helping you?"

I stuff my hands into the pockets of my jeans. "Nothing. You still owe me one for killing that cross-road demon so you could sell his souls to buy that little red-haired woman for your pleasure."

"She was my servant," he corrects me.

"Servant. Sex slave. Is there a difference?"

"That was a long time ago, brother." His nostrils are flaring as he folds his arms across his chest, the fabric of his black T-shirt crawling farther up his stomach. "And you can't talk. You think I can't tell that the scrumptious little thing you brought to hell has you tripping over your feet? What is so special about this girl that two of my brothers are willing to risk everything? Is her cunt made of gold?"

"Shut your fucking mouth," I growl. "If you're going to help, then do it, otherwise fuck off out of here. Or have you forgotten how deals work? I do you a favor, and you pay back when I call it in."

Except, the way he's staring at me, I can tell he *wants* something from me too. But trusting him is a mistake I won't make. He might be my closest brother, but that doesn't mean I would trust my life in his hands. Far from it, but sometimes it's the whole better-the-devil-you-know. And it couldn't be truer in our case.

"Are we doing this, or what?" I ask him, my voice darkening, glancing down at the blood on his hands dripping over his clothes. "By the looks of it, you've got somewhere to return to."

"Nothing that can't wait. I'm helping out Lorcan in the torture cellars and just needed some escape from all his moaning about not being allowed to hunt, as Father's put a ban on it for now. And I'm that bored and going bat-shit crazy that I'm visiting him."

I lift my gaze to the bruise on the side of his neck. It's faint and it won't last long. We heal fast, but the only person capable of leaving such marks on a sin demon in Hell is our father.

"What did you need help with?" I ask, and curse myself instantly for asking. I must be getting soft by living here on earth, but it's hard to ignore the same signs of abuse I received regularly.

He strides around the room. "Tell me what you find in Father's diary."

I freeze, staring at Nix, trying to see through him and if his words are a direct order from Lucifer.

When I don't respond, Nix turns to me. "I used to sneak into his quarters and take a sneak peek into his diary, but fuck if I could work out what it said. Not like I could ask anyone without it getting back to him, you know."

"I don't have it."

"That's not what Father told Torryn."

My shoulders curl forward, an ache racing through me like a spear had been plunged right through my chest. I shouldn't be surprised by his revelation, but I had hoped Lucifer wouldn't be onto me that quickly.

"I'm on your side, Brother," Nix tells me. Except, I don't fucking believe a word he says.

"Get me out of this room," I command with steel in my voice.

Nix drops his arms by his side, his fingers splayed. "All I want is a shield against him. Like you and Cain have; there is only so much you can take of torture. How long before he locks us all up, or throws us out of Hell, or shit knows what?"

A soft groan rolls in my chest. I'm familiar with how Nix plays his games, how he uses pity to get his victims. You'd think with his power of lust, he'd gain who he wanted with ease, except all my brothers are predators who loved to hunt. But if Nix has any intention of reporting this to Lucifer, then I have every intention to keep my enemy close.

So, I nod once, giving him hope where there is none. My alarm bells are off the charts. I might have just made a grave mistake, but too late for regrets. That's why there's a saying in Hell that one should hug their enemies, so you know how big to dig the hole for their graves.

Nix claps me on the shoulder. "Good, now let's get you out of here, shall we?"

While he goes to the door, I can't stop the dread churning in my gut. A flicker of fear lingers at the back of my mind...not for me, but Aria.

Nix pushes the door open, which does resist him, and he scuffs his foot across the mark, creating a gap in the salt and soil. Of course Cain would have created a protection barrier personalized to only affect me. What a prick!

"Done," Nix calls out, glancing back at me. "I'll be speaking with you soon, brother." Then he fades and vanishes in a blink.

It irks me that he visited, but at least it served two purposes. One, it let me know Lucifer knew about the diary, meaning we had to keep our guards up. Me specifically. Two, I'm free from this dull basement and I can track down my girl.

I step out into the quiet hallway and make my way upstairs just as Elias storms outside into the yard. I wait for him to vanish from sight, then I turn up the steps quickly and make my way to the upper levels of the mansion.

ARIA

I run a comb through my wet hair as I stroll back into my bedroom after *another* much needed steaming hot shower. Since arriving back home from Illinois with Elias, I've been exhausted. My thoughts are on overdrive after finally speaking with my mother, discovering how much of a douche my father was, and despite all of that, Elias knew exactly how to put a smile on my face afterward.

I still tingle all over as I think back to the things Elias did with his tongue on the hotel's balcony. That guy never ceases to amaze me with what he does to me, leaving me constantly craving him. Even now, I can't forget how his hands felt all over my body, how he pounded into me, over and over. I already miss him, feeling partly empty with him not by my side.

When we first met, he scared the hell out of me, but now everything about him fills me with arousal and admiration. Funny how initial perceptions of people can be so wrong. I put the comb down on my bedside table and search for my socks as there's a chill in the air. It's then that Cassiel trots into the room like he's a show pony.

"Where have you been?"

He responds with a half groaning sound, then hops up on my bed and lays on his belly, his front legs stretched out in front of him and his chin propped over them. But his eyes follow me around the room. With all the new furniture in the room and having salvaged my clothes, everything is all over the place. Finally, I track my underwear and pants at the bottom of the chest of draws and hop around the room to pull them on. Then I begin sorting through the huge bag of clothing I still haven't put away.

I hit the power button on the radio and start folding to the dance song that is playing.

It's only when I'm tucking my underwear into the draw that I notice someone standing in the doorway.

I glance up and lock eyes with Maverick, eyes widening appreciatively at me. Hastily, I toss the panties inside and slam shut the drawer with my hip.

"Aren't you supposed to be in the basement?"

He pushes forward, strutting his stuff, and well, he is freaking gorgeous in every aspect. Those strong shoulders, biceps that make me want to curl up against them, and kissable lips, that I recall all too well how they taste. "Is that really where you want me to be, or here with you?"

He sweeps right past me, his arm sweeping across my stomach as he crosses the room. His touch leaves me tingling, and I turn to find him chuckling as he's staring out the window.

"It's not about what I want, but where Cain believes you are safest," I answer.

He turns and lounges against the wall, arms folded across his chest. "Safe for me, or the rest of you?" There's something almost antagonizing about his tone, and I'm not sure why but it irks me. Perhaps it's all the bullshit we've been facing lately, or that I had been craving some alone time.

"I was thinking this might be a good time to pick up from where we left off down in the basement." He casually unfolds his arms and collects a blade from the back of his jeans. Standing there, he spins the knife in his hand effortlessly.

I'd be lying if I say the temptation of his offer doesn't linger on my thoughts. The memory of the excitement he brought out in me, the impulse to play dirty, the exhilaration of cutting him excited me. I don't quite understand it, but even now, my gut buzzes with the adrenaline of what we did.

Except what came afterward with Elias and him was an explosion I don't ever want to experience again. I swore he was going to kill Maverick, and I was powerless to stop him. I'm shaking remembering how hard I screamed and beat my fists into them with no effect.

I've just found happiness with three demons, and of course I go and find myself drawn to a fourth who's bringing chaos to our lives. Maybe the mistake is mine for letting myself go there with Maverick, with believing anything could happen.

"It's not a good idea," I answer. "If Elias catches you again, he'll murder you this time. And I'm exhausted from the fights. I just want you all to get the hell along."

With a final spin of the blade, he tucks it into the back of his belt. "You really think it's that easy? Elias is a mutt and has hated me since forever. Dorian is a wannabe sin demon, so my hopes are on making peace with my brother. He's the one who calls the shots here, but that will take time."

My shoulders rear back, and I hate the way he speaks of

the men who destroy me with their love, and I won't let anyone talk shit about them.

I grind my jaw as fire licks across my skin, and my words come flying out. "No wonder Elias wants to rip you apart. Maybe it's better if he does find us together, and then I'll be sure to grab myself some popcorn and enjoy him beating your ass instead of making him stop."

His eyes narrow and his face goes still, as he watches me with serious eyes. "Want to give it a try yourself? You and me. Take this anger you have out on me and let's move past this point."

My insides tremble. "You want to know what I really think?"

"Be brutally honest. I can take it." Darkness sweeps over his gaze, and if I look too close into them, I am convinced I'll find the darkest pits of Hell.

"Deep down inside, you're lonely and want to make peace with the guys desperately. You see how hard they've fought after being tossed out of Hell, and now you wish you would have joined them instead of taking Lucifer's side. But your ego stands in the way of just being honest and admitting you made mistakes."

He arches a brow. "My ego isn't that big. Do you even know Dorian?"

I roll my eyes. "Your head is so inflated, I'm surprised you even fit into this mansion."

He chuckles, the sound forced and fake.

"And you want to know my truth?" he replies.

I brace myself, expecting the venom as I see it swimming across his expression.

"You are terrified of how much you crave the darkness. From me, from Sayah. Because if you accepted it, then you'd have to admit that maybe you're not so innocent.

Maybe it's not Sayah who's been making you think these terrible things."

I stare at him as fury climbs through me at his words. Something in my chest soars with anger. "What the hell is that supposed to mean?"

He pushes off the wall and strides across the room. "You've been living with that thing inside you most of your life. You don't think that she might have shaped who you've become as a person?" He reaches my side and takes hold of my chin, lifting it, forcing me to look into those deep brown eyes. "I accept what I am, Aria. That inside me flows a river of darkness that drives me to hunt, to fuck, to take what I want. What about you?"

Everything about him annoys me, and I hate his words. I shove his hand away. "You don't know what you're talking about."

He laughs and strolls out of my room. The strike of his heavy boots on the floorboards fades as he heads downstairs.

Panic surges in me, that part of what he said is right. What if the attraction I have toward these demons, toward Maverick's darker side, is because even without Sayah, I've become something dark myself?

DORIAN

"Well, that didn't turn out how I'd pictured it," I say, crashing down on the couch in the parlor. The blaze in the fireplace crawls over my freezing body. Even though I've been on Earth for what feels like forever, the cold is still something I haven't fully acclimated to.

"It turned out better than we could have planned." Cain rubs his hands by the flames. "You checked on Maverick?"

I nod. "He was asleep on the bed down in the basement." I had noticed the salt and soil ring looked slightly thinner in one part, which could have been the cat if it went down there to explore. I fixed it up regardless.

Thumping steps coming from the hallway has me glancing over my shoulder to the parlor doorway.

Elias appears, all serious and stiff. "We have a visitor."

I laugh beneath my breath at how much he reminds me of a butler, but before I can mock him, Miranda steps into the room with a small bag under her arm.

I stiffen in my seat, curious why she's here.

She's wearing black riding pants over her long legs and a cream knitted sweater. Something about her looks... normal. I'm used to seeing her in a witchy dress or wearing crystals. No one would ever suspect she's a powerful seer looking like she's just come in from a round of Polo.

She only has eyes for Cain, not even acknowledging Elias and I as she goes to stand by the small table in the middle of the room. Cain moves to join her, and I recall the tense conversation in her tent when we dropped off the diary. I hurry to my feet and stroll over to join the pair, as does Elias.

This woman has been playing us from the beginning, her sights and claws aimed at Cain, wanting a spot right by his side, ruling over Hell. Fuck, she has balls to set her sights that high, but to also think she could control a deranged place like the underworld, well, she has to be partly crazy.

"Is it done?" His words are direct.

She nods. "It's fully deciphered," she tells him.

Sure, Miranda and I had a thing way back when, even if I left her high and dry. But I have always appreciated her directness, and right now I want to hug her. Fuck, she got Lucifer's deepest secrets from his diary all translated.

"What's it say?" I ask.

Her gaze remains glued to Cain. She's lucky Aria isn't with us now, or she might have ripped out Miranda's eyeballs for staring lecherously at Cain.

I'm sure Miranda isn't really that into him, but more into his power. The energy radiating off her isn't a command of arousal, not like Aria. With Miranda, this is strategic and calculated, and I wouldn't be surprised if her plan involved gaining favor with Cain to get to the throne, then stabbing him in the back.

Elias has his hands on the table, leaning forward, catching Miranda's glare.

"Give us space. Don't you have something better to do, like fetch a stick?" she taunts, snapping her attention back to Cain.

"There's plenty of space," I reply, standing across the table from Elias, and he grins my way. "Now, talk. What did you find?"

She still grips onto the diary, holding it close to her chest now. "You remember our terms, right, Cain?"

Shadows slither over our commander's face, his eyes darkening, but he hasn't shifted over into his demon form either. He's in control, like he always is. But the air might as well be molasses from how thick it's become.

And I love every second of it…the tension, the uncertainty, the games. There are many things I don't miss about Hell, but watching others play their political games was something of a favorite pastime for me.

"I never go back on my word. Now, what did you find?" Cain's words are sharp and clipped, carving through the tension. It's clear he hates the situation, but what's the human saying about the captain going down with the ship?

Part of me wonders if that's his backup plan, should things ever reach that stage and Miranda forces him to fulfill his end of the bargain. Except, Aria would never let it happen…she would murder Miranda, that I have no doubts about. My girl is a hellfire, and maybe that's what Cain is counting on.

Now that is something I don't plan on missing.

We're all silent, watching Miranda, waiting.

She grins, taking her time to lower the diary from her chest and slowly opening it, flicking through the pages before she shuts it and slides it across the table to Cain.

He grabs it quickly and checks it, then looks up at her. "Where's the translation?"

Miranda taps her temple. "I figured you were in a rush and didn't want me to waste weeks typing everything up, especially based on my findings."

"And that is?" I usher her to speak. This drawing out bullshit and waiting has me itching to force her into speaking. But I also don't want a seer on my ass.

"Are you going to tell us, or is that going to take a few weeks too?" Elias asks through clenched teeth.

Miranda huffs, put out by having to deal with minions like Elias and myself. Fucking arrogant bitch.

"In all honesty, the majority of the stuff in there were ramblings," she began. "Repeating the same stuff over and over. He was basically using it as a notepad to collect information on types of creatures. A few things in Latin about holy water, but not much else. Think of it as a monster manual." She laughs, but no one is laughing with her and then she quiets down. "Tough crowd."

I stare at her, wanting to remind her that when she showed her claws at our last visit, she made it very clear where she stood with us. And it sure as fuck wasn't on any friendly levels. "Is there anything in there mentioning Aria?"

"Once only, and it was a title to an empty page. But you know what I think?" she asks, sucking in a deep breath. "To me, the rest of the diary almost read like a list of possibilities, like he was writing down his thoughts on what she could be."

"What makes you say that?" Cain asks, his narrowing gaze piercing into Miranda.

"Well, for one thing, there were a lot of pages where he'd scribbled origins and features of a monster, but then crossed them out. They were ridiculous ones, like shifters for example. Even I could have told him that's not what's going on with the girl."

"And the ones not crossed out?" I prod, feeling like we're having to pull the answers from her excruciatingly slowly.

"They were varied. One was a Shadow Caster."

"That wouldn't be it," Cain interrupts. "Those things produce regular shadows, not living ones. And they can't possess anyone."

"Exactly," she agrees with him, then shuffles the chair back to sit down, making herself comfortable. The three of us follow suit. "He listed a fallen angel as a possibility, with only a few features and lots of scribbles that made no sense. "There were quite a few things like Shades, Wraith, and even Nightmares, which I don't know much about, but again, he only made notes of their features that could relate to Aria I assume."

"It sounds like he has no fucking idea," Elias mutters the obvious.

"He doesn't know enough about Sayah to determine the best match with the monsters," Cain answers, then glances over to Miranda. "I'd like the typed-up translation sent to me by next week for me to study."

Cain knew Sayah better than Lucifer, so he might find something in his notes to help control Aria that the devil himself had missed.

"It's a research journal, really," she tells us. "And it comes with no conclusion. Just random thoughts and information he's discovered."

"Well, guess it's something," Elias says, leaning back in his chair. "Not sure it's information worth dying over, but that's your brother's problem, not ours." He's looking over at Cain, who doesn't answer. By the distance in his eyes, I'm guessing he hadn't even heard what Elias said.

"Anything else?" he asks suddenly.

"Yes," she admits. "It's not a lot, but toward the back of the book there are notes that talk about torturing someone to extract their soul, or maybe in this case, whatever is inside Aria. It doesn't mention her, but what else could he be talking about?"

I straighten in my chair and my chest tightens, my sudden catch of breath fills the room.

"He really is a depraved soul, isn't he?" she answers, her mouth thinning. "There is no discovery on those pages aside from his own thoughts on torturing someone. I'll let you read those when I supply the full transcript."

That's not what I want to hear, and I tense, my hands by my side curling into fists. It shouldn't surprise me that Lucifer would turn to torture. It's his go-to with everyone.

Miranda's on her feet. "Well, that's all I found. There's nothing else, but just because it doesn't give you the answer you seek, it doesn't change our deal."

Cain's brow furrows but he doesn't argue the point. "Walk with me. I'll show you to the door."

Once they leave, I look over to Elias, who's tense as hell,

his shoulders curled forward like he carries the world on them.

"He can't get his hands on her," he says. "We've both seen Lucifer's tortures in action, and no one comes out of them alive. Look how fucked up the sin demons are, all because of him. If he gets hold of Aria, he'll break her and she'll never come back. We'll lose her forever."

I swallow hard and drag a hand through my hair. My chest aches with his words because he's right. If we let that sonofabitch get his claws into Aria, then we've lost everything.

CHAPTER EIGHTEEN

ARIA

My eyes fly open at the sound of a thud by the door.

Night cloaks my room and I stare at the door, slightly ajar, still lying in bed silently, trying to hear the sound again. If someone is in my room, then I want them to think I'm sleeping…at least for now.

When nothing comes for a long pause, that feels more like fifteen minutes, I crane my head up gently to see Cassiel isn't on the bed with me. And I'm certain I know what woke me up…him jumping out of bed.

I breathe easy, hating that I've become so jumpy lately. I seriously need to chill. Taking a deep inhale, I flop my head back down onto the pillow and wonder if one of the guys would be awake.

Closing my eyes, I settle in and let sleep take me.

The floorboards groan, and I roll onto my back, my eyes opening groggily, and I wait for Cassiel to hop back up and settle down. Instead, a blur comes toward me from the corner of my eye so fast, I know it can't possibly be Cassiel.

I flinch to get up, but a heavy weight crashes into me, shoving me back to the bed. What the fuck? I fling my arms to get up, but it's so huge, so heavy.

The cold bite of a blade is suddenly at my throat. "Quiet down, dark one."

"W-Who the hell are you?" I'm stiff in bed, terrified to move. One slip of the blade, and I'll bleed out all over my bed sheets.

And really, dark one?

Talk about the pot calling the kettle black.

The fuckwit is straddling me, and like a mountain he towers over me. All I see in the dark is the silvery glint of his eyes.

"Who I am is of no consequence. It took me a long time to finally track you down."

My mind is buzzing and I'm rolling through all the sin demons in my mind wondering who the hell this one is. Clearly not Nix. But that doesn't stop the furious quiver that runs through me at being attacked in my bed at night.

"So, which one are you?" I ask brazenly, even if my life hangs in the balance. But if there's one thing I know about demons, it's that they love to talk, especially about themselves. "So, the hellhounds have failed and you're the backup? You know that means you are just one step up from those hounds according to Lucifer."

"Don't you dare speak his name in my presence!" he hollers, his whole body shuddering, and that pinch of the blade pushes harder against my skin. I press myself into the bed, as if willing myself to slide right through the mattress. The glow of his eyes intensifies, and shit, but this guy is freaking me out.

"Okay, chill. We all have daddy issues."

"Listen carefully. You are *The First*, and I care not for

your love of Hell or your decision to become Lucifer's concubine, but—"

"Um, excuse me, but let's back up a bit. There is no concubine happening with that sadistic asshole. Ever. I mean, is that what he told you?" Geez, I really don't need the psychopath who rules Hell to suddenly decide he is going to claim me. That would be the worst scenario in this entire damned world. In that circumstance, I'd purposefully allow Sayah to take me over just so she could have a go at him. And knowing my luck, she'd love his brand of bat-shit crazy.

But the beast on top of me hasn't shifted or loosened his blade from my throat.

"What do you mean, I'm The First? Like, I'm your first mission and it's the first time you've been allowed out to play?"

"You talk too much."

"And you haven't killed me yet, so what do you really want?"

He lifts his head, laughing, the sound terrifying and exactly what I'd expect from a serial killer finding out he just got away with the perfect murder. The moonlight hits his face, revealing the grinning sneer painted on his face. "You are like the rest of them, even if you don't know it yet."

"Like who? Your hellish brothers?"

His head lowers, the darkness stealing his features once more. "I can't exactly deny that. My brothers are frustratingly annoying," he hisses.

"That's putting it mildly. More like arrogant asses."

His head tilts to the side, studying me for a long pause. "Are you ready to die, fiend?"

"Well, no, the answer is no to that. And why am I the fiend when you're the one from the pits of the most depraved place in the universe...*Hell.*" Everything about this dude feels like the opposite of the spawn of Lucifer. He's asking me if I want to die, and there's no lecherous flirting. What am I missing?

He flinches at my response, his shoulders curving forward. "Do not insult me."

The blade presses to my neck harder, and I freeze, a quiver rushing down my spine.

"Look please, you don't have to do this. Let's talk about it, hash it out, anything."

"Oh, but I do. This is my mission."

Mission?

The light to the room flicks on and blinding light burns my eyes. I squint just as the blade eases from my neck. The bulky thing on top of me groans, shading his eyes with an arm.

I squirm and shove his hand with the blade away from me, which fails miserably. Shit, is this guy made of steel?

"Gabriel!" Cain growls as Dorian and Elias burst into the room behind him. "What the fuck are you doing here?"

My mind is reeling at the name Gabriel. There are no sin demons by that name. The only Gabriel I've heard of is...I gasp. No fucking way! There is no way in the world the man on top of me is...

"Please don't tell me an archangel is trying to kill me," I say, getting really tired of being everyone's punching bag.

No, it can't be. Angels are our protectors and do good deeds. It has to be another demon with a similar name.

I blink to clear my vision and slowly the man on top of me comes into view. I gape at the sight in front of me. The guy is glowing. It's the only way to describe it.

Soft curls the color of sunshine frame his strong face, all sharp jawline and cheekbone, prominent nose, and those pillow-like red lips. There's something almost cherub-like to this man, and then there's his piercing silvery eyes that hold that same glow.

I don't even have to ask because there is no way this man is a demon.

Shit!

"Now Heaven's involved?" We're in so much trouble.

"This isn't your business," Gabriel orders, the angry glower on his face deepening as he glares at Cain. "I am here to slay the dark one."

I fake cough, though on the inside, I'm trembling. "You have me mistaken for someone else."

Here I always assumed angels would have voices of... well, of angels. Except, that's not the case with Gabriel. His voice is gravelly, like he's just finished chewing on a bag rocks. Damn, he's huge, and incredibly intimidating. Guess he'd have to be if his task is to keep humans protected from demons. All those images I've seen of angels are misleading.

They're painted as vulnerable, almost fragile, while this guy looks like he's made of two quarterbacks, his muscles bulging against the sleeves of his white tunic.

My men don't look impressed. "It's very much my business," Cain growls, his shoulders rising as he steps forward. "She is ours, bound by blood. She is not yours to take. Whatever reason you have for being here comes to me." A growl rolls out of his throat, Dorian and Elias on either side of him. They're a terrifying fighting machine when together like this.

In a blink, Cain's eyes darken, as do the veins under his skin.

I swallow hard.

Three demons against an angel, and I'm in the middle of it. Not good.

I'm sort of terrified to have them fight. And it has

nothing to do with the whole good-versus-evil thing. All the men are large and powerful, but I suspect Gabriel here can unleash some terrifying holy shit against them. And I don't want my demons hurt.

"Umm, how about you get off me before you squish me to death, and we talk about this misunderstanding over some coffee?"

Gabriel glances down at me, his eyebrow arching like I made a stupid joke. Wow, he has no sense of humor.

Suddenly, he shifts and climbs off me smoothly like he's well versed in getting off victims he's knifed to death while they sleep. I move to get up when his hand grabs me by the shoulder and forces me to my feet. Searing pain shots down my arm at how hard he grips me, and I wince.

"Ouch. You don't need to jab your fingers through my bones."

He releases me and turns to Cain.

"Sin Demon of Pride, exiled Son of Lucifer, speak," he demands.

Wow, that's quite the title there.

"Your conflict isn't with us." Cain steps forward, his chin high. Nothing scares him. Hell, I freaking adore him and love seeing him so powered up.

It's probably not the best thing to be thinking about, considering the situation.

"*She* is our concern," Gabriel states. "And you know it, son of Lucifer. She is The First and needs to be vanquished."

I blink at him, my mind catching up with his words, realizing he must be referring to Sayah as The First. "Wait a second...I need to be vanquished?"

My earlier levity evaporates instantly.

When no one responds and my guys look as confused as me, Gabriel breaks out into one of his over-dramatic laughs, and even places a hand to his chest for extra effect. "Oh, you have surprised me today, demon."

I am so confused right now, my gaze swinging between the angel and demons. "Did I miss something?"

His eyes widen as he glances around the room. "None of you know, do you?" he continues. "How can this be?"

"If you're going to keep talking in circles, get the fuck out of our house," Elias says.

But Cain lifts a hand to silence him, studying the angel. "Enlighten us."

"You are harboring a Leviathan creature in your midst, a ticking time bomb for all angels and demons, for all humanity, and you've been protecting her."

Did he just call me a Leviathan creature? "What the fuck is that?"

Gabriel swings toward me swiftly and has his hand around my throat, squeezing.

Panic spears through me, and I claw at his hand.

"It's a filthy creature. The very first monsters God created. You were a mistake, an abomination, and I was ordered to clean up the mess. I did my job, eradicated the beasts, but one got away."

In a flash, Cain is at our side, his fist colliding right into the angel's head, unlodging him from me. I tumble backward, tripping over my own feet. But I fall right into Dorian's arms, who's there to catch me in a flash.

The battle with Cain and Gabriel sets off like an explosion, moving so fast I can't see where one begins and another ends.

My heart is thundering in my chest, and I turn to Dorian. "I don't really understand what a Leviathan is, but it's bad, isn't it?"

He nods and pulls me to my feet, and brutal fear trembles through me now. I've wanted to know for so long what Sayah is, but now I take it back. If it's brought down the wrath of an angel who wants to kill me, I'm literally in the worst-case scenario of what could happen.

Gabriel is hurled into a wall, leaving a gaping indent.

Cain zips over to him in a blur and grips him by the throat. His demon is out, black wings spread, the claws tipping the ends curling in toward Gabriel. "Neither of us will win if we keep fighting, you know this. You need to understand there is a greater danger on Heaven's doorstep, and Aria might be the only thing that can help all of us. Now back the fuck down!"

Gabriel's nose wrinkles in disgust, then he shoves a fist into Cain's chest, sending him reeling back. "Speak then, demon."

They face each other, each of them tall and formidable.

Dorian and Elias are on either side of me, holding me close, ready to fight to keep me safe, and my heart beats for them. They are everything to me. But I'm seriously scared right now.

"Lucifer is set to unleash war and overtake Heaven, killing as many angels in the process as possible. He believes he needs Sayah...I mean, the Leviathan creature as the weapon that will aid him."

Gabriel's chest puffs out and he's exhaling loudly. "Then we strike down the monster now, just as I had intended."

"Except, she is *our* weapon to stop him. He won't see it coming."

There's something not reassuring about them talking about me as if I'm not even in the room. From the intensity of their words, the power radiating from the two power-houses, they both seem to have forgotten they aren't alone in my bedroom.

"Explain!" Gabriel barks, folding his arms over his beefed-up chest. "How will you do this?"

Cain doesn't miss a beat. "We are ironing out those details, but when it comes to Lucifer, we are all on the same side. We need to stop him."

"So, what is stopping you from dethroning him right now?"

Cain runs a hand through his dark hair. "We haven't found the last two relics for Azrael's harp to give us entry back into Hell."

Gabriel watches him intensely, then glances over to me, leaving me covered in goosebumps. How is it possible that an angel scares me more than a demon? Except, as Cain said, he's on our side. Well, except for Sayah...the first creature God created. Fuck, that sounds horrible and she's inside me. No wonder she wants to take me over. And here I was, suspecting the entire time that she might be some kind of demonic beast or curse.

Except, she originated from Heaven.

Does that make me God's mistake, or weapon? I really prefer to be neither, in all honesty.

"If she really is a Leviathan, as you claim, then she is the only one who can dissolve Lucifer's plan and bring him to an end," Cain goes on.

Gabriel hasn't said anything for a short while, but has his eyes shut like he's decided to take a brief mediation. When they flick open I flinch, and did I mention the guy freaks me out?

He finally speaks. "Since I was the one to destroy the harp and scatter it's pieces, I will reveal the location of the last two parts for you to dethrone Lucifer. You fail, and I will personally hunt you down, Cain, and your demons, smothering you into oblivion."

Cain doesn't seem disturbed by the threat. He's

standing tall, staring directly at Gabriel, but then again, he's always had the best poker face.

"Deal," he states.

Gabriel shifts closer to him, talking to Cain, but his hushed words are undecipherable.

Cain gives a nod, and the two break apart.

"What will you do with Aria?" Dorian asks out loud. "She's free and in our care." He states this as a matter of fact.

Gabriel twists in my direction, his gaze burrowing into me.

No word.

No expression.

No movement.

He's a goddamn freak and reminds me more and more of serial killers with their laser focus on their prey.

In a flash, he pops out of existence, a whirlwind blowing against us while half a dozen white feathers swirl through the room.

Cassiel suddenly appears from who knows where and lunges to catch the feathers with his huge paw, batting at them as they fall.

"We're in so much shit, aren't we?" I ask.

But no one answers. Elias pulls me to his chest and I press into him, waiting to be wrapped up and whisked away.

Cain moves to stand in front of me, his hand on my cheek so tenderly that my next breath hitches all the way to my lungs. The passion in his eyes is everything to me.

"This might actually work in our favor. We have Gabriel on our side for now," Cain states. "We are going to speed things up. We have my father to dethrone. And now we know where to go next."

Absolutely nothing about what he just said has put me

at ease. Especially the fact that Gabriel never answered the question about what he plans to do to me. "But what about what Gabriel called me. Leviathan. Someone please tell me more about what the heck that is. It's freaking me out."

Cain sighs, and I already know I'm going to hate his answer. "They are rare and never encountered. All I've seen about them are what's in the Bible, and since it was written by man, it's not very reliable. It basically says all Gabriel gave us—one of God's first creations that he accidently made too powerful and had to destroy."

"Great."

"At least now, we have a name for Sayah," he says in an attempt to make it sound better.

I want to believe that what we've just discovered is a good thing, but then why is there apprehension flashing in Cain's eyes?

CHAPTER NINETEEN

CAIN

Our first stop is Iceland. To the Kirkjufell mountain to be exact.

According to Gabriel, this is where the harp's foot is located, while the last piece resides at the bottom of the Atlantic Ocean. So, while Aria and I hopped on the next flight across the world, I had ordered the closest of our search teams to charter a boat and retrieve the skull.

I would've asked Dorian and Elias to go, but with the Nightwalker and hellhound problems still looming over us, they're of better use at the mansion and Purgatory. Plus I don't trust leaving Maverick home alone still. Even if he seems to be keeping to his promises for now. I know my brother, and he's like Houdini, the way he can break out of all my restraints. Magical and non.

As the tour guide drives us through the icy and rocky terrain, I find myself staring at Aria again. She sits next to me, gazing lazily out the window, and much like the plane ride here, she's spoken very little to me. Despite my poor attempts to strike up a conversation, she's remained cold and distant.

I sigh, remembering how not long ago I'd put such a gap between us on purpose. It'd taken time, but we'd gotten past that and opened up to each other. So why did it feel like we were back to square one? Why were we ignoring each other, waiting for one of us to bend our stubborn ways and apologize?

She doesn't need chocolates or flowers, like Dorian suggested. I need to just talk to her. Explain everything—why I did what I did. She needs to know that I only have her in mind.

Sucking in a deep breath, I open my mouth to say something, but her excited squeal cuts me off. Pressing her cheek to the window, she points outside where the sky is ablaze with neon greens and yellows, colors flashing and moving as if they're alive.

I let out all my breath, entranced by the sight myself. I've never seen something so amazing. Especially on earth. "The aurora borealis…"

She glances over her shoulder at me. "The northern lights?"

"Mhmm." I never thought earth could offer anything so breathtakingly beautiful. Until I met Aria, of course. And now, being here, watching two of the most magnificent wonders this world has to offer at the same time, I'm practically speechless. In awe.

"I feel it," Aria says suddenly, jarring me out of my daydreaming.

"Feel what?"

She glances at the driver, who is undoubtedly human, and lowers her voice. "My toe…"

Ah. She's feeling the dark magic of the harp's relic. Perfect. "That means we're in the right place."

The car bumps along the dirt road until we reach a chained-off area with signs saying to keep out. The driver throws it in park and shuts off the engine. "This is as far as we can go," he says.

"It's far enough." I throw open the door and on the other side, Aria does the same.

"No one's allowed past the chains. It's too dangerous of a climb," the man begins.

"We'll be fine," I call to his rolled down window and join Aria at the rear of the car. When I drape my arm around her, she side-eyes me. "Just a bit of…romantic sightseeing."

She snorts a laugh.

"We'll be back in a few minutes," I tell him, and guide Aria past the chains before he can say anything more. My hope is that this will be a quick venture, certainly less eventful than the time we'd gone to Missouri on Maverick's wild-goose chase.

The land is frozen over and slippery. Aria clutches my arm as her shoes slip and slide. She struggles to stand, let alone walk up the steep mountain. If I didn't need her gift to tell us where the foot relic is hidden, I'd make her stay in the car.

"Do you hear anything yet?" I ask her.

She shivers against me but nods. "A high whistling, I think. Like a flute. But I'm not sure if it's the relic or the wind whistling past my ears."

"And your toe?"

"It's twitching like mad. I think it wants us to keep climbing."

I sigh. "Of course it does." I secure my grip on her waist as we round the back of the mountain. Slowly. Very slowly. At this rate, we'll make it to the top by dawn. "Would you be opposed to me flying us to the top?"

She grimaces. "What about the driver? Won't he see?"

"The mountain will be blocking us mostly, and I'll stay close to it. The darkness should help as well."

Still, she looks unsure.

"Even if the human did spot us, I doubt he'd believe his own eyes," I assure her. "Humans have a way of convincing themselves of things to ease their fears."

"That's true. People see what they want to believe."

"Precisely"

She nods, giving me the okay, and I press her body against mine as my demon bursts out of me. My wings tear through my shirt and jacket, hellfire spinning through my veins, and wasting no time, I push off the ground. Aria's arms clutch me around the neck as we ascend, and I make sure to keep as close to the mountain as I possibly can, even with the wind pounding into us.

Peeking her head out, she points to the very top.

The moment we touch ground again, my demon shrinks away and my wings fold in. I roll my shoulders to ease the discomfort restraining my monster always brings.

Aria stops at the crest, and her face falls.

"What is it?"

"Do you feel that?" she asks. "The ground? It feels like it's…pulsing."

I glance around us but see no signs of movement. Feel nothing too. "Pulsing?"

"Maybe breathing? I'm not sure how to explain it. But it feels like the mountain's alive under my feet."

"It must be the relic."

She nods. "My toe agrees. Although, the flute has stopped." Her gaze drops. "How are we going to get the thing if it's under layers of ice and rock?"

Not a problem. I wave for her to step back and summon the demon part of me again but concentrate the raging fire inside me to my enclosed fists. They glow an orangey red. Crouching low, I position myself over the rock and punch down with all my strength and power. Sharp pieces of earth and ice fly out in all directions, causing Aria to leap back a little further. I do it again and again, pain ricocheting up my arm but getting deeper each time.

"Keep going," Aria says. "I can hear the music again. You're almost there."

Another three hits and the rock breaks away to a hollow cavern. Air rushes out at us, hitting me in the face and smelling like decay and stagnant water. Carefully, I reach inside.

Once my fingers brush against something solid and icy cold, I seize it and wrench it out of the hole. Under the lights of the aurora borealis, I can just make out the wrinkly gray scaly skin and clawed toes of a creature's foot. Not human-like at all. No, this thing looks to be from some animal.

As I examine the thing in my hand, green light flashes before my eyes, stunning me. I hear Aria gasp somewhere close by, but I can't see anything past the brightness.

I'm blind.

ARIA

*M*y eyes burn against the harsh green light. I can't see Cain; I don't even know if he's still on the mountain with me. Or if *I'm* on the mountain, for that matter. There's no way for me to know when I can't see a damn thing past my nose.

Dark forms begin to take shape in the distance, and I blink rapidly to help them come into focus. The lights shift and dim, and gradually the shadowy blobs gain more of a form—human forms—until the scene before me becomes clear.

I'm standing in the middle of a large room, medieval in style but made up of black polished marble and draped in red and gold. There's a colossal stone fireplace, one I remember, and a dais set up with an altar and throne fit for a king.

A king of Hell, that is.

My breath freezes in my lungs. I'm in Lucifer's castle again.

How the fuck did I get down here? And where's Cain?

I glance around desperately, wondering if the foot relic managed to transport us somehow, but when I see Cain, he's crawling up the few steps, clothes torn as if he'd just been in a vicious battle, and blood painting every inch of him. His wings are out, his black veins decorating his skin, and I can feel acid burning its way up my throat. He's hurt. Badly. I want to run to him, but my feet are somehow glued in place. I don't have any control over my body.

"Cain!" I try to yell, but my voice is trapped inside me, too. Panic surges forward. Is it Sayah again? It must be. She's taken me over again, and I'm powerless to regain my control.

That's when I notice that he's trying to get to another person who's laying on the other side of the throne. With silvery white hair and equally pale skin…

I gasp, my heart thundering. Maverick.

He's on his back, clutching his stomach, which has been torn open and is bleeding profusely.

But he'll heal, right? We're in Hell, and demons are immortal here. It should only hurt like a bitch for a bit, but he should be okay.

When Cain reaches him, he lifts his hand and the

candlelight around the room glints on something metal in his hand.

A dagger.

And not just any dagger. An angel blade.

Cain's going to plunge it into his brother's heart.

"No!"

But it's no use. They can't hear me.

"I'm sorry, brother..." he whispers, pain lacing his voice.

To my horror, Cain does exactly as I predicted and stabs Maverick straight through the chest. My head fills with my screams, but none of them leave my mouth. I can only watch as Maverick's body jerks before going completely still. Dead.

Oh my god...

I can't even process what's happening. And when Cain grips the blade again, points it to himself, and raises it again, my brain completely fogs over. One of my greatest fears is about to play out before my very eyes, and there's nothing I can do to stop it. He's about to kill himself too.

Cain's black eyes flick my way and automatically change to their beautiful crystal blues. This time there's a great deal of sadness reflected in them as he looks at me, but not a hint of remorse, telling me he knows what he's doing. He just wishes he didn't have to.

My heart twists. *"Please. Don't."* I beg him silently, hoping somehow he knows what I'm thinking. But it's clear in his expression that he's made up his mind.

The moment he thrusts the angel blade through his chest, I lurch forward with all my strength and somehow my feet are able to leave the floor. The neon green lights flare again, blinding me, and suddenly, I'm sliding on slippery ground, my sneakers unable to get a grip. Disoriented,

I windmill my arms and grasp for balance, but it does nothing. I feel myself falling.

"Aria!"

Strong hands seize me and wrench me back. Colors burst in front of my eyes as the strange light fades away, and once I can see again, Cain's face is there, as perfect as can be, but creased with worry. No blood. No wounds. Just my demon prince breathing hard and holding onto me like he's afraid to let me go.

When my gaze drifts to the right, I see why. I almost fell down the side of Mount Kirkjufell.

I leap forward, slamming into his chest, and he wraps his arms fully around me. I can barely feel the fear of almost dying myself when all I can see is the image of him killing Maverick and then himself playing over and over in my head. As vividly as if I was there in Lucifer's throne room.

I can't hold back the tears that come rushing forward, or the sobs as they wrack through my chest.

Cain tightens his hold on me, and his fingers begin to comb through my hair. "You saw it too, didn't you?" he whispers against the top of my head.

I squeeze my eyes. At that point, I couldn't even form words if I tried.

"It has to be from the relic," he goes on gently. "Some kind of…moment of fear or something."

I peer up at him. As I struggle to regain my composure, my voice cracks. "But you were holding it. Not me."

His head tilts in thought. "You're right. And killing my brother isn't a fear of mine."

"How about killing yourself?"

"A fear? No."

"Then what the heck was that? And how did I see it, too?"

"My guess is that it has something to do with the link between us now," he explains. "The magic was able to transfer through the bond we share."

On cue, Cain's cellphone rings. He pulls it out of his pants pocket and glances at the screen and says, "It's Dorian," before holding it to his ear.

"Yes?"

"What the fuck was that?" I hear Dorian saying.

Stepping back, I put a little space between us but make sure it's not too much with so much ice underneath me.

"So you saw it as well." Cain nods my way to say this only confirmed his theory.

Dorian goes on loudly. "Bright green light? Popping into Lucifer's throne room? You offing your brother and then—"

"Yes, yes. *That.*"

"What the fuck, Cain?" Now there's concern in his tone. Of course there is. He just witnessed his closest friend stab himself to death. "Is there something you want to tell me?"

"We found the foot," he says, and then clarifies. "The relic. I believe whatever we saw was part of its dark power, and it transfers through our bond. Aria saw it, too, and I'm guessing Elias will be calling me next to say the same thing."

There's a tense moment of silence on the other end of the phone before Dorian speaks again. This time, in a lowered voice. "You don't think that was a flash into the future, do you?"

The thought sinks like a boulder in the pit of my stomach. "A flash into the future? What? That's actually going to happen?"

"I'm not saying that," he replies in his normal overly calm manner. "We won't be able to tell if that's what it is until..."

"Until you run an angel blade through your heart." My voice is rising; I can't help it.

Cain's about to take a step toward me but then remembers he's still on the phone with Dorian and hangs up without saying goodbye. He pockets the phone and then reaches out to me.

"Aria, please."

The sorrow in his eyes reminds me too much of what I saw in the vision—or whatever it was—and my chest squeezes.

"Can I..." He lets out a breath, almost annoyed at himself. "Can I...hold you a little longer?"

His question throws me off guard. It's so unlike him to ask such a thing, but after what we've just seen, how can I say no? It feels like my insides are shaking, and all I want is for him to hold me close and tell me he'd never do something that insane. No matter what the relic says.

I close the distance between us and welcome his embrace again. He squeezes me a little tighter this time, but I don't care. It's the comfort I need right now.

Drawing in his cologne and fiery scent, I let it wash over me and calm my raging nerves. Above us, the northern lights have vanished, leaving only an inky-black sky dotted with stars. It's almost as if the relic was causing the magical light show. And maybe it was. When it comes to these relics, nothing much surprises me anymore.

We stay locked together like that for a while. Saying nothing, only enjoying each other's company and warmth. Whatever anger I'd felt towards him before about my mother is gone now. Long gone. And there's only the pain and absolute grief that comes with possibly losing him again. It engulfs me.

I want to ask him if he's been planning on doing what I'd witnessed in the vision, if it really was a glimpse into the future, but I'm almost too terrified of the answer to ask it. I rather not think about it ever again.

I love him so much it hurts. Physically *hurts* to think that he won't be with me anymore. I never thought I'd ever feel like this towards anyone, especially a demon.

But I do.

After more time passes, Cain finally releases me and steps back. Then he shrugs off what's left of his torn jacket and uses it to pick up the foot relic without touching it again. To our relief, no more bright lights flash or haunting images appear.

Wings unfurling, he's about to grab me around the waist to fly us off the mountain when his phone rings again. Sighing, he takes it out of his pocket and answers it without even looking at the screen.

Through the speaker, a familiar deep voice booms, "What the fuck—"

"Yes, Elias. I know."

CHAPTER TWENTY

DORIAN

Elias and I are still rattled by the vision.

I mean, how could we not be? We just witnessed our closest friend sacrifice himself in the middle of Lucifer's throne room. And for what? I'm not sure. But I have a sneaking suspicion it has something to do with what Aria and I discovered in Storm's library about Lucifer and his son's souls being connected.

It may have been just a faulty flash of something not real, a way to spook us as part of the relic's magic. Or it could be something more. A peek into a future event, and that's where my fears lie. Knowing Cain for as long as I have, I wouldn't put it past him either, so you bet your ass the moment he and Aria walked through the front door from their trip to Iceland, I waved Aria up the stairs to sleep off the trip and steered Cain right into the parlor to talk more, one-on-one.

The second I assure we're alone, I whirl on him. Before I can even get a word out, he holds up his hand.

"Where's Elias," he asks, voice as emotionless as stone.

"Hellhound duty," I say dismissively. I know he's

avoiding the inevitable conversation, but he can't hide from me. He paces in front of the fireplace and I cut around the couch to stop him. "Cain."

He frowns.

"Please don't tell me what we saw was a vision of the future," I say. "Don't tell me you are planning anything crazy like that."

He glances down at his jacket in his hands, and it's then I realize that it's wrapped around something. Most likely the relic.

His silence irks me. He's not answering my very simple question, and that's not a good sign.

"Cain…"

"I don't know," he replies finally and draws in a deep breath.

But that's not good enough for me. "What do you mean you don't know? How do you *not* know whether or not you're planning on killing yourself? That's what I'd consider a big fucking thing and not something you're on the fence about."

Sighing, he runs his fingers over the jacket before looking up at me again. "I've been thinking…"

"Uh oh. Never a good sign."

"Listen to me," he begins again more sharply, "if what you and Aria discovered is true, and my soul is somehow linked to Lucifer, then there may be a way to weaken him."

"You mean by killing yourself." I can't believe what I'm hearing here. "And your brothers."

He nods. "The more of us that die, the weaker he'll be. And then you and Elias can take him out. For good."

I blanche. He isn't serious; he can't be. "Look, I know Miranda is a handful, but there has to be another way to get out of the demon contract than offing yourself."

He's deathly quiet. Not a flicker of humor on his face.

"What I'm *trying* to say is, abso-fucking-lutely not. You're out of your damn mind if you think I'll let you kill yourself."

"Do you want to take Lucifer off the throne?"

"That's a fucking stupid question."

"Then this may be the only way."

"I severely doubt that," I snap. "Why do you have such a death wish all of a sudden? We've done everything to survive. Fought, scraped, and clawed to stay alive, and you want to just end it? Just like that?"

He doesn't respond, only continues to stare at me grimly.

I clasp my hand on his shoulder and lock gazes with him. "Cain, listen to me. I told you I'd follow you to the end of time, and I will. I'll do whatever you ask of me. Hell, I'll spike an angel blade through Maverick myself. Even Lorcan. Or Val. Fuck, even—"

"I get it." He cuts me off as a small smile curls his lips.

"Sorry." Got a little too excited at the thought of killing those ass-wipes. "You get the point. But the one thing I'll never do is let you die. Never. It's nonnegotiable."

He pats the arm on his shoulder. "You're a good friend, Dorian. I'd be lost without you."

"Ain't that a true statement," I scoff and step back. "Now, I'm guessing what you're holding there isn't just a pile of dirty laundry?"

He nods. "I need to put it with the others in my room."

"I'm supposed to be giving Elias a break for a few hours. I've convinced him to finally take a shower. Although the stink may be what's keeping the hounds at bay."

Another crack of a smirk, but he hides it well. "And Maverick?"

"Still in his hidey hole in the basement. Throwing knives at your portrait or something."

"Good, that means the magic's holding," he says.

"For now, yeah, but you and I both know he's an escape artist."

"Not if he's trying to prove his loyalty to us."

I don't know about that. I don't trust Maverick at all. He's scheming down there. I'm sure of it.

"Go relieve Elias of his guard duty," he says. "I'm sure he'll want to talk to me too."

I watch him walk out of the parlor and up the stairs before heading down the hall and out the back door myself. Right away, I spot Elias huffing it up the hill toward the mansion. When he sees me, he rolls his eyes.

"You were supposed to meet me a half an hour ago," he barks in annoyance.

"Cain and Aria are home."

His eyes widen. "I need to talk to—"

"He's waiting for you," I say. "In his room."

He pushes past me and heads inside.

"Don't forget to bathe!" I shout to his back. "You smell like a barn."

He holds up a middle finger before slamming the door behind him.

Turning back toward the dark woods, I make my way down the hill and head for the lake at the edge of the property. As I pull off my shirt and chuck it into the brush, I release my demon form and let the hellish power race through me. It warms my skin, chasing away the bitter winter cold. Part of me wishes I'd run into a hellhound tonight, just so I can stretch out these wound-up muscles and get the chaos and destruction my demon craves. But the other part of me wants a smooth and easy stroll so I can get it over with and pay my sweet little Aria a visit tonight before she goes to bed.

When I reach the lake, I gaze upon the silvery ice coating the top and shimmering in the moonlight. It's almost poetic. Especially how a light haze clings to the frozen ground and among the trees on the opposite side.

Sights like this you could never get in Hell. This peacefulness. This ghostly glow and calm. It's...dare I say...*heavenly?*

The crunch of my footsteps in the snow coupled with whistling of the wind are the only sounds in the night. I don't know how long I've been out here or how many times I've walked around the mansion surveying the land for anything suspicious, but when I reach the lake once more, the chill starts to seep into my bones. I don't have fur; I'm not made for this type of work, so it looks like it's time for Elias to switch with me again. Hopefully the dog took his bath.

As I'm about to make my way back to the mansion, a low hum vibrates in the distance, somewhere behind me. I stop dead in my tracks.

Another sound, louder this time, and I realize it's not a hum, but a growl, and every hair on my arms stands on end. I spin around to see a pair of glowing yellow eyes through the haze, staring at me from across the lake.

Then another pair.

And another.

Until every shadowy place between the trees is shining with predators' eyes. Hellhounds.

There aren't a few of them, but dozens, and that's only from what I can see. Fear spikes through me, and their snarls and growls rip through the silence.

Fuck. It's an ambush.

ELIAS

*T*error weaves through the invisible bond that connects all of us, and simultaneously my hound senses approaching danger.

Dorian. Shit. He's in trouble.

I rush out of the shower butt-ass naked and head into the hall, only to find Cain there, his face reflecting the worry I feel. He'd sensed it too.

A clatter of footsteps, and Aria hurries down the stairs. "Something's wrong. Dorian—"

"We know." Cain's already flying down the remaining steps to the first floor.

I take the easier route and leap over the railing. "We're under attack."

"Aria, you stay here. Go to the basement with Maverick. He'll protect you," he orders.

As much as I don't like the idea of Maverick anywhere near Aria, she should be safer with him than alone if our enemy gets past us. It's a risk, but one we need to take.

"What? No!"

"Stay. Here." He grinds out each word before dashing out the front doors. It's not up for negotiation, and I can't stand up for her this time. Cain's right. If Hell's come back to play, it's too dangerous for her.

I glance at her one last time and growl, "Go downstairs," then sprint for the back door, releasing my beast mid-stride.

The moment I burst into the frigid night, I spy Dorian running up the hill toward me and the army of giant wolves thundering after him, too big to be from this plane.

Really? I leave for ten minutes and this is what happens.

They must've been hiding and waiting for me to leave so they could make their move. Dammit. I should've known better than to let Dorian's pestering get to me. And besides, I didn't smell *that* bad.

A shadow swoops down from the skies, and suddenly fire erupts, blazing through the darkness and knocking several of the hellhounds out of the line. Cain's wings beat against the wind as he drops low, pick up one of the massive animals, and shoots back into the air with it. The hellhounds snaps its powerful jaws at him, but Cain spins and uses his momentum to launch the thing across the grounds. Squealing, it disappears somewhere far off past the trees.

I thunder down the hill, my beast wanting blood and nothing less. Dorian halts suddenly, drops to his knee, and turns his arched back to me. I'm confused for a second, but then I realize he's created a ramp for me to jump off.

Smart, I'll give him that.

I rush for him. Once my paws hit his back, he thrusts himself to his feet to give me even more lift. I sail through the air, the wind cutting through my fur, and when I land, my claws sink into the flesh of two hounds. We roll together, and during the tussle one of them manages to latch its teeth into my hindquarters. Pain slices into me and I lash out, fangs gnashing at anything I can get ahold of. I get the soft underbelly of one and tear. Warm blood fills my mouth. The other hound lets me go and I buck my wounded leg back, nailing it in the eye.

When I look up again, Cain is flying low and circling the pack, throwing balls of fire into the chaos. Dorian's joined in too, his silver hair and glowing rune tattoos like a beacon in the darkness. He jumps and dodges any animal who gets too close, using his long nails to rip through muscle and flesh.

But there's too many of them. As many as we take

down, there's still a herd of hellhounds sprinting for the manor. We can't get them all.

"Don't let them reach the house!" Cain shouts. He sends a blaze of hellfire, creating a temporary wall that makes the hounds stop. But with so much snow around us, the flames are quickly extinguished, the creatures on the move again.

Shit. He's right. We can't let them get to the mansion!

Heart hammering against my ribs, I speed back up the hill, clamp my jaws on one of their legs, and drag them back down to me. Tearing into its jugular, it dies, and I lurch for the next one.

There's still too many of them. And they're almost at the back door. Some even break off and around to the front in a divide-and-conquer maneuver.

We're in deep shit here.

I take down another hound, but a dozen more are still racing ahead of me. Only feet away from barging their way in.

Glancing over my shoulder, I find Dorian's too occupied taking down the lot by the tree line, and Cain's following the group heading for the driveway and trying to stop them from busting through on the front doors.

We've failed.

MAVERICK

There's a thunder of footsteps upstairs. More dust and who knows what else rains down on me as I lounge on the bed and I leap up, sputtering and coughing.

Fuck this room. Fuck the basement. I was getting tired of spending my time down here while Cain and his Brady Bunch lived nice and comfy in their rooms above.

Fucking ridiculous.

Of course, I could leave this room whenever I felt like it. The little smudge in the demon trap circle is still there, since the reinforcement job Dorian did was half-assed. He missed a spot. And it seems Aria has kept my visit to her a secret, so, really, the only thing keeping me in the room is me.

And my need to get on Cain's good side and defeat our father once and for all.

Although, I will admit, it is getting rather boring.

Where's the excitement? Where's the danger? The action? My brother's been swimming in it lately, and I want a piece of that pie.

"Maverick!" Aria's fear-filled shriek comes from somewhere upstairs. "Maverick!"

My stomach instantly drops and before I know it, I'm hightailing it up the steps to meet her in the foyer. Alone.

I glance around. Something's not right here. I can sense trouble nearby, see the fear in her eyes…but why is she alone?

"We're under attack," she says in a rush. "I'm not sure by what, but from all the commotion outside, I'd say it's not going well."

A symphony of growls, animalistic snarls, and all too familiar sounds of fighting erupt outside, getting louder by the second. Closer.

Uh oh. Looks like the boys are having a hard time winning this one.

"Hellhounds," Aria says. "Has to be."

"Where the fuck is Elias? Can't he control his kind?"

"Something must be wrong. They're all out there, and I can feel their panic through the bond."

"The hounds must be closing in." I glance around the room, looking for some kind of weapon we might be able to use if it comes down to it. There's a shield with two crossed swords hanging on the wall near the staircase—a priceless antique, no doubt—and I rip them down.

I had asked for excitement, hadn't I?

"What are you doing?" Aria asks, eyes wide.

"Getting us something to defend ourselves," I tell her.

More terrible sounds come from outside, and shadows move outside the windows. I push one of the sword's handles into her hands. It's heavier than she expects, and she struggles to lift it. "Time for you to put those fighting skills I taught you to good use."

"Skills you taught me?" Her voice rises. "We only ever had one lesson. Barely a lesson at all."

"Time to put whatever you know to work."

With two hands gripping the sword, she manages to lift it to a fighting stance. Well, sort of. I take the other sword and hold it in a firm grip. I also have my daggers strapped to my belt, just in case they're needed, too. I'm more accurate with them anyway.

More shadows pass in front of the windows, closer to the front door. Then a blaze of fire and light.

Has to be Cain. My brother is the only one of us seven who had the ability to control hellfire.

Better go out the back then.

"Let's go." I spin and, together, we run down the hall. I kick the door open, and we leap into the snow and right into the middle of the insanity.

Hellhounds as big as cars are scattered throughout the grounds, with Dorian doing his best to battle them off at the tree line. Fresh claw marks tear across his chest, bleeding profusely, but they don't seem to slow him down. He's fast enough to bounce around most attacks and snap the animals' necks before they even know where to lunge.

The main carnage is coming from just yards in front of us, where a massive black hellhound is bulldozing into the ones charging at us, throwing them left and right. Blood spurts as its powerful jaws tear into necks and stomachs—really anywhere it can reach—and paints all the wintery whiteness with crimson.

"Elias," Aria gasps beside me, confirming my guess that the one ramming into the crowd like a bull is the big oaf.

But despite his outdated fighting style and Dorian's quickness, there are too many hounds for them to take on and a few are slipping through. If Cain's dealing with his own problems at the front of the house, that means we're the last defense back here.

"They want the relics. We can't let them get into the house," Aria says, widening her stance and lifting her sword. Even with all the danger surrounding us, I can't help but marvel at how incredibly sexy she looks with the weapon in her hand and the look of determination on her face. She may be scared, but she's not going to back down either. Not when it comes to defending what's hers.

"Relics? I'm more worried about them getting to you." The words slip out before I've realized what I've said, and she side-eyes me. I quickly come up with a clever explanation. "Cain will kill me if you get hurt again."

One of the hounds break out of the scuffle with Elias and head for us. Quickly stepping in front of Aria, I swipe my sword and cut the beast down. Easy enough.

Two more race towards us, and I grab my daggers with one hand and unleash them. They spin through the air and nail the fuckers right in the middle of their foreheads. They drop instantly. Dead.

With a slight flick of my wrists, the daggers fly backwards and find my hand again.

Aria stares at me in disbelief. "That's a nifty trick," she says.

"What?" I chuckle, loving the impressed and stunned

look on her face. I show her the crystals along the handle, which are laced with some heavy-duty magic. A special gift I got from a warlock whose soul I had in contract. "I wasn't going to tell you all my secrets."

From over her shoulder, I see a hound rounding the corner from the front of the house, coming at Aria full force. Its eyes glow yellow when it spots her, and my lungs squeeze in panic. I try to move in front of her, but sharp teeth sink into my calf at the same time and pull me to the ground. Twisting, I see another pair of amber eyes latched onto me as one of the beasts bites into my leg.

Pain hits me like a semi-truck, and my vision goes black for a second.

Fuck, that hurts!

Lifting my hand, I realize I dropped my sword during my fall, and it's become lost somewhere in the snow. That's when the hound decides to shake its head, tearing muscle away from bone. I roar with anger.

Screw the sword. I'm better with my daggers anyway.

Grabbing them both in my one palm, I plunge them into the creature's eyes. It squeals, bucking, and rears back but lets me go. My victory is short lived, though, because another hellhound wants to take its place and comes at me.

My leg is a bloody mess of skin and tissue, and I know standing, let alone running, is going to hurt like the dickens, if possible at all. But I'm a sitting duck otherwise. I can't just lay here.

As I call my daggers back, the hell-thing pounces. Right before it lands, there's a glint of silver that comes down with it.

As its full weight lands on top of me, I feel the warmth of its blood seeping into my clothes. But I hadn't been the one to stab it and end its wretched life.

Then I see Aria standing over me. Her sword's blade is

coated in red, she's breathing hard and her shoulders are shaking.

Holy shit. She killed it. She saved me.

She blinks, and that's when I notice the eerie white film over her eyes. It's starting to fade back to their naturally brown color, but it was definitely there. I'd seen it with my own two eyes.

The shadow creature wants to come out and play.

I know I should be worried, and part of me is, but another part—the darker, twisted part—is incredibly turned on.

When I shove the dead hound off me, Aria offers her hand. I don't need it, but I take it anyway and let her help me up.

"You okay?" she asks.

She *sounds* like Aria. No weird mingling of her and Sayah's voice yet.

"Yeah, are *you*?" I press back.

She nods slowly, slightly unsure. But that hunger for death lingers on her face. Especially when she turns back to the chaos raging before us. Sayah wants more blood, more destruction, and letting her have it could make Aria go fully dark again, like the other night after the ritual. We could lose her.

"What are you doing? Get Aria inside!" Cain flies overhead, his huge, bat-like wings blocking out the light of the moon. More hellhounds thunder up the hillside, and Cain throws another stream of fire at them to try and hold them off.

"Inside!" he bellows. "Now!"

I whip around to Aria. "Come on. We'll barricade the door." I grab her by the arm, and her head jerks toward me, her movements too stiff.

"They need our help," she snaps. There's an odd rumble

lacing her voice now. A twist of the dark entity within her coming to the surface.

Uh oh. We may be too late.

I tug her back, but her feet don't move. They're planted in place.

"They're big boys," I tell her. "They can handle it themselves."

Her hands whip out, making me jump back, and the earth begins to quake under our feet. A warning zips up my spine.

I may be no Cain, and sensing darkness isn't really my thing, but evilness is radiating off Aria in dense waves. So much so that I can feel it even from where I'm standing.

"Aria!" Cain shouts, voice full of fear. "Don't let Sayah control you. Fight her. You have to fight her."

She ignores him and flicks her wrists. A shadow shoots from the ground straight into the air, creating a dark wall in front of us that rises like an opaque skyscraper. I can't do anything but gape at it, shocked and thoroughly impressed.

"Ar-Aria," I try instead. "Cain's right. You can't let this thing rule your life. You can control it."

Arms still out, her fully white gaze flicks my way. The venom in her stare makes me shift back. The hellhounds smash into the makeshift wall at full speed to try and break through. The audible crack of their necks breaking comes next, and Aria's mouth ticks up in a wicked smile.

She's loving this.

I love death and carnage as much as the next demon, but this is a little freaky. Even I can admit it.

Cautiously, I approach her. "Aria...I know you're in there."

"She knows her place, demon! And you'd be wise to as

well," Sayah barks back. It's Aria's lips moving but their mingled voices coming out.

Another flick of her wrist, and another tall shadow wall appears at the bottom of the hill. The ground trembles again, and suddenly both walls begin to move toward each other, pushing any hellhounds or demons that were in between to the center. And I say demons because Elias and Dorian are in that mess, and now they're being shoved along with the rest. Cain shoots upward to escape being crushed by the rapidly moving walls, but Elias and Dorian are having a hard time running for the ends with so many hellhounds in the way. They're being tossed about and trampled as the walls slide closer and closer to each other.

They're going to be crushed.

"Aria!" Cain shouts down to us, but of course she's not listening. Her mouth is split into a full-on grin now.

What do I do? Do I take her out? That may save Dorian and Elias, but it'll hurt her. I grip my daggers. Is there any other option at this point?

"Aria, listen to me. You can control Sayah. You can. You've been doing it your entire life, and you can do it now." My words tumble out in a rush, but Dorian and Elias only have seconds before being flattened into demon pancakes. "She's working off your fear. Off your insecurities." I should know. My power allows me to do the same.

Wait, shit. My power.

Without another thought, I slap my hand against Aria's shoulder, dive into her and Sayah's tangled and chaotic emotions, and shift through until I find Aria's confidence. It's small, fragile, and overwhelmed with so many other negative feelings surrounding Sayah, but I yank it out and fill her with enough ego to make Elias jealous.

Aria blinks and her outstretched hands begin to waver.

Sayah's losing her grip.

My hand stays firmly on her. "If you don't push Sayah's ass out now, you're going to kill Dorian and Elias. Shove that shadowy bitch back in her hole."

The shadow walls flicker, and I watch the transformation on her face. Her eyes lose the milky whiteness, and her features soften. Her shoulders slump, and the walls start to slow down.

"That's it, Aria. Sayah can't survive without you. You can call the shots. You have the strength to do it."

Again, the walls flicker in and out. Dorian and Elias rush for the exits on opposite sides, leaping over hellhounds and fighting their way out. Finally, they make it out just as the two sides speed up again and collide in a huge plume of smoke. Every hellhound trapped inside? Gone. Poof. Smashed into oblivion.

Elias shifts back into his human form, and he and Dorian look at each other, breathing hard and bleeding from their battle wounds. That was fucking close.

Aria's knees buckle and she goes down, but I quickly grab her and pull her against me. Her head tilts up, her gaze roaming my face.

"Thank you," she whispers.

I snort a laugh to cover the worry, fear, and regret warring inside me. As much as I don't want to admit it, I hate seeing her this way. So weak. "Thank you? For what? You did all the work."

Cain lands in front of us with a loud thud. His wings fold in, and as he looks Aria over, he frowns. "Are you okay?"

She tries to nod, but she's too weak to even do that. Cain moves and takes her from me, cradling her in his arms. When he looks up at me, anger and uncertainty pass over his face. But, to my surprise, there's relief there, too.

"Thank you," he says, with a firm dip of his chin.

My brother...thanking me. I never thought I'd see the day.

Then, without another word, he turns and walks Aria inside the house. Elias and Dorian stride past me, Elias with a slight limp, and follow Cain inside. They keep the door open for me to come in, too.

Before I do, I gaze out onto the mansion's acres of land and try to absorb everything that just happened. Hellhounds, Sayah, the incredible and terrifying powers Aria possesses... Adrenaline still pumps through my veins, and I'm having a hard time settling down. Now we know for sure there's a way for her to control them. Not sure how exactly, but at least we know there's a way.

And that makes all the difference.

CHAPTER TWENTY-ONE

ARIA

Morning light drenches my bedroom, and outside the woods are peaceful. Not a creature stirs. Who would have thought that last night this was the scene of a bloody battle with hellhounds…with Sayah?

Not me. But I am starting to learn that I shouldn't be surprised anymore by the things that happen in my life.

A leviathan. One of the first things God ever met. Before angels? Before demons?

I've seen Sayah's immense power. I can understand why God wanted to snuff all of them out. They must've been too powerful. But somehow, Sayah got away and hid for centuries. Hell, millenia. Until she latched herself to me.

There's so much more I want to know about her, now that I have a name for what she is. But that'll be a job for another day. There's still so much I'm unpacking.

I shake my head and drag myself into the bathroom, stripping down on my way.

The hot shower sprays over my head, steaming water rushing down my shoulders and body. I close my eyes and tilt my head up at the hot stream, washing away all the aches, the worries…I want them all gone.

Is it too much to have a day where I'm not being hunted down?

Today, I will be lucky!

I laugh to myself, otherwise I'll end up crying at how fast things got out of control yesterday and how quickly Sayah came over me. On the bright side, I seemed to gain some control over her, so I'm going to take the small wins where I can.

I grab the soap and lather my body until I resemble the marshmallow man from *Ghostbusters*, then let the hot water roll down my body, creating a pool of suds around my feet. The stress from the day threatens to wrap me up like an anaconda squeezing the life out of me. And maybe that's been my problem. I'm overthinking things.

Look at Elias and Dorian. They don't seem to care about most problems and deal with them as they come. I need to be more like them.

The swishing sound of the shower door sliding open has me snapping open my eyes.

Speak of the devil…Dorian is sticking his head inside, smirking, his eyes narrowing in on my breasts. "Hey beautiful."

I instantly smile back. Something about him just melts away the tension, and butterflies burst through my stomach, beating their little wings.

"You feel like having sex?" he asks bluntly.

I can't help but burst out laughing at how candid he asks the question. It's only when he pushes open the steamed-up shower door that I see he means every word. He's stark naked, his heavy cock already erect.

I narrow my gaze at him. "How long have you been watching me?"

"Wouldn't you like to know. Now, is that a yes?"

I step back in the large shower that easily accommodates two people. "How can I possibly say no to your crazy-butt-naked-ass? As you're practically in here already."

He chuckles and steps inside, only to make way for Cain stepping in behind him, also naked.

My eyes might have bulged out of their sockets, like one of those ridiculous cartoons.

"Oh, did I forget to mention I meant both Cain and I?" Dorian remarks, then loops an arm around my waist and tugs me up against him, his cock cradled between my ass cheeks, which he purposefully rubs against me. He holds me tight as my sin demon climbs in to join us.

"It might be a tight squeeze," I say, watching Cain step in sideways before sliding the door shut and moving under the spray of water, his cock just as hard and erect. Water splashes down his body, his muscles bulging, and I'm utterly mesmerized how beautiful and sexy this man is.

"That's what we're hoping," Dorian whispers in my ear.

I do that thing where I'm half rolling my eyes, and half laughing at his terrible pun.

Cain is facing me, dripping wet, the wounds he gained from yesterday's fight sealed, but they still blush red and look painful. He cups my face and says, "Do you feel like being shared?"

I'm unable to really find my words. I've been with Elias and Dorian at the same time, but Cain…he's always been more of a lone wolf.

"We figured you could use some pampering," Dorian tells me, while I'm still lost in Cain's eyes, in the seduction flaring over his face.

"Oh, I see," I finally say, and clear my throat. "So does this session come with a foot massage afterward?"

Cain moves even closer to me, and now I'm sand-wiched between both men, their rock-hard erections against me, and I'm gasping for air suddenly.

His gaze roams over me before he leans in and kisses me with the kind of passion that weakens my knees. Dorian has his mouth on my neck, his hands on my ass.

"I'm going to fuck you until you scream, gorgeous," Dorian whispers in my ear, while Cain licks my lips.

"She won't have a chance to scream," Cain teases, looking me in the eyes, promising me all the filthy things I can't get enough of.

Right now, I am having trouble focusing on anything but my men and how quickly things have escalated. They weren't kidding when they said they want to have sex, like, *now*.

"We've come to the conclusion that we haven't been showing you enough attention," Cain tells me.

"You two have been conspiring about having sex with me?" I gasp the words, as it's especially hard to concentrate with Dorian's tongue running the length of my neck and his fingers sliding across the crack of my ass. My chest flames with how hot I'm feeling, how hard my heart is beating. I'm soaking wet and aching, and I'm not talking about the spray of water splashing over us.

Cain smirks with a wickedly evil grin. There isn't much room to move in the shower, but we're managing perfectly well.

"We are going to make you ours over and over," Dorian breathes in my ear while Cain runs his hands down my breasts, follows the curve of my waist and down my legs. When his fingers sweep back up on the inside of my thighs, I moan.

I'm tingling all over with how feather-soft his hands feel.

He finds my pussy with his fingers and teases my swollen folds. His lips press to a hardened nipple and he sweeps it into his mouth, devouring me.

I moan, arching my back, clawing at Cain's strong, round shoulders to hold myself upright.

"I adore your body," Dorian says gruffly against the soft skin behind my ear, and there's something dark and erotic behind his words. The heat inside me sparks alight into a bonfire, and my skin pricks with goosebumps. Every inch of me grows extra sensitive to every touch, every stroke of my skin, every kiss.

When I look over my shoulder at him, his eyes are partly glazed over, like he's so lost to arousal, there is no coming back. And I know he's using his incubus power on us all, heightening the already inflamed arousal between us.

The sensations are suddenly so much more erotic, their moans sexy, the way they tease me primal and raw.

Dorian suddenly pushes his finger into my ass unceremoniously and without warming.

I moan louder at the unexpected flare of sharp pain that quickly morphs into the most exhilarating sensation.

Cain moves onto my other breast, his two fingers now pushing into my pussy.

The sounds pouring from my mouth, the cries of pleasure, are the most delicious sounds I'm certain I've ever made. I'm floating, unsure how much of this is me and how much is Dorian's influence, but my core is tightening and I need more.

"You keep making all those sounds and you'll have Elias joining us," Dorian warns, except I'd welcome him. Well, he may not fit into the shower with us, but there is no way I'd exclude my huge sexy hellhound.

My hands are threading through Cain's hair as his

tongue flicks over my nipple. These gorgeous, dangerous men are driving me mad with lust.

Cain releases me with a popping sound and straightens…though he keeps his fingers deep inside me, fingering me, while Dorian does the same from the rear.

I'm barely standing upright with how much my body hums.

The moment is just absolutely perfect.

I am being turned on by two gorgeous hunks, and my body burns up, while the water pours down our bodies. Why haven't we had sex in the shower before? This is sexy as hell.

Cain pulls back his fingers and puts them into his mouth, savoring me. "You are so beautiful and perfect."

His words mesmerize me and I lean in against his chest. My hands slide down his rock-hard chest to where my fingers brush over his heavy cock.

Dorian pulls out from my ass and has his hands on my hips. "I want you bent over," he demands.

I glance up at Cain, completely smitten by him. How did I get so lucky?

"I would do as he asks," Cain teases me, but the lust behind his eyes carries him to a place of explosive pleasures. I palm his cock, stroking him up and down quickly now, which only has him groaning. And I love the way he looks like this.

Completely under my influence.

Dorian has his mouth on my ear, a hand on my breast, squeezing. "I need you, beautiful."

I twist my head around and our mouths meet, our kiss made of hungry arousal, of unbridled need. His teeth scrape my lower lip and a growl rolls from his throat.

"Fuck! You're made for me…for us!" He pulls back,

stepping to press his back to the wall, then runs a hand down my spine, forcing me to bend forward.

Cain steps back almost instantly, falling into rhythm with Dorian's instructions. And I take that as my cue to bring Cain the kind of pleasure he serves to me. Leaning down, I slip the tip of his cock into my mouth.

He growls, his hands fisting my hair in a dominating manner that has me buzzing with excitement. I love being dominated and I won't deny it.

Dorian rubs the tip of his cock across the soaking wet folds. I part my legs to give him more room, to accommodate us in this tight space.

He pushes into me and a moan escapes my throat as he grips my hips, his fingers digging into me.

I slid my lips lower over Cain's erection, loving his musky, salty taste.

Dorian pushes deeper into me, building his momentum, rougher, quicker. His greedy hands adjust his grip and he's rocking in and out of me, our fiery flesh slapping.

The three of us quickly fall into a pattern of fucking and sucking, our groans escalating.

I hungrily run my tongue along the base of Cain's dick and cup his tight balls with my hand, my other resting against his thigh to stop myself from falling over.

In that moment of raw ecstasy, I forget everything. I shiver as these men bring me to the ultimate state of euphoria, and I want to give back just as much. My mouth works over Cain's erection, needing him to lose himself just like the buzz claiming my body.

Dorian's growling, plunging into me, while his fingers tease over my clit. I'm shuddering under the explosive climax pushing me over the edge, I never saw it coming. It erupts through me so fast, that my pussy clenches tight around Dorian. I'm groaning, shaking.

"Fuck!" Cain snarls in response, as if my orgasm has set off a chain effect. His cock stiffens in my mouth and he's pumping his seed into me. I swallow everything he gives me.

Dorian is fucking me wildly and groaning. Suddenly, he's twitching and pulsing his own climax into me. The sounds he makes are so damn sexy. Thick, sticky cum fills me from both ends, while I'm floating on air, unable to get enough.

I have no idea how I'm even still standing, seeing I can no longer feel my body. I'm breathless and release Cain, coming up for air. Licking my lips, I swallow what's in my mouth. Dorian collects me into his arms, my back pressed to his chest, while he's still buried deep inside me.

He's growling in my ear, his dick pulsing still, his hot seed seeping down the inside of my thighs at how hard he's come.

Cain watches me, smiling. "I love watching you get fucked."

And I can't help it, but hearing him say that turns me on so much. My pussy squeezes, clamping down on Dorian. He howls behind me, while I reach over to Cain's growing erection.

"It's your turn to take me," I purr. "I want more. Please."

His lips pull into a wicked grin and he closes in against me. "Aria, my love, I'll give you the world if you ask for it."

Cassiel bumps into my leg as we both emerge from my bedroom at the same time. I ruffle the fur on his head and he groans at me.

"Hey, *you* shoved out at the same time as me." He rushes up ahead of me, and I shake my head at how pushy he's become, like he thinks he owns the house.

A thunderous wind howls and the mansion creaks as it's battered by the snowstorm raging outside. I went to sleep early last night, and I am certain I could sleep for twenty-four more hours.

After the recent events I'm embracing a calm day, considering there is still the last relic for us to hunt down. But today I want no end-of-world problems. My e-reader is in hand, and I have every intention of crashing in front of the fire downstairs to curl up with a good story.

Sadie is coming up the stairs, her head up and eyes wide at seeing me approach. She smiles at me warmly, and I find myself doing the same. She's wearing her long black frock with the white apron looking every part the maid.

"Miss, Cain requests your presence down in the dining room for lunch."

"Luckily, I was headed in that direction," I say, jokingly. The girl smiles shyly and nods, then heads down the stairs. Cassiel races down, thinking she is racing him. I giggle to myself as he practically bowls her over to reach the bottom of the steps first.

Sadie straightens and pats down her dress, seeming slightly perturbed.

"Sorry, Sadie. He's a bit stir-crazy being stuck in the house."

"It's fine," she says, tight-lipped, then sweeps her hand toward the dining room for me to proceed. The double doors are shut, which is unusual, but maybe they are keeping the room warm. The demons aren't particularly fond of the freezing cold.

Sadie has already left so I step forward, then pull open the doors.

I'm instantly bombarded by so many visuals cues and colors that I'm unsure where to look first.

A giant Christmas tree towers in one corner, the tip bent at an angle from being too tall to fit into the room, and every branch is blinking with ornaments and lights. A mountain of food and a plump turkey adorn the long table. Then there are the greeting cards hanging from ropes strung across the room. Oh, and the oversized red ribbons plastered to the walls. Bowls spilling over with Hershey's Kisses chocolates all through the room, and for some reason there are red Coca-Cola cans and bottles everywhere. Like, I'm even talking about an actual crate in the far corner with the bubbly stuff. What is that about?

I turn on the spot, loving the room, and I'm smiling like a crazy person that my demons remembered Christmas. I love the festive colors, the roast turkey has me salivating, and everything they did is just adorable. Though I want to know what is with all the soft drinks.

So much has happened that it never occurred to me that it's Christmas Day. In all honesty, most years I ignored the day, hating that I had no real family to celebrate it with. Murray would go out with his buddies to play poker.

But this is…everything. My throat chokes up that they made this for me.

It feels like I've just walked into a room where Santa might have exploded and all his cheery goodness has splattered over the room.

When a soft version of the song "Carol of the Bells" starts playing from a speaker in the room, I look around for the guys, but the room's empty. I step inside, blown away at the creation, when someone clears their throat from behind me.

I twist around instantly, and my mouth might have just fallen open.

Cain strides into the room dressed up in a Santa suit. I am not sure if I should be laughing or strip down naked for him. He's wearing baggy red pants very low on his hips, revealing those V-dips at his hips that make girls go silly, and his red Santa coat sits open, revealing a bare chest beneath. Ripped muscles are all I can stare at.

A half-strangled moan falls from my lips at the sight of this delicious hunk. Sweet hell! Does he want me to eat the food or him?

From either side of the doorway, Dorian and Elias emerge, each of them dressed in a polar bear onesie, complete with hood and ears.

My heart might have just melted into a puddle by my feet. And seeing these powerful men dressed like that for me destroys me.

I half laugh, half start crying like a baby. Geez, I feel stupid for overreacting and probably looking like a mad person as I wipe away the tears.

All three guys surround me quickly, Cain taking me into his arms. "What's wrong, Aria?"

"Told you we should have brought in real polar bears," Dorian states.

"And have it maul your ass," Elias answers. "My vote was for those beastly Clydesdales from the Budweiser ads. Then we could have gone on a ride."

"In the snowstorm?" Dorian barks back.

I'm watching them, laughing, while more tears run down my face.

Cain is looking at me with a confused expression. "I'm not sure what we did wrong to upset you so much," he says.

I'm shaking my head as I say, "You did everything right. These are happy tears." I have my hands plastered against his solid chest, his skin is on fire, and there are so many emotions vying for attention inside me. From the ache in my chest that they did this for me, to wanting to study every inch of my men in their costumes, and then the notion of finding out if Santa Claus goes commando play heavily on my mind.

"Y-You did all this for me." I hiccup my next inhale as my throat thickens some more.

Cain wipes away the tears from my cheeks with his thumbs as he cups my face. "I would bring Krampus himself to kneel before you, if that would bring a smile to your face."

Tears slide out from the corners of my eyes, not at the notion of him bringing anti-Santa to me, but that I know without doubt that he would if I asked him to.

"Why are you crying?" Elias asks genuinely.

"You all remembered Christmas while I completely forgot about it." Who exactly is the real demon in this room, anyway? I break from Cain's embrace and turn on the spot to face the room. "This is perfect. I mean I don't fully understand the giant bows or the crate of cola, but I love it." Turning to face my three demons, I smile softly. "And what I love more is that you made this happen, and you even dressed up."

"We are here for you," Cain says.

Dorian crosses the room to the tree, bends over to collect something, then strolls back with a small wrapped gift in his hands. "You've got something to wear too." He's grinning especially wickedly. All three of them are, as a matter of fact.

"Wow, you got me a gift. Thank you. I didn't know or I would have got something for you all too."

"Open it," Dorian insists, more concerned with my reaction to the gift.

Curiosity has me ripping off the green wrapping paper

and I pull back the lid to the black box. I peer down at the red silk and lace folded within pink tissue paper. I pick up the piece of clothing as Dorian collects the box from my hand. I'm holding onto a sexy, one-piece lacy bodice that really doesn't conceal much at all. It is mostly made with thin white lace that sparkles like it's been woven from diamonds, and a few well-positioned red streaks of ribbon to cover vital parts. Thin shoulder straps, a low V-neck, and the bikini line looks like it might reach my armpits. This is extravagant and so revealing that it almost makes me blush.

I glance up at the guys, who stare at me like they're wolves. "This is beautiful. Extremely revealing, but just stunning."

"Will you put it on?" Elias asks mischievously, their gazes already devouring me.

They're nodding and I'm laughing almost hysterically now because I shouldn't be surprised it's what they want. "You know what, after lunch, you got yourself a deal."

If there's one thing that never gets old, it's the delicious look on my men's faces that show me how turned on they are by just thinking of me. That stuff does things to a girl, like how my nipples harden instantly, and when I squeeze my legs together, heat flares between my thighs.

Lust sweeps over their gazes, and I fold up the gift and place it back into the box in Dorian's hands. He sets it aside like it's a precious crown. On the inside, I'm giddy with anticipation at seeing how they'll react to me dressed in it, along with exactly what's going to come right afterward.

That's when Cassiel suddenly bursts into the room, half knocking into the back of Elias's legs. He wobbles, arms thrown outward to balance himself, while I laugh.

Cassiel is already at the food, front paws up on the table

and he's got his nose in the bowl of gravy, splashing it everywhere.

"Cass," I call out and we all rush over to stop him in some chaotic crazy moment of pulling a full-grown lynx from delicious gravy.

He growls at the guys grabbing him, and they back up, then he shoves his nose back in there.

I can't stop laughing in all honesty. "Just let him have the gravy." I'm gripping my middle, unable to stop laughing at how crazy Cassiel looks, but it's his first Christmas too.

The rest of us take a seat at the table. Cain at the head, Dorian by my side, and Elias across from me. Cassiel is at the other end across from Cain, slurping away.

Cain does the honor and carves the turkey, and I'm still tingling all over to think that the first time I've ever felt so completely content and at home is when I am sharing Christmas with three demons and a lynx. Who would have thought? And that's when my thoughts travel to Maverick.

"Should we invite Maverick to enjoy Christmas lunch, too?"

"No," all three say in unison. Okay, well that's a unanimous decision.

"Saw him settled down in the basement," Dorian confirms. "He looks content."

I want to push back at his comment, but I also don't want lunch to end up in another fight between the guys.

With my plate filled with turkey, roast potatoes, and greens, I dig in. Elias has the turkey leg in his hand and he's eating it like a beastly king sitting on a throne.

Dorian and Cain are enjoying their wine, watching me.

"I've never had a real family, and Murray avoided Christmas, so you guys doing this for me means everything. Thank you. But I gotta know...what's with the ribbons and years supply of Coke?" That's when I spy a pile of toy boxes for Hess trucks near the tree. "And are we donating toys to kids later on?"

Dorian strains to look around and follow my line of sight to the trucks.

"These are all the things humans enjoy at Christmas," Cain tells me. "For years, we've seen the human television ads push the same things every year, and we wanted it perfect for you. The huge ribbons are always on cars at Christmas, which I assume is a good luck thing. Though it does surprise me that so many people buy their significant other a car for Christmas."

"And there are constant ads with Santa and his polar bears drinking Coke. They are what humans seem to enjoy," Dorian says.

"Hmm well—"

"Told you the bear costumes were too much," Elias says, smacking his lips with a mouthful of turkey. "I could have just shifted forms."

"Really?" Dorian answers. "Is that so you in your hellhound form and the lynx can both fight over the gravy?" He bursts out chuckling.

"I didn't mean full transformation, but to show a bit of our real selves."

"I don't mind either option," I reply instantly, which is completely true. I take a bite of a roast potato, then sit back, chewing, and stare at them. Hell, I love everything about these men.

The way they squabble always makes me laugh.

They might have come from the underworld, but they aren't above showing the kind of affection I never expected from demons. And they adore me more than anything. They barely let me out of their sight, they protect me with their lives, and I feel like I can talk to them about anything. The whole being sexy as sin goes without saying. These three devour my body and own every inch of me.

Sometimes they are so loving and kind to me that it makes me want to cry.

I keep eating as the conversation turns to a polar bear shifter they knew in Hell, and I'm mesmerized. Cain reaches over and places a hand on mine.

"Happy Christmas," he says, and my heart is close to breaking at how adorable he is. I can't even bring myself to correct him that it's *Merry* Christmas. I just smile and soak up everything he tells me, wanting this moment to last for eternity.

That's when I realize that in truth, I can no longer live without my men. I need them.

CHAPTER TWENTY-TWO

ARIA

Goosebumps cover my bare skin, but nothing compares to the fire pulsing between my thighs. I'm not exactly naked, but looking down at myself in the skimpy, sexy bodice from the demons, I might as well be. The strip of red ribbon barely covers my nipples, then between my thighs it's just a strip of fabric that leaves nothing to the imagination. And from behind, I am practically butt-naked.

My face is on fire, yet my mind fills with filthy images of what the guys will do to me, the porn-star kind of naughtiness that has me burning up.

Butterflies tingle in my gut in anticipation, and just thinking about it already has my pussy soaking wet.

Down girl!

A soft knock at the door to the bathroom has me flinching. Geez, why is it so hot in here?

"Won't be long," I reply.

"Okay, babe," Dorian replies, and I can hear his eagerness from just those two words. Seconds later, he's back.

"Just in case you need any help getting dressed, I'm here for you."

"Ha, I don't think so. You can wait and be surprised like everyone else."

I turn back to the mirror and am almost shocked at the girl staring back at me. Okay, girl is not an accurate word. More like sex-kitten bomb. Who would have thought that a lacy ensemble could completely change the way I look and even how I feel about myself?

I grab the headband that came with the outfit. I slip it on and stare at the cute little reindeer antlers. How this outfit is in any way meant to resemble a reindeer is beyond me, but I'm willing to play along. It's Christmas after all.

I take a deep breath and reach for the door handle. "You got this. You're going to go out there confident and get fucked by Santa and his two polar bears." I roll my eyes at how bad that sounds. Yet, the thrill of their promise flares over me.

Outside in the hallway, there's no sign of Dorian. Whispers from the guys float from the parlor, so with a quick look left and right to make sure Sadie and Ramos aren't around to see me, I dart forward. The floor is freezing against my feet.

My heart is thumping so loudly that I fear I might pass out. Then I pause in the doorway, my face flushed, but I tell myself nothing I do right now would turn off the guys. Not dressed like the reindeer queen of all sin.

I drape an arm against the doorframe, half leaning against it, staring at the guys with their backs to me.

"Is this a bad time?" I purr, putting on my best sexy voice.

They turn around at the same time and Elias trips over his own feet as he tries to move around the couch.

I grin devilishly, bathing in the lustful looks, at the way their eyes devour me…all of me.

Cain has his Santa jacket off, standing only in his red pants, with a pressing erection tenting them. Dorian and Elias are almost gobsmacked, which isn't like them at all.

I laugh at their reactions.

"Fuck me!" Dorian growls, coming toward me as he peels away the onesie to sit very low on his hips, revealing a sculpted body, lines of muscles. My sights are locked on the peek of dark hair skimming to the fabric over his groin, and I'm suddenly breathing heavily.

My nipples harden at the sight and his powerful arm loops around my waist, hauling me against him. His erection presses against my stomach and his lips lock to mine, his tongue plunging into my mouth. There is no ceremonial dance. Dorian is horny and he's going to take what he wants.

DORIAN

*A*ria moans out loud against my mouth and I lose my mind seeing her dressed up this way. She's fucking beautiful.

When I first saw her in the doorway covered in strips of fabric, my cock hardened so fast it made me dizzy.

That insanely hot image is forever imprinted on my mind.

The curve of her breasts and her tight nipples poking the red ribbon covering them, her hour-glass figure, the length of her sexy legs. But I can't get the image of her sweet pussy out of my mind. I don't want to. That sliver of fabric just barely covers her slit, the soft outer lips of her shaven pussy exposed.

Fuck!

I press her against me, deep throating her with my tongue, my cock already leaking pre-cum from how much I need to fuck her, and hard.

I'm a damn incubus, but with Aria, I'm losing all control.

Her hand slides down the front of my onesie pants, her small hand wrapping around my swollen cock. I'm so fucking huge and thick, and to feel the softness of her touch, the eagerness of how she squeezes me, undoes me.

I growl as she pumps her hand up and down my shaft.

Our brows are touching and we're looking into each other's eyes. Everything about her makes my body react, and I slide the strap off her shoulder easily, the fabric rolling down and revealing a gorgeous breast, tipped with the pinkest of nipples. I reach over and cup it, then knead it.

"You are everything to me," I groan, barely able to catch my breath from her touch. "And go harder. That's it, gorgeous."

She's making that delicious moaning sound again, the one that lingers on my mind long after I'm finished with her.

Fuck!

Footsteps sound upstairs, from one of the maids no doubt, but it's enough to draw Aria from my embrace. Her hand releases my cock and I growl, needing her touch back. She glances over her shoulder, and I sidestep past her to slam the rolling pocket doors shut.

Aria's licking her lips and staring from me to Cain and Elias, who both look ravenous. Cain has his hand down his pants, stroking himself. He doesn't make a move toward her, just watches.

She strolls past me and goes toward Elias, swinging her

hips, and from behind her the view is spectacular. That luscious ass moving with each step is perfection.

She is too much. I'm going to fucking lose it today and nothing will be enough until I sink my cock into her.

ELIAS

The sight of those perfect tits have my balls tightening. Slowly, my little rabbit prowls toward me. She knows exactly what she's doing…when the fuck did she become such a temptress?

When she looks at me there's only raw hunger behind her eyes, and my hellhound rises to the occasion. He wants to come out and play. I sniff the air, drawing in her sex. Fuck, I'm barely holding it together.

"This is how I want you…naked and wet for me."

She almost misses a step at my words, and I adore the faint blush of pink on her cheeks. Every inch of her turns me on. My breath catches in my throat and I take her into my arms, my hands falling to the back of her thighs. She's off her feet in moments and wrapped around my waist, just how she should be.

She fists the ridiculous polar bear outfit and pulls herself closer, finding my lips. Her kisses are the sweetest candy, but when she bites down on my lower lip, I snarl in response. My cock twitches at the pain, at the fucking agony that I'm not slamming into her yet.

Cain and Dorian are near, they're watching, but my focus is on my Aria.

She's mine.

Every inch of her I own.

I walk her over to the table as those delicious lips glide over to my ear. Her breath is warm and like a feather tracing over my skin. The fire inside me roars to claim her and remind her she is ours…and only ours.

"Tell me how much you want to suck on my pussy," she whispers in my ear.

My vision blurs at how fast my blood jolts down to my cock at her words. All I can smell is her sweet nectar, so to hear her teasing me breaks me. There's only so much a man can take.

I lower her carefully onto her back on the table, her legs still spread and on either side of my hips.

Dorian and Cain are there, watching, stroking their cocks. Their eyes are only on Aria, and that's my focus.

"You are spectacular," I say. "But it's time we unwrapped our present."

"Do it," Dorian groans.

I want every inch of her.

I peel back the strap from her other shoulder, releasing the other breast, and she gasps quietly, staring at each of us. My eyes move to the softness of her stomach as I slide the fabric over the curve of her hips. She raises them as I tug on the lace, and she raises her legs into the air for me. In slow motion, I drag the lace to her ankles and slip it past each of her gorgeous little feet, which I kiss.

Cain is growling, his impatience as harrowing as mine, but we have all day and night. An eternity to enjoy Aria… so for the first time, I want to take it slow and savor every part of her.

"Elias…" she purrs, squeezing her breasts and pinching her nipples. My cock hurts at how desperately I need release.

I pry open her legs wide and run my fingers lower on the inside of her thighs.

She trembles under my touch.

My gaze lowers, and her pink little pussy is glistening

with excitement, her inner thighs so wet from how turned on she is.

Dorian and Cain are on either side of me, their heaving breaths loud like beasts. Aria spreads open for us, moaning as her hand slides down between the valley of her breasts, over her stomach and to her fiery core.

She's stroking herself, rubbing her clit.

My body tenses and I drop to my knees, pushing her hand away and pressing my face between her thighs. She's so wet, her scent intoxicating. A growl snarls possessively in my throat.

I take her into my mouth, rolling my tongue over the soft folds of her pussy. Her moans escalate, her hips rocking, pushing herself against me.

I love when she's so turned on she shoves her pussy into my face. I'm an animal and devour all of her, the wet licking sounds only escalating. I lose myself eating her and let myself get carried away as her hips rock and her moans intensify.

Her body tenses and I know she's close. I want her screaming but not yet. So I break away and lick my lips. "It's not time."

She cranes her head up toward us, her cheeks flushed, her eyes lost in arousal. "Are you kidding me…why are you stopping? Please keep going."

I laugh, getting to my feet. "I love it when you beg."

CAIN

She is a goddess.

Soft curves, perky breasts, an unparalleled beauty. She's so much smaller than the three of us, yet she has us all eating out of her hands.

Her lips pout at Elias holding out on her, and when he moves aside, glancing my way, I take my position between my love's legs.

"Cain, please don't make me wait."

"I love you like this." The words roll from my lips as my fingers glide down her thighs.

She's nodding, her gorgeous breasts bouncing from the gesture. "Uh-huh. Now are you going to do something about it?"

I slide my fingers down her swollen pussy and press two thick fingers into her wet softness. She moans and tilts her head back, her chest rising with burning arousal.

"Yes. Yes!"

Dorian and Elias are breathing loudly, their gazes locked on our girl. The things she does to us is unimaginable. She's curled herself around our hearts and there is no escaping her hold.

I pump into her furiously, her hips rocking, her pussy sucking down on my fingers, her eagerness so fucking beautiful.

An abrupt knock comes from the doors to the parlor.

I growl and Elias snaps at the intruder, "Leave us."

But the persistent knocking comes again. "Cain, I apologize for interrupting. Please, I must speak with you urgently." The hoarse voice tells me it's Ramos, and the tightness in his tone tells me something's wrong. He knows better than to interrupt me unless the reason is dire.

Groaning, I pull my fingers from Aria. Her disappointed moans are blades to my heart.

"What-What's going on?" She blinks up at me.

I lean over her and kiss her, then whisper, "I'm not finished with you. Don't go anywhere, my love."

I cross the room, feeling disgruntled at the interruption. I'd promised myself today would involve nothing but spoiling Aria, giving her anything she wants. And that doesn't include work getting in the way.

Swiftly, I step out into the hallway, pulling the doors shut behind me. Ramos is sanding there, bouncing on his feet anxiously. The dhampir is usually calm and relaxed, no matter the situation, so the fact that he can barely stay still has worry spinning through me.

"What is it?" I ask him.

The air around him is charged though with tension, and the bitter cold air is blowing into the mansion from the front doors being wide open. He must've burst in here, frantic. He doesn't even acknowledge my nakedness in front of him.

My anxiety ticks up a notch.

He licks his lips before he answers, "The Nightwalkers have taken over Purgatory."

I stare at him, unsure if I've even heard him right. "Excuse me?"

"Their master and his followers barged in, kicked out the customers, and locked down the place," he goes on, his words picking up speed in urgency. "They say they own it now."

Laughter bubbles up my throat.

This vampire clearly has a death wish. Did he really think he could just waltz into my club, put down his flag, and claim it as his own? That's not how things work around here.

What an idiotic and amateur mistake. One he will end up paying for with his life.

I built that club from the ground up. *I* did the work to make it what it is today. It's one of the things that propelled us to the top. And no one—*no one*—is going to take it from me. Especially some new-age vampire with an entitlement complex.

It's laughable that he'd even try.

But I did have other people to think about. Like Antonio, Sting, and the rest of my employees. "What's happened to the staff?" I ask.

"They've been tied and locked up for now, but from their talks, it sounds like they have plans to either turn or feed on them."

The amusement within me dies and is replaced by anger. Stephan wants to make a meal of my people? I don't think so.

"Were you there?"

He nods. "They tried tying me up like the others, but I was able to get away."

He means he used his special skills with pressure points to knock out his assailant.

"And what of Viktor and Charlotte?"

"Gone. They had left before the attack."

Getting into more trouble, no doubt.

I'm about to head out the door, where I see the Town Car and Holmes waiting for me, but then realize I'm still only partly clothed. I turn abruptly and race up the stairs. When my demon begins to push out of me, I let it, my wings bursting out of my back and my vision darkening.

"My Lord, what would you like me to do?" Ramos calls from below.

On the landing, I spin abruptly, and he jumps back at the sight of me transformed. "Tell the others." My deepened voice echoes off the walls. "Get them to Purgatory. We finish this tonight."

I bound up the rest of the stairs, push into my room, and quickly change my pants. Seconds later, I throw open the balcony doors and step outside. My wings stretch out and beat against the wind.

I had a feeling Stephan was going to retaliate after Viktor decimated his Hush supply, but going after Purgatory? He's going to regret this.

My black heart pounds with brutal hatred as my wings carry me higher. I speed toward the edge of the city, right toward Purgatory, knowing Elias and Dorian won't be far behind.

As the treetops and dirty roads give way to blacktop and high-rises, I notice billowing black smoke in the distance filling the night sky. The air reeks of fire, reminding me of Hell, and as I swoop down lower, the immense heat coming from below scalds my face. Red and orange flames consume one of the corner lots.

But not just any lot.

It's Purgatory.

And it's been set ablaze.

CHAPTER TWENTY-THREE

CAIN

*E*verything I have worked for. Years of my life, money, time and energy. Gone. Up in smoke.

I stumble through my landing, unable to take my eyes off the inferno raging through the building, practically swallowing it whole.

I had put my heart and soul into this club; I'd built an empire from the ground up. And now, all I can do is watch as it burns.

Sorrow grips me unlike anything I've ever felt before. I'm paralyzed with it, only able to stare at the flames and know there's no way I'll be able to salvage anything, even when the human fire department comes.

I don't know how long I'm frozen there, but when I hear the frantic pounding of wings and the scratching of nails on pavement, I know I'm no longer alone.

"Shit…" It's Maverick. He must've flown here.

Although he hadn't been one of the people I'd wanted Ramos to tell to come, I don't mind him being here.

"What the fuck happened?" he asks, strolling up to my side.

I don't answer.

The violent and painful sounds of bones breaking and realigning come on my other side and soon Elias stands at his full height, completely naked.

He glances at me, waiting for the next command. When I don't give any, he says, "What do you want us to do?"

Tires screech in the distance, and suddenly light floods the parking lot as the Town Car whips around the corner. No Holmes driving this time. It's Dorian behind the wheel, driving like a madman, and the moment he throws the car in park across three parking spots, he flings open his door.

"Fuck me," he mumbles, the bright colors of the fire dancing off his face.

Now dressed for the freezing weather, Aria and Ramos get out next, and for some reason, seeing the devastation on Aria's face almost undoes me. Purgatory may have started just as a way to keep her busy while she was under our contract, but it had turned into much more for her, too. A second home. A place where she had some freedom and could be with friends. I can see the grief and torment clear on her face.

"Cain," Elias repeats, a little louder this time, "what do you want us to do? The fire department will be here in minutes."

That's when I remember that Ramos had mentioned Antonio and the others being tied up somewhere inside.

"Ramos, you and Elias run inside and see if any of our staff members are still in there," I order, and without even a flicker of hesitation, they both rush into the building.

Aria steps forward, her face contorted with fear.

"They'll be fine." Dorian places a hand on her shoulder. "Remember, we're made from hellfire, and Ramos is too smart to die."

But despite his somewhat comforting words, she still seems unsure.

We all wait, every second feeling like hours. It's impossible to hear anything beyond the fierce hissing and crackling of the flames. When neither Ramos or Elias return, my concern begins to grow. It shouldn't be taking this long.

This blaze has reached a dangerous level. Even for Hell creatures. Let's not forget that we're weaker on this plane; we can die.

That's it. I need to go in and get them. I pull my wings back into my body and trudge toward Purgatory, the heat and smoke intense enough to make my eyes water.

"No, Cain!" Aria shouts behind me.

I have to. I can't just leave them in there.

But just before I reach the threshold, the roof folds in and collapses, causing an explosion of hot air and flames so large, every window shatters and pieces of ash and wood and glass fly everywhere. Throwing my arms over my face, I'm pushed backwards from the power of the blast, my bare feet sliding across the pavement.

Aria's screams fill my ears, followed by Dorian's curses. Panicked, I rush toward the fire again, this time with Dorian on my heels, but a massive shadow suddenly darkens out the light and a black hellhound bounds out of the wreckage, five people clinging onto its back. Ramos appears next, stumbling out and shielding his face. He drops to the ground and I rush over, dragging him further away from the club in case of another collapse. He's coughing and hacking, his eyes bloodshot.

Despite his weakened state, he pats my arm, a silent way to tell me thank you and he'll be okay.

Rising to my feet, I look across the lot to see Elias dropping off the five very shaken up Purgatory employees,

Antonio and Sting among them. Aria is there, checking them all over for any life-threatening burns or wounds. Besides being rattled and a bit knocked around, they seem okay.

"Good job, you big oaf," Dorian teases, swatting at the smoke that radiates off Elias's fur. He snorts at him in response.

"What's a-matter, demons? Afraid of a little fire? Isn't that, like, your thing?" A male's voice floats down from somewhere above us, somewhere hidden behind all the thick smoke. Laughter rises, and instantly the sadness of losing my club is gone. Replaced only with immeasurable rage.

I unfurl my wings, ready to take to the sky and find who's speaking, but the smoke parts as a man leaps through and lands in a perfect crouch before me. Slowly, he rises, and I realize I was wrong to call him a man. He's too young. Barely looks over twenty-five with short buzzed hair, a wide nose, and a clean shaven face. A boy.

His mouth splits in a cocky grin, fangs on display, as he saunters across the parking lot. "No hard feelings, I hope," he says as he closes the distance between us. He hooks a thumb toward Purgatory still engulfed in flames behind him. "You took something very important from me, so I had to take something from you. Fair is fair."

Dorian comes to my side and snorts a laugh. "Wait, you're Stephan? *You?*"

When the vampire bows, Dorian's laughter bursts out of him. "This is a joke. It's a joke. It has to be. Are we on one of those stupid reality shows? Where's the camera?"

Something he said must've struck a nerve because Stephan's confidence seems to waver. "You've lost, old man." He spits the last words as if it's an insult. "It's time for a new generation to rule this town."

Elias steps up to my left and growls, lips curled over sharp teeth.

"What's with these millennials?" Dorian teases. "Always think the world owes them something, and that they can just take what isn't theirs."

Maverick shouts from somewhere behind us, "What's a millennial?"

"Hell if I know. I just hear it used a lot."

Unamused, Stephan rolls his eyes. "You're pathetic. Really," he says. "And if you're hoping for the fire department or police to swing by, I wouldn't."

That means he has his hands in both, influencing them behind the scenes. He's even extended his reach to the human side of Glenside. Not just the supernatural.

Fury pumps through my veins like molten lava.

"Maverick, Aria, get Antonio and the others somewhere safe," I order, my eyes never leaving Stephan. The thundering of hurried footsteps tells me they have no problem doing so.

Good.

My wings stretch out, my demon growing restless with this pointless back and forth. I want blood. I want revenge. And no prepubescent little vampire child is going to stop me from getting just that.

Stephan looks at his nails, seeming bored with this whole thing, and I don't know what irks me more. His nonchalance or the fact that he's still able to breathe, let alone talk. "Before we kick this party off and things get bloody, I have a proposal for you."

I grit my teeth. Now he's just toying with us. "A proposal."

He raises his hands. "Hear me out. I know deals are usually your biz but I got one you'll want to hear."

Dorian glances at me. "Did he just say biz?"

"Not interested," I bark. My nerves are running low.

"Yeah, take that proposal and shove it up your *biz*," Dorian shouts back.

"You've run this city for a long time," Stephan goes on, ignoring him. "You obviously know what you're doing. It's only because of that I'm offering you a place on my team. To become my ally, not my enemy."

Elias snarls, spit flying.

"That's 'fuck you' in dog language, if you couldn't get that from the context clues."

"Took the words right out of my mouth," I push through my clenched teeth. "This city is ours. Always has been. Always will be."

"It's a shame you feel that way." Stephan flicks his fingers and more vampires drop from the smoke. Behind us. All around us, until we're completely surrounded by them. They bare their fangs at us.

I look from Elias on my left to Dorian on my right, whose horns curl back on his head, nails grow into claws, and runes glow underneath his shirt. They're bouncing on their tiptoes, ready for the fight.

"Like old times?" Dorian asks, a wicked smile on his face.

I nod. "No survivors."

Head tilting up, Elias lets out a mighty howl, and then the three of us are tearing off in opposite directions.

ARIA

I run with Antonio, Sting, and the other crew members of Purgatory down the dark street when a warning of danger wiggles up my spine. I stop in my tracks when I realize it's not from me or Sayah, but from the tether that binds me and my demons together. Something's wrong.

I glance up and spot danger leaping from the tops of buildings, heading back in the direction we'd just come. To Purgatory.

More vampires.

Oh shit. Stephan's brought back up. And from the looks of it, he brought an entire army.

Fear churns in my gut. The last time Cain, Dorian, and Elias had been up against vast numbers like this, they'd almost been beaten.

They're going to need help.

Maverick notices I've stopped and skids to a halt. "What are you doing? We have to get everyone out of here."

"They know that. They don't need us anymore." I switch directions and start running back toward Purgatory. It's not long before Maverick's beside me, keeping up with my strides.

"We were given orders, you know," he says.

"Oh, that's right. I forgot. You are all about following orders from someone else, regardless of the consequences. You did it with your father."

His eyes widen. He's stunned by my words, but I don't fucking care. If my demons need me, that's where I'm going to be.

He's quiet for a bit, still running at my side. Then, he says, "Fine, then I'm coming with you."

That's a bit obvious now but okay.

"And you're going to need this." He unsheathes the sword at his hip. During all the madness of Ramos telling us what was going down at Purgatory and us all rushing over here, I hadn't even noticed Maverick had it. Slowing down, he passes it to me. It isn't until the weapon is in my hand that I realize it's the same sword from our fight with the hellhounds.

"You brought this?" I ask, turning it in my hand.

"You did pretty well with it before." He shrugs. "Besides, you *never* want to go into a vamp fight empty handed."

"Right."

He nods toward the next street where the club's raging fire is still lighting up the night. "Let's go."

We pick up our pace again. I'm no expert swordsman by any means, but I did feel a little safer with a weapon to battle vampires with than nothing at all. Especially since Sayah is such a wildcard nowadays. Calling her for help could lead to disaster.

When we make it to the empty parking lot, we're halted by the sight before us. Bodies litter the ground. Even though most of the snow's been plowed into mounds, everything—from the pavement to the benches and parking meters—is painted red with blood.

In the background, the fire rages on, providing light on a very dark scene. Elias is ripping out a vampire's entrails and throwing them across the ground while Dorian claws his way through a crowd of them, impaling one with his taloned fingers and launching him across the way.

Cain's in the air, holding two vamps by the neck and then flying full speed into a neighboring building to crush their skulls against the stone. I hear the crack from all the way down here, and it makes me nauseous just to think about, so I try not to.

"There!" Maverick calls and points to the closest rooftops. The shadows I'd seen before are hopping closer to the brawl.

Panic seizes me. "We have to stop them!"

"Here, hold on!" Maverick scoops his hands under my arms and before I know it I'm being lifted into the air. His wings aren't as strong or large as Cain's but he's able to fly me onto one of the rooftops with no problems.

The moment our feet touch the rooftop, the vampires veer in our direction, coming at us in a maddening rush from the shadows.

My skin crawls at the sheer number of vampires, my grip tight on the sword.

Maverick unleashes a war cry and charges, moving with unimaginable speed. Pulling out his daggers from his belt, he throws them through the air with deadly precision and takes out two vamps in one go. With a flick of his wrist, the blades are sailing back into his hands, only for him to cut down three more vampires.

I've seen Dorian, Elias, and Cain fight many times, but Maverick is almost beautiful in the way he skillfully uses all parts of his body to fight with his weapons. Whatever it takes to finish off the enemy—and he's good at it too.

At the sight of carnage, Sayah rises up, wanting a piece of the action. I can feel her darkness seeping into my muscles and clogging my veins. But, as I learned during the hellhound attack, her presence helps me, makes me stronger, faster. I can use her to my advantage...

If only I could control her.

I'd managed to keep her from taking full control of me before, but that was with Maverick's help. He'd been able to bring out confidence in me, more than I'd felt before on my own. Would we be able to do it again if things got too out of hand?

I don't have time to think any more about it because a vamp lands in front of me from somewhere above. It's a woman with a short blond bob and a pink cardigan sweater. If it weren't for the red staining her teeth and rapidly healing bruise under her eye, I'd swear she was a

PTA mom or running some soccer fundraiser. Not a bloodthirsty creature of the night.

Stephan was turning housewives too?

I raise my sword and she hisses loudly, fangs flashing. She pounces and I swing the weapon. In a blur of speed, she dodges my blow and comes at me again. A warning zips up my left side—a warning from Sayah—and I spin sharply, whirling my blade. It slices the vamp clean through her middle. She blinks, stunned, before her top half separates from her bottom, and she drops.

Sayah rejoices at the death, and my excitement grows. Maybe I can do this after all.

The thud of another enemy landing nearby has me whipping around, sword slicing through the air. I move only on instinct, and when warm blood splashes over my face and chest, I know I've delivered another fatal blow. A smile tugs at the corner of my lips.

I'm enjoying this. Maybe a bit too much.

The vampire stumbles backward, clutching his neck. I fall into my attack, bring the sword down into the center of his chest. I watch the life drain from his eyes, and something inside me ignites with excitement.

When I yank it back out, I kick him for good measure.

Someone grabs my hair and pulls it hard. I cry out, pain shooting through my skull and making my eyes water. My assailant tugs it back again, jerking me into his chest. His arms come around me, and his rancid breath spills over the side of my face.

"Hmmm, you're a fiery one," he purrs in my ear. "I wonder if you taste as good as you figh—"

There's a swoosh of air and a flare of pain at the top of my ear, and suddenly, the vamp's arms loosen on me. I jump away from him to see Maverick's daggers embedded in his forehead. Shuffling back, his eyes cross as he tries to look at it.

Another whoosh as Maverick's other dagger whizzes past me and nails him in the heart.

In a flash, Maverick is at my side. I touch my stinging ear, and when I glance at my fingers, they're glistening with blood.

"Shit!" I gasp.

"Sorry about your ear," he says with a playful wink.

"Just a scratch. Could've been much worse." I lift my weapon again and swing it toward the next bloodsucker coming at me, while Maverick darts into battle.

He calls over his shoulder, "The heart. Remember to aim for the heart for a sure kill."

The heart. Right.

This time, I grip the sword with two hands, heave the hilt back, and charge. I ram it into the first vamp who spins in my direction, and I drive it hard into his chest, getting it as close to his heart as possible.

When the thing convulses, eyes widening, blood dribbling from the corners of his mouth, I figure I've done right.

Pushing a foot up against his leg, I heave the sword out of him. He collapses to the ground in a heap. Boots slap the floor behind me, and I whip around to the oncoming monster. I charge forward and lash out my weapon, taking him out.

Maybe it's the adrenaline of not dying, or having Maverick close to me destroying these vampires, but I am feeling more confident than I ever imagined myself to be with a sword.

Cain soars overhead and uses his wings to push a huge gust of wind across the rooftop. The vamps lose their footing and are thrown back, some rolling off the roof and plunging to the ground below.

I look up, happy to see Cain unharmed, when a dark figure climbing up a neighboring fire escape catches my eye.

"Cain!" I scream, just as Stephan leaps through the smoky haze and lands on one of his wings, dragging it down. Unable to wrench it free, he spirals out of control and together, they tumble through the air. Cain's punching and clawing at any piece of Stephan he can grab, but Stephan's grip stays iron-clad. I run to the edge of the rooftop, drop onto my knees, and watch as they fall straight for Purgatory and the fire.

My heart stops beating, terror paralyzing every inch of me. Just before the flames can swallow them up, Elias in hellhound form appears out of nowhere and leaps across the inferno, knocking both men out of harm's way.

The three of them land in a dark alley, out of my line of sight, but from the vicious snarls and sounds of fighting that follow, it's safe to say they have things handled.

"Aria!"

At the sound of Dorian's voice, I spin on my heel and drop to the ground as another one of the Nightwalkers swings something at me. It isn't until he tries to swing it down that I realize it's a lead pipe. My hands jut out in reflex, his blow meeting my sword instead.

He snarls at me, fangs out, and leans into his weapon. Inside me, Sayah's hold on me increases, and my mind starts to drift. She wants to take over me; she wants control.

But I can't let her have it. But without it, I may die.

Dorian appears behind the vamp in a blink of an eye and taps on his shoulder. "Um, excuse me."

Confused, he glances over his shoulder, and that's when

Dorian slashes him across the face with his long nails. It isn't enough to kill him, obviously, but he does pull away the pipe and lashes out Dorian's way with it. He dodges it effortlessly. Sways left then right, back and down. With the gashes across his face already closing, the vamp growls in frustration.

"Okay, you're right. Enough playing around," Dorian says. When he swipes the pole at him again, Dorian grabs it and rips it out of his hand so fast, both the vamp and I are stunned. Then he stabs the thing directly through his chest.

The vamp sputters, blood bubbling out of his mouth, before dropping like a sack of potatoes.

Dorian steps on the corpse to get to me and offers me his hand. He helps me stand. "You're not too bad with that thing," he says, nodding toward the sword.

I smile. "Thanks."

"Oy! Dorian!" Maverick calls from the opposite end of the roof. He's leaning over the edge and peering down at the street below. "Looks like we're getting a second wave!"

Dorian and I rush over and follow his gaze to see even *more* Nightwalkers coming to join the fight.

"Holy fuck. How many of these fuckers did this high school dropout make?"

"Looks like another fifty or so," Maverick answers, even though the question was clearly rhetorical.

"He couldn't just stay in his mom's basement and be addicted to internet porn like the rest of this generation?"

Maverick wipes the blood splatter from his forehead with the back of his hand. "Is that what you did as a kid?"

"I fucking wish," he says, then jump onto a nearby drainpipe and begins to climb down. "Keep her safe," he barks Maverick's way.

"She's pretty capable of taking care of herself, if you haven't noticed," he shouts after him. Glancing up at me, he offers me a smile and butterflies flutter awake in my stomach. At least someone believes in me.

A loud battle cry shakes the night. Maverick and I exchange puzzled looks before gazing back down. Out of the shadows comes a man dressed in a gold chest plate and leather skirt. With his dark hair and tanned skin, he looks like he just stepped out of a time machine from ancient Rome.

"What the fuck is that?" Maverick asks in disbelief.

I only know one tall, dark, and handsome vampire like that. I laugh. "That's Viktor."

He throws his head back and lets out another warrior shriek. The darkness behind him shifts and moves and suddenly, more vamps rush out, spilling into the parking lot and clashing head on with Stephan's horde. It looks like he's brought some friends from other covens.

"He brought the cavalry," Maverick says. "But why is he dressed like…"

"I wouldn't ask," I reply.

"Gotcha." After twirling his daggers in his hands, he sheathes them in his belt. "Well, hopefully that means all this can be over with faster."

Taking in the space around us, I notice the rooftop is scattered with dead bodies, mostly Maverick's handiwork. "You didn't have fun?" I ask him, because it sure looks like he did.

He smirks as his answer.

The savage sound of screams and death from down below has us both leaning over the roof's edge again. Down below, the lot and the remains of Purgatory are a chaotic mess. They look like a swarming nest of ants from up here, spreading out over the land, consuming everything in their path.

There are so many vampires against my demons, and

from the looks of it what Maverick and I did up here has barely made a dent. My stomach drops.

"Stay here," Maverick commands, and before I can argue, he jumps off the building, wings out, and glides right into the heart of battle.

"Maverick! Wait!" But he doesn't hear me and vanishes into the masses to combat the enemy.

This is insane.

I thought the hellhounds were bad, but this is an all-out war. How many casualties will be caused by this? Will my demons survive?

My heart twists. There needs to be another way to end this bloodbath. A sure way.

The shrill wind blows past me, tossing up my hair, and rising goosebumps on my arms. My skin tingles, and I realize the chill rushing around me isn't natural. It's super-natural.

Sayah.

Across the rooftop, my shadow wiggles and grows and Sayah leaks out of me. At first, my pulse races with fear—I know what she's capable of, after all. She's a leviathan, a monster, and she wants to use me like her puppet to do whatever she wants.

But then, I remember fighting the hellhounds and Maverick's encouraging words. He'd said Sayah *needs* me. I don't need her. And that's the key, isn't it? She's protected me all these years in a symbiotic relationship. But we're more than that.

I've controlled her before, when I thought she was my friend. Then, when I saw how strong she really was, I deemed her my enemy. Maybe I've been looking at this all wrong.

It's not her versus me. Her power is mine, and what's

mine is hers. If I'm weak, she'll step all over me. But if I call the shots, she'll have to listen.

We're…one.

Can this work?

I draw a deep breath in through my nose and try to draw on that confidence I'd felt under Maverick's touch. It's not as easy to find within myself like when he did it, but I repeat to myself that I can do this. Like with the sword, like with finding the relics and outsmarting the necromancer, and escaping the dragon, I keep surprising myself. And I can do this too.

I am a survivor. It's what I've always been. But this time, I am going to be more than that.

I'm going to be the ruler of my own destiny. And no one—not a demon, a leviathan, not even Lucifer himself—is going to tell me otherwise.

This is my life, and I'm taking back the reins.

CHAPTER TWENTY-FOUR

ARIA

*P*ower surges through me, unlike anything I've ever felt before. Wind rushes all around me in a mini tornado, throwing up my hair and through my clothes. I feel strong, invincible, immortal, and it's not Sayah doing it to me; it's me. I'm in control.

I drop my sword. It clatters to the ground, but I don't care. Hopefully I won't be needing it anymore.

Slowly, I lift my hand and Sayah's shadow mimics my movements and lifts from the ground. She stands tall before me, like a ghostly stretched-out version of myself.

Sayah is a force alone, but I wonder how far I can take it.

I continue to lift my hand even more, and to my surprise, every shadow on the rooftop darkens and grows before peeling off the ground to stand freely on their own, too. Like miniature Sayahs, complete with glowing red eyes and all. Their opaque forms float closer to me as if waiting for my next command.

Holy shit. This is absolutely terrifying. A nightmare in the making.

But I can't be scared. Right now, they're obeying me, and I can use them to end this battle with the Nightwalkers once and for all.

I ball my raised hand into a tight fist.

Shadows? I call to them mentally, like I used to do with Sayah. Hearing my command, they all perk up. *It's time.*

Their red eyes shine brighter, and then they're off, zigzagging down the building and weaving in and out of Viktor's men. One by one, they seek out Stephan's vampires, covering them in their shadowy essence, engulfing them, until nothing remains. Once they move on to the next, there's nothing left of the vampire before. Not a trace. They've been completely swallowed up by their darkness.

I watch with a mix of horror and excitement as Sayah and the others take out the Nightwalkers with little effort. I spot Cain, Dorian, and Elias among the crowd, watching the whole thing unfold but unsure what to do about it. When Cain lifts his head and sees me standing on the roof, he leaps into the air.

His wounded wing doesn't go unnoticed by me, especially since he has a hard time directing himself to land on the roof. He misses the edge and slips, causing my heart to skip a beat. I rush over to the side to see him still there, only holding onto the bricks.

One good heave up, and he's over the top. The moment he stands, I throw myself into his arms. He pulls me close and tucks in his wings.

"It's still you..." he murmurs against my head.

I tilt my head up to him and find his baby blues staring down at me. "Who did you think it'd be? The Queen of England?"

"But...the leviathan..." He glances over his shoulder at the scene below, where my shadows are doing a good job cleaning up the place and fewer Nightwalkers litter the parking lot. Some are even fleeing now after seeing what they can do.

"I think I'm getting the hang of this now," I say, but his gaze is searching my face, looking for any signs of Sayah controlling me.

"Your eyes are still white, but you sound like my Aria."

"That's because I *am* your Aria."

Still unsure, he continues to stare at me.

I let out a nervous laugh. "Cain, it's me. Really."

He waits another long moment before asking, "Then how did you summon more creatures?"

"I'm not quite sure exactly… But I realized that I have the ability to control them. And Sayah. Thanks to Maverick."

"Maverick?"

I nod. "Yeah, he helped me see that I don't need Sayah. She needs me. And she was only able to take me over because I was letting her. If I'm the one calling the shots and believing in myself, she has to listen to me. I mean, I think so anyway. It seems to be working so far."

He glances down again. "I'd say so. But I think you should call them back to you now."

His words surprise me. "Call them back? But why? They haven't taken out all the Nightwalkers yet."

"They've done their job more than efficiently," he says. "Most of Stephan's coven was only under his command because of their allegiance to him for turning them. Now that he's gone, Viktor can take over again as Glenside's master vampire and reform his coven."

"He's dead?" I ask eagerly. After all the shit that vamp's put us through, it does give me some sick satisfaction to know he's done for. I just wish I could've been the one to do it myself. Or with the shadows.

"Yes, he's dead," Cain confirms. "So you can recall the creatures. The fight is over. We've won."

Problem is, I don't want to stop them. The energy buzzing inside me is intoxicating, and the thought of me being the reason all those bloodsuckers are dead…it fills me with pride.

Little Miss Aria, now able to kill so many without so much as lifting a finger. Or sword.

Little Miss Aria, no longer needing to cower or run or need protecting.

I have power, *real* power now. I can fight back.

"Aria…" A warning rumbles in Cain's throat as he shifts toward me.

"But your club… They destroyed it. And what about your wing? They all deserve to die," I try to reason with him.

"I'll heal with time. And my club is replaceable. You're not."

"But I'm fine," I tell him. "Better than fine, actually. See?"

He keeps walking toward me, making me shuffle backward. "It's done," he says. "Call the monsters back."

Everything inside me is saying no. Don't do it. Every one of those bloodsuckers deserves the horrible death coming to them. But the way Cain's looking at me, like I'm becoming the enemy instead of his love, has me rethinking everything.

He's right. I don't want to go too far either and sink into that dark mindset Sayah can put me in. I need to be aware and find the balance.

Like before, I lift my hand and find the power inside me that is attached to Sayah.

Return. Your job is done.

On command, Sayah zips up the side of the building

with the other shadows in tow. Cain and I watch as the others take their rightful spots and become the rooftop's natural shadows once again.

Once Sayah shrinks back into me and my normal shadow returns, the power radiating off me ceases and Cain smiles.

"There she is. Aria. My love." He wraps me in his arms again and leans down for a kiss. It's sweet and gentle and everything I need to calm the adrenaline still rushing through me. It helps douse the fiery need for more death and destruction.

Once he pulls away, I whisper, "Thanks for keeping me from losing my way."

"Anytime." Then he glances around the rooftop and concern wrinkles his forehead. "With my wing, I'm not sure it's safe for me to get us both down from here. Dorian may have to carry you…"

Chuckling, I hook my thumb toward the rooftop access door. "Or we could always just take the stairs."

He laughs, his eyes sparking with amusement.

"Walk down stairs to the ground floor? You mean like normal people?" he says as we walk toward the access door.

He's a prince of Hell. I'm a leviathan—whatever that really means—and shoot shadows out of my body, and we just finished killing an army of vampires together. What about any of this is normal?

"Yeah, sure. *Normal.*"

Whatever the fuck that means.

I collapse into the back seat of the Town Car, completely exhausted, but my pulse is buzzing. Cain is in the front, while Elias and Maverick climb into the back snug seat with me and Dorian drives.

It's a tight squeeze, but we manage. There's no argument from anyone, we just make it work, like somehow after what happened, it's become clear we are not the enemy to each other. Maverick is more *us* now then he's ever been.

We're all splattered in blood, covered in wounds and cuts, clothes torn, but we're smiling.

"Fuck Stephan and those vamps," Elias growls. "My little rabbit, you demolished so many. Fuck, do you know how sexy and terrifying that was to watch?"

I can't stop smiling, which is odd, feeling such satisfaction after leaving a bloody war zone. But for the first time ever, a sense of belonging and satisfaction flares over me. For the first time, I don't feel like the freak I've always been.

"You were mesmerizing," Dorian adds and glances at me from the rearview mirror. "You controlled Sayah again."

I'm beaming on the inside. I catch Cain watching me from the front seat with a proud look on his face. Is it strange to love bathing in their acceptance and compliments?

"It's thanks to Maverick for showing me how to control her, really." I lean forward, glancing over to him, grinning at him. Adoring how damn sexy he looks with blood over him. All my men mean everything to me, and right now, I'm including him in that lot.

Every demon turns to look at Maverick, who shrugs nonchalantly. "It's nothing."

Dorian chuckles. "Maybe you're not all that bad."

I roll my eyes at his attempt at a compliment, but Maverick smirks at that. "Maybe."

"So, what's next?" Elias asks.

"Nothing," I say in unison with Dorian.

"I want a damn break from all the end-of-world stuff," I admit truthfully. "At least for a day or so, especially since we never finished celebrating Christmas completely."

"What happens during Christmas?" Maverick asks.

"For you," Elias answers hastily. "Absolutely nothing."

I giggle to myself at his possessiveness, adoring when they go all macho. These demons are mine. There are no take-backsies. I'll fight tooth and nail to hold onto them as they do for me. Now when it comes to Maverick…it's still a work in progress, but I have a feeling he'll be the decent guy he's showing himself to be of late.

I lean back against Elias and just enjoy the peacefulness for a change. I know there's a big mess waiting for me with Gabriel and the showdown with Lucifer. I also still want to find out more about Leviathan, if I can. But that can all wait until later.

Once we pull up in front of the mansion, we all peel out of the Town Car and stumble into the mansion.

"I'm going to sleep for a week straight," I joke, though in truth, I crave it so badly. Along with foot massages and breakfast in bed.

Cain is already dragging himself into the parlor, Dorian behind him, and they're dripping blood over everything.

"Hot shower and food," Elias responds, and loops his arm around my waist, drawing me toward the parlor. I'm guessing we're going to chat about what happened first.

I glance back to Maverick, who's already strolling away and down toward the basement instead of joining us.

"Maybe he needs another room. The basement is so

doom and gloom," I suggest, to which Elias grumbles but he doesn't outright say no either. I smile to myself, knowing that as much as Maverick is growing on me, he's slowly gaining acceptance by my three lovers as well.

Inside the parlor, I make my way toward the fireplace. The warmth of the blaze against my skin is like heaven

On my next breath, the hairs on my arms lift.

A current of power races down my spine. But with it comes the tingling in my toe…the power I feel when I'm near the relics, when they are activated.

I freeze and glance at the three men at the same time they ice over too. "Did you feel that?" I ask.

They're nodding. "What the fuck now?" Elias growls.

"Magic!" Cain answers, his face panicked.

My stomach knots because we barely got home and it started again?

"Fuck, now?" Dorian snarls.

"My toe," I gasp out, the sensation dancing heavily across all my toes now. "The relics," I barely say, when the three demons rush out of the room.

I'm on their heels, and we're flying directly into Cain's room.

There's soil strewn everywhere like someone's been tossing earth in here, covering every piece of furniture.

"What the heck happened here?" I ask.

Cain darts across the room and throws open the closet door. Then he drops down to his knees in front of a latch door in the floorboards that's already open. There are piles of dirt all around the closet, like someone's been digging for a bone.

And I know instantly it's where he's been stashing the relics. The earth keeps their power at bay.

My blood turns to ice as I close in and find the gaping

hole empty of relics. Cain is digging furiously through the soil with his bare hands.

"Fuck!" he roars, and rears back on his heels. When he lifts his gaze, there is a look on his face I never thought I'd see, and I want it gone because it doesn't belong to him.

Defeat.

"They're gone. All the fucking relics are gone!"

My heart thunders and terror wrenches through me.

"You are fucking kidding me!" Dorian's pushing forward, needing to check for himself.

"How? Who?" I ask.

Elias's thunderous growl has me turning toward him as he tears out of the room.

My knees are trembling as I stumble closer to the closet, and my wide eyes greet Cain as he gets to his feet.

There are no words I can find to ease the ache of what they've all lost. What we've all lost...our chance to eradicate Lucifer from our lives.

Shock hits me hard, and I'm stumbling backward as the world stands still for those few moments.

Cain's face reddens with fury, and Dorian is digging through the earth desperately. But it's true. There's nothing there. Someone's stolen the relics.

Movement rushes across my back, and I twist around to Elias bursting into the room. His livid, his eyes on fire, and his hands fisting.

"Maverick's gone," he snarls breathlessly. "The fucking weasel is nowhere in the mansion. He took the relics!"

Dorian scrambles to his feet as a rush of breath expels past his lips. "That sonofabitch! I'm going to rip his spine out with my bare hands, then feed it back to him."

Cain doesn't move, doesn't say a word. He's shaking with rage, and his silence is terrifying. I can't even begin to know how it feels to have his brother betray him this way.

But this disaster destroys everything we've been working toward.

I can't catch my breath as only darkness sweeps over me, stealing the earlier hope I'd been clinging to. Stealing everything.

Maverick...what the fuck have you done.

THANK YOU

Thank you for reading When Hell Freezes Over
Reviews are super important to authors as it helps other
reader make better decisions on books they will read. So if
you have a moment, please do leave a review.

HELL ON EARTH

BOOK 6

This is it. This is where it all ends.

It's me, my shadow, and my demons against Lucifer.

With the relics stolen, the only way to get them is to go back into the hellfire--back to Hell where Lucifer awaits. Defeating him may mean making the ultimate sacrifice, but even with so much at stake, I don't know if I can.

Things heated up fast with Cain, Elias, and Dorian, and now Maverick, but I'd sell my soul a hundred times to keep them as mine. Forever.

What if that's impossible?

There's so much danger ahead of us, but I'll bring Hell on earth to save the ones I love. I just wonder that when all's said and done, who will be the one wearing the unholy crown?

Read the hotter than Hell finale to the Sin Demons Series! Find out how it all ends today!

Hell on Earth is book six in the Sin Demons Series.

Find out how it all ends today!

LOST WOLF

SAVAGE SECTOR

Being rejected by my fated mate is the least of my problems...

I'm a half-breed, a Cursed. The wolf half gets me an alpha for a fated mate...the witch half gets me killed.

Or so they think.

Now four Viking Alphas are all that stand between me and certain death. They need my powers to take over the Savage Sector, and they'll hold my sisters as leverage until they get what they want from me.

My wild magic, my heart.

My wolf calls to them, but I can't trust them to keep me alive once this is over.

I'm just an Omega to them, but that mistake may cost us all our lives

What the Viking Alphas want, the Viking Alphas get...

...and right now that's me and my wild magic.

START READING LOST WOLF TODAY

HIS HAVEN

Free on Kindle Unlimited

She was never meant to be his...

Avrum Brenin should have died in the same fire that claimed the lives of his mother and brother. Instead, he was granted immortality by the powerful vampire, Lord Henri. Under his diligent care, Avrum revels in the world's most lavish splendors. But as payment for this extravagant lifestyle, he must look after Haven, Lord Henri's human rescue. A task that proves far more complicated than it seems.

After stumbling onto Haven barely clothed and bound at the wrists, Avrum discovers that Lord Henri may not be the salvation he once believed. While the more time he spends with Haven, the more determined he becomes to protect her.

When the passion between them ignites, Avrum finds himself caught between honor and loyalty. Will he stand with the man who rescued him? Or risk it all to save the woman who captivated him?

ABOUT MILA YOUNG

Best-selling author, Mila Young tackles everything with the zeal and bravado of the fairytale heroes she grew up reading about. She slays monsters, real and imaginary, like there's no tomorrow. By day she rocks a keyboard as a marketing extraordinaire. At night she battles with her mighty pen-sword, creating fairytale retellings, and sexy ever after tales. In her spare time, she loves pretending she's a mighty warrior, walks on the beach with her dogs, cuddling up with her cats, and devouring every fantasy tale she can get her pinkies on.

Ready to read more and more from Mila Young?www. subscribepage.com/milayoung

For more information...
milayoungauthor@gmail.com

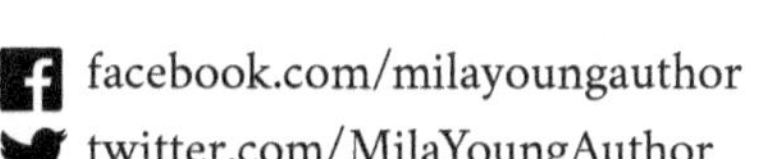

facebook.com/milayoungauthor
twitter.com/MilaYoungAuthor
instagram.com/mila_young_wicked

ABOUT HARPER A. BROOKS

Harper A. Brooks lives in a small town on the New Jersey shore. Even though classic authors have always filled her bookshelves, she finds her writing muse drawn to the dark, magical, and romantic. But when she isn't creating entire worlds with sexy shifters or legendary love stories, you can find her either with a good cup of coffee in hand or at home snuggling with her furry, four-legged son, Sammy.

She writes urban fantasy and paranormal romance.

RONE AWARD WINNER
USA TODAY BESTSELLING AUTHOR

Want to read more from Harper A. Brooks? Subscribe to Harper's newsletter and get *Halfling for Hire* for free! http://BookHip.com/MCBDCN

Join Harper's reader group for exclusive content, sneak-peeks, giveaways, and more! www.facebook.com/groups/harpershalflings

www.ingramcontent.com/pod-product-compliance
Lightning Source LLC
Chambersburg PA
CBHW060759190726
48285CB00002B/488